Standstill

J.A. Marley

AVOCADO BOOKS

Avocadobooks.com

First published by Avocado Books in 2016

© J.A. Marley

ISBN: 978-0-9935658-4-7

J.A. Marley asserts the moral right to be
identified as the author of this work

A catalogue record of this book is
available from the British Library

Cover artwork and formatting:
Matt Trollope / JaxEtta.com

A strong spirit transcends rules
- Prince Rogers Nelson

Sally!
You should enjoy this...
Arsenal get a Mention!!

Sept '16

This book is dedicated to my parents. Thanks to Dad for his love of pulp fiction and to Mum for the Hollywood movies...

CONTENTS

1

✧ A Rude Awakening ✧

With a sound like a whip crack, the front door of the flat exploded. The slam of the battering ram tore through it just below the dead lock.

Danny Felix was instantly reminded why this four room wonder was his latest home, not because the rent was low and the landlord lowlife, but because he could see the front door from his bed, once he had removed the bedroom door. That was a 'unique selling point' for Danny, and with the sight of 'uninvited guests' about to arrive, he was pleased all the DIY had paid off.

Four or five burly men came cramming through the remains of the door, like a pack of crazed sale shoppers bursting into a department store on Black Friday... trying to get that 800 quid telly for twenty.

He had spent the previous evening convincing the nice blonde lady with the shapely backside that he was a 21st century knight in shining armour and she should come home with him...which she had. Any thought of some morning glory had been shattered along with his front door.

Danny just stayed put.

He just lay there, his tall frame cool beneath the sheets, his deep set, dark eyes watching, his breathing even despite the immediate threat before him.

Soon enough, a face pushed its way through the melee of bodies. Danny did not recognise it but assumed instantly that it belonged to the main player.

Fuck me, he's big, Danny thought.

And then The Tall Man spoke.

"Good morning Danny...pleased to see us? Or maybe not, eh?"

Turning to the girl. "Put something on love, I haven't had breakfast yet. Danny here has to come with us for a chat, while we search the place. So you might want to fuck off...alright?"

The blonde girl didn't need a second invitation, practically sprinting into the bathroom gathering up her clothes as she went.

Once she was dealt with they hauled Danny out of his bed, standing there naked, all six foot four of him, not feeling exposed or embarrassed, just matter of fact. It was his gaff after all, so why shouldn't he be?

Danny caught sight of himself in the mirror on his one wardrobe, taking in the scratch marks the recently departed young lady had left on his side and back. Well at least she'd had a good time.

He was, at 28-years-old, in his prime. A slim waist with a strong torso vee-ing up to broad shoulders and muscled, strong arms. His blue grey eyes, the most striking feature in a face that was oval, with a strong jaw. All this was set off by early morning stubble with hint of auburn in it that matched his close-cropped hair. And last, but not least, was a small quarter inch scar just by his left eye, right where he would probably develop crows feet in a few years. This was the only giveaway that he was taking this developing situation seriously. In times of excitement, stress, arousal or all three it usually glowed a little pink, and right now he could even feel its hot presence without having to study it in the mirror.

Maybe, Danny thought, it's time to break the silence…

"Morning officer…shall I put the kettle on?"

The Tall Man, smiling now, took a long slow look around the room.

"A brew would be most welcome…but what makes you think I'm Old Bill?" The Tall Man winked as he said it, and then nodded to his accomplices.

And suddenly they were tearing the place apart…

Danny Felix is a thief.

He didn't feel proud of the fact, but neither was he embarrassed by it.

He also knew he was very, very good at the dark art of blagging.

Betting shops, post offices, cash in transit vans, he'd even had a crack at a bank a few times. He had pulled off jobs in them all and not had so much as a single day in the grey barred hotel.

So he had always known that a day like today would roll around at some point.

They were all a blur around him, while he now stood impassive. It reminded him of one of his favourite films, *Heat*: DeNiro cool as fuck, telling Val Kilmer (the pre-fat, good looking and also cool Val Kilmer) that as a thief he shouldn't own anything that he was not willing to walk away from in thirty seconds flat. In the film it was meant to be just cool, but actually Danny had thought it was pretty good advice. Hence, his small flat didn't sport much more than the basics: Bed. TV. Small sofa and some kitchen stuff, no faff, no paraphernalia, no excess.

Just stick the spoils of your light-fingered fun some-where and don't over complicate. Except after his most recent little bit of misappropriation Danny had not yet had time to do the sticking away. Not that he hadn't been clever, just that it was closer than he would have liked.

So watching the various kitchen drawers being emptied and the mattress being ripped apart was all rather amusing but for the hunters it was unfruitful. At first he thought he might just get away with it this time...they looked like they couldn't find their own dicks in the gents without help, but then his heart sank. A yelp. An excited bark. A flurry of furry.

Bollocks.

A Springer Spaniel, all tail wagging, sniffing and eager to please. Still, Danny mused, if you are going to take one on the chin, losing out to a cute dog was just about bearable. At least it would be fun to watch because the dog was about to get a dose of sensory overload.

"Anything you want to discuss with me before this little Hound of the Baskervilles gets busy?"

The Tall Man, who Danny had noted was yet to give himself a name, was now standing in the living room looking down with barely concealed mirth in his eyes that soon spread to a full on smile.

Danny thought a shrug would suffice for now. Why get chatty? Why make their lives any easier? And so the Springer went to work, and as Danny expected, went bananas. Like, apoplectic bananas. Barking, growling, dancing round in circles, like he was trying to chase his tail but couldn't. Next it was shooting from the kitchen to the bedroom to the living room to the bathroom and generally looking like a kid on about three million E numbers.

Everybody stopped.

The amusement on The Tall Man's face faded.

The dog's handler became flustered, repeatedly

calling the dog's name "Jiffy" in a vain attempt to gain some control.

"Fucking hell, Jim. Get furry balls down to business will you?"

But now Jiffy was just panicking. The poor dog didn't know which way to turn and Danny couldn't hold on any longer. He started to laugh.

The sound of the heavy flat handed slap The Tall Man delivered to Danny's face even gave Jiffy pause. Kicking out at the dog, he grabbed Danny by the hair, his reddening face right there, spit flying.

"Think this is a fucking joke, do you? Where is it? You know what we are looking for. Now do yourself a favour and just tell me or do I have to wipe the walls with your face?"

"Guv...Guv."

The Tall Man backed away long enough to look where the dog handler was pointing. Jiffy was licking the wallpaper like it was made of beef gravy.

"What the fuck is the bloody dog doing?"

Danny knew. He knew only too well, and as his head was swimming and his eyes watering he couldn't do much to mask his gathering disappointment. The dog was good. Give the little shit some credit.

The Tall Man and the dog handler were now crouched at the spot where Jiffy had been sniffing and licking furiously. Using a knife (from Danny's own kitchen; so much for heeding DeNiro's advice on minimalism) they began to peel away at a corner of the wallpaper. The game was up, at least for now, as it revealed a fresh and additional layer of insulation between the actual wall and the wallpaper. Made exclusively of 50 pound notes the new insulation was stuck there temporarily using a very old fashioned mixture of flour and water. No wonder the poor dog had gone nuts. Sensory overload indeed. At least two walls in each room were indulgently decorated this way.

The Tall Man, now back to his original good humour, stood up and crossed to where Danny was just about ready for another not-so-happy-slap.

"I'm Detective Inspector Harkness. You are Danny Felix and that…" - pointing to the wall of money - "…is much, much more like it. Clear out lads. Danny and I need a chat…"

Surprise, surprise, Danny thought, a fucking copper, a big one at that, and now he's got what he was looking for. Jiffy got a meaty treat and I'm going to get what? A chat? This will be interesting.

Oh and another thing; someone else must have been chatting too. A little too chatty, or else why was Danny standing here now with ringing in his ears, sick to his stomach and nowhere to skip off to before the shit hit the fan?

The flat emptied almost as rapidly as it had filled up, and the newly revealed detective looked squarely at the thief before him.

"Let's do a little redecorating before we talk, shall we?"

2

✧ Chance ✧

The young couple stood outside the boutique jewellery store in Wheathampstead for the umpteenth time.

And it was still there, twinkling beautifully in the window; the engagement ring that had been the subject of 75 per cent of the girl's waking thoughts since she first laid eyes on it.

There was no price tag but her boyfriend had managed to find out the bad news on the quiet; just shy of £2,000. He supposed it wasn't much to ask, it was a once in a lifetime purchase. And what she didn't know was that he had managed to offload his motorbike and his old man had weighed in with a loan of sorts to tip the balance. And so, here they were at the shop window; looking.

Today, he was going to take her into the shop and buy that ring for her. That was the adventure he had planned for them.

Except today was not to be a romantic day.

Not in the slightest.

As the young man gently whispered into her ear that they should go in and maybe try that ring on, as the surprise spread across her face, a huge motorbike roared up the street and all the romance in the world rushed to some place else.

The bike, a beast of a Suzuki, with a rider and a pillion passenger, flashed up onto the pavement right by the window. The passenger was wielding what looked like some kind of gun, and just as that thought struck the young man...BANG.

Suddenly the window had gone, and now the bike passenger rifled through the shattered glass, and had his hand on the ring, their fucking ring, and everything else around it.

The bike revved up in pitch and intensity about to scream off...except now three cars had arrived, tyres screeching. Acrid burnt rubber hung in the air, shouting, men in peaked and chequered black and white caps dived out of cars, also holding guns. The front biker thought it's time to do one...

The Suzuki had a big engine, with a big kick when the throttle is pulled right back, causing the whole bike to leap.

LEAP.

Forward it goes, just five feet from where he has pulled his girl behind him, trying his best to shelter her from this fucking craziness.

The front wheel of the motorbike met the front end of the BMW 3 series that tried to block its way, the heavy engine block under the bonnet enough to send the bike up.

UP.

People talk about such events unfolding in front of them in slow motion.

Crock of shit.

He saw what happened next in a series of flashing, shiny, heartbreaking moments. The bike tipped up and the two riders flew with it, backwards. As they do the shotgun that had been used so expertly to destroy the window was now spinning, first up, then with gravity

playing its part, it dropped

Right in front of him.

Asked many times after that day, he still can't remember the next bit, except he knew his soon to be fiancee is screaming her head off, and he suddenly cannot stand. The glass and gravel is soon digging into his face and he felt an unrelenting heat in his legs. He could smell a bitter mix of firework and burning flesh in his nostrils and his thoughts. And then more burning to a level of intensity he hadn't thought possible. He did the only thing he could then. He started to scream.

Suddenly there were lots of people. A flurry of activity and the nearest of them, a woman with one of the chequered caps on, told him to take it easy, stay where he is, not to move his legs if he could at all help it.

And that was all Detective Inspector Christine Chance could say to the man…she didn't want to be the one to tell him.

If only the shotgun had landed facing the other way. If only they had not removed the trigger guard when they had sawn it down. If only the blast from the shotgun had not been close enough to blow this poor blokes foot clean off at the ankle.

Christine Chance, or CC to her friends and colleagues, had experienced bad days on the job before. All coppers had. The days that really upset them were the random, meaningless ones. Ones like today. Should've, would've, could've…

So when she had one, she couldn't help but turn the events over in her mind again and again, just as she was doing now.

In all other respects, 'the job' had gone off

perfectly. They kept the would-be robbers in their sights, nobody got clocked. Textbook follow and foil.

Except for the accident, she thought. Was it that? An accident?

Once the thieves had pulled the gun and the shout "robbery robbery robbery" had gone up Old Bill had to move in. Gun, job on, members of the public nearby, game on.

For someone who considered herself a proud-to-serve, lifelong, career copper today was like a thumb in the eye. Still, the bad guys had been taken out on the pavement. It was better than allowing these bastards another chance and another set of bystanders to crash through.

No, Christine felt proud of what she did. She understood that sometimes there were pay offs and compromises, but what she really loved was the sound of a set of cuffs biting into a wankers' wrists. CC knew in her heart that hers was a big job, a big set of responsibilities and she loved doing it, especially the action-packed stuff.

And now that she had answered all the follow-up questions from the police oversight team, signed the statements and taken her own for the arrests, she had to deal with the smaller stuff.

The really difficult stuff. Personal stuff.

Christine Chance got out of the car and started towards the building that held everything in her life that she held dear but was now heartbreak made solid in brick. The weight of the walk threatened to push her under, drowning her under the wash of her own anxiety, but she kept going, kept walking. It was funny, in life or death moments, ones that involved crime, random fate, violence and, sometimes, sheer luck, she never doubted her next step. She never wavered, always propelled herself forward. How about here?

Well, here she felt continually unsure. Off balance. Sliding towards a certainty that she would try and deny with each and every breath she took, despite the futility of the effort.

CC stood at the entrance to the hospice. She had to go and spend some time with her dying daughter.

3

✧ Q&A Harkness Style ✧

They had only just finished stripping the walls of one room and already there was a stack of crisp, or rather crispy, 50 pound notes on the floor between them. Danny was giving it the broken TV treatment - all picture, fuck all sound. But as long as they were peeling money from behind the wallpaper, D.I Harkness seemed content enough.

Now that there was only the two of them left in the room, it seemed the huge policeman had decided he had seen enough.

"How much...?"

Time to have that chit-chat.

Danny looked at him with flat eyes, trying to keep all emotion from his face, trying to channel DeNiro in *Heat* when he had to look Pacino in the eye. The two of them measuring the size of their respective robber/detective dicks, like two actors sharing their first screen time together.

"I don't know anything about anything...I only rent this flat."

Harkness cocked his head to one side, like a dog listening to the sound of his food being poured into a bowl, a smile breaking across his big flat wide face.

"Now Danny, you don't think I'm here through

simple detective work, do you? No! You're already trying to figure out who gave you and your little private bank up. So let's just say, let's pretend, that I'm not your run-of-the-mill 'inspector plod'. Alright? Now how much did you scoop from that cash transit van?"

Danny gave him nothing back.

"It was you and two others. A driver. Someone else to do the lift work while you used the charm and guile of a pair of Glocks to convince the poor dumb shit in the helmet to hand the bags over. Your driver was a big Polish lad, Janusz Piesakowska. Done time once before for a botched bookies' job. The heavy lifter was a sweaty jock, Nelson...Frankie, I believe. They were interesting old pros."

Were? What did he mean "were"? Danny was beginning to feel anxious about this supposed policeman. He was starting to feel like a rat that had just nibbled on the wrong bit of cheese.

"Let me see your hands."

Danny didn't quite compute first time round so the cop repeated the demand, this time grabbing Danny's wrists and flipping the palms upwards.

"Now Danny, didn't your old mum ever tell you that your hands are supposed to be used for good? These are supposed to be God's hands. To do the Lord's work. Hands can give, not just take all the time. Didn't your mother ever tell you that?"

And suddenly Harkness had one of Danny's wrists in a vicelike grip. One meaty fist twisting his palm upwards and into place, the other hand slapped down on top. But this was no handshake of peace.

Harkness had a sharpened door key between two of his fingers. The fat end was just visible between his knuckles. The toothy, business end of it was pointing downward.

And Harkness started to grind.

21

Danny was instantly shocked at how much pain such an everyday, seemingly innocent object could inflict. His breath caught in his chest, holding it there so as to show no weakness to the big copper.

The key felt like it had been stuck in a furnace, scorching hot, twisting, digging, gouging into Danny's palm. All the while Harkness just looked straight into Danny's eyes, not smiling, not blinking just looking. He was taking the measure of the man in front of him.

Danny could feel blood drip at his own feet. Try as he might, he could not squirm free of the grip. Just as he thought the red-hot burn of the key might make its way clear through to the bone Harkness let go. He palmed the key away, almost as magically as he had made it appear between his fingers and finally stood back.

"Danny, I am a very determined man. Motivated you might say. Just give me an approximate figure for your fancy wallpaper and I will give you the lay of the land."

Staring at the bloody hole in the centre of his hand, Danny didn't look up...

"Twenty five and change. Maybe thirty, I haven't counted."

Smiling again, a playful light in his eyes, Harkness passed Danny a dishcloth for the blood on his hand and then clapped his big meaty hands together, letting out a short laugh.

"Take a drive with me."

And with that, Danny was shown the door of his own flat, taken down the stairwell to the front passenger seat of an Audi and driven off into the early morning light.

The buildings of Central London were whipping by at seventy miles an hour. At around five in the morning, the sun was already extending light and benevolence into the June sky, making this particular joyride almost a pleasant one.

The burning in the palm of his hand was a simple refrain that was anchoring Danny to the gravity of his situation. Right now, sat in the car next to Harkness, the pull seemed to be getting heavier by the second.

The big copper had not said a word since firing up the engine of the car and taking off like he was piloting in a rally championship.

And now here they were heading towards London's West End theatre district at 100 and illegal miles an hour.

Harkness finally broke the silence.

"I love the sound of a great, dirty big engine telling the world to fuck right off...don't you Danny? Or are you too full of questions right now to appreciate the Vorsprung durch Technik? Tell you what, just sit back and enjoy the revs, Mr Felix."

And with that, Harkness pushed the accelerator even flatter to the floor, and now the Marylebone Road was flashing past them, Harkness stealing only glances at the road while staring at the side of Danny's face. Even at this time of the morning and despite the traffic on the London thoroughfare, Harkness handled the German car like a pro. To a chorus of horns and gesticulations only glimpsed in the rear view mirror the car blew every red light between Tottenham Court Road and Baker Street. Traffic cameras flashed like paparazzi as they went, but his driver didn't seem to mind, and as they climbed the elevated section of the road, Danny could have sworn they would take off as they crested the rise. And as they did, Harkness let out what can only be described as a feral howl, filling the interior of the car with noise and his breath.

Just eight minutes later they reached an exit off the dual carriageway leading to a cluttered industrial estate that sat cheek by jowl with rows upon rows of council high rises, a journey that at the wrong time of day could take the guts of an hour. But now they were slowing.

The Audi found its way to the gate of a construction site where a new set of high-rise somethings were emerging from the scrabbly ground. Flashier, classier, the latest part of this city to get the gentrification treatment.

The car came to a rest.

"Out." Barked like he was talking to a dog.

As they stood in front of a gate at the entrance to the site, Harkness motioned for Danny to go through first. As they walked, Harkness talked.

"Cities are amazing things aren't they Danny? Living. Breathing. Constantly changing. Refreshing themselves in the image of some corporation or billionaire developer at the skyline, while the little man does what he can with his shop front or a window box hanging off a shitty flat at street level.

"What cities don't do is stand still. If you do you might as well die my fine young thief. Orders change, circumstance shifts and that is why we were supposed to meet. Today."

Harkness had Danny's attention. Fuck knows he had got it from the moment he had walked into his flat. But this crazy bastard gave him the feeling that if you were to just write him off you would be doing so at your peril.

Danny took this moment to take him in again, assessing the man who was jerking his chain like the owner of a puppy at a behaviour class.

Harkness was big, yes, but not bulky or fat. He was

just...big. He looked cut from granite, standing there, all six foot something of him, broad in the shoulders but with a head that still managed to look too big for his body. He might even have been considered handsome, except at the last minute the head size robbed him of that particular gift. He had a wide flat face that was perhaps a touch Slavic or Eastern European, but his accent was pure London. His hair was all swept back and dark, no greying, not even at the temples.

And then there were his eyes.

That was what bothered Danny the most. The eyes were dark with big wide pupils. They looked like they were dilated, almost devoid of an iris, just deep dark pools of 'God knows what' potential.

No doubt. This was a crazy bastard in front of Danny now, but one that you had to handle with care.

"And so, Danny, just like this great city of ours, the part you play in its rambling, rumbling history is about to change."

They were now at the foot of one of the new high-risers, walking around it to an expanse behind, where an area about the size of a house had been staked out on the ground. Next to it a cement truck, its round body gently turning, a load obviously sliding around within.

"This will, when it is done, be a security station, a place for small men in blue uniforms to sit in and watch TV and get fat, all so that the wealthy homeowners who will fill up this space can feel safe at night. Yes, a security hut, but a fucking fancy one mind, all CCTV and alarm systems going full pelt. What better place to secure one's own, changing future?"

They were looking down into the ditches now, the cuts in the ground that would receive the foundations for this outbuilding. Trepidation was building in

25

Danny's always-to-be-trusted gut. Was he about to meet a clichéd, cement bath end? For pulling a bank van job? Had he stepped on some kind of organised crime toes? Upset some Eastern European gang? His mind raced through the possibilities as fast as a synapse can snap, but no, he couldn't come up with a reason for being executed.

Harkness grabbed Danny's shoulder, interrupting his mental checklist. They were now face to face, the tall copper looking into him with those eyes. He spoke gently, almost in a whisper as if worried someone might overhear them.

"Now, Danny, what we found at your gaff earlier. Not a bad little haul, one might say, enough for all of us. The word is that you are excellent at what you do. I like excellence. Whether it is in my wine, my football team or my women: I like excellence. And that little pile of money pretty much proves your reputation of having a cracking set of light fingers.

"So here is your future. You are now working for me. We will treat the wallpaper as my consultation fee, as I guide you to bigger and better things. Don't worry about paperwork and red tape. Every single copper who ruined your sparse abode this morning also works for me. I say the word, and stuff gets forgotten, or lost...or both.

"So welcome to your new life son. I know most people hate change, they resist it. But the ones that do, often they are the ones who don't make it in their own cities. But I can help you and you can help me, this change will be good for us both...you'll soon see.

"A wise man once said, "All great changes are preceded by chaos"...well, Danny, here we are. I. Am. Your. Chaos."

Harkness accompanied his last words with a big meaty hand on the back of Danny's neck, jostling his head at each syllable.

A black Ford Transit van crept across the site towards them, pulling up alongside them. Two men got out and went around the back to open the doors of the van.

"And just so that you know that I am very serious, and indeed, committed to our future together, Danny Felix, I thought I would give you something, a little signing on gift...so you wouldn't doubt my sincerity."

And at that the two men came from behind the van, each carrying a body on their shoulders, heading straight to the foundation trench that was directly beside the cement lorry.

Harkness guided Danny by the neck over towards the same spot, only letting go when the two heavy lifters had caught up with them.

And there it was: the reason for the anxiety in Danny's oh-so-ever-reliable gut. He couldn't keep the shock off his face, as the two bodies were unceremoniously flopped into the dug-out channel, landing face up, blank-eyed and staring.

Danny was now looking at the recently deceased bodies of Janusz Piesakowska and Frankie Nelson, the two men who had most recently helped him rob a cash-in-transit van. Both had been garroted, blood had cascaded all down their fronts, eyes still bulging from sadistically brutal deaths.

Dragging his gaze from his two ex-partners Danny looked over to where Harkness was standing by the cement lorry.

"You see? I'm very serious about the pursuit of excellence. I'll be in touch soon, Danny."

And with that Harkness pulled a lever on the big cement truck and its contents began to pour onto the staring corpses.

4

✧ Little'un ✧

Just before entering the ward Christine Chance went to the ladies loo.

After splashing a little water onto her face, she gripped the sides of the sink and took a long, deep breath as she raised her eyes to meet her face in the mirror.

She looked tired. But that was no surprise. Crows feet were just beginning to make their presence known around her clear, green eyes to add to her exhaustion. Her mousy blonde bob framed her almond-shaped face, a face that was once quick to light up with a smile, but now wore a heaviness that was nothing to do with her job and all to do with the fact that she felt daunted.

She pulled herself up to her full five foot nine inches and in her head she counted to ten.

It was this way every time for her. One last attempt to steady herself before facing her fears.

It was, now, very late at night, but the nurses had long ago worked out what she did for a living (her daughter had helped here) and so never seemed to mind that her visiting hours bore no relation to any kind of common sense. She was never challenged, never asked to leave or given even so much as an odd look. Sometimes, when her child was having a rough day, Christine had wished they would stop her at the heavy rubberised doors, but that had never happened.

CC made her way to the furthest corner of the small ward. The rectangular room housed just five beds, five souls waiting for their last step into whatever next life they chose to believe in.

And there, in a bed that at once seemed regular size but now appeared giant by the way it dwarfed its occupant, lay Christine's daughter, Shauna Elizabeth Chance. The bed only seemed to swamp Shauna because of how frail she had become. This was the most telling sign, in Christine's mind at least, of just how ravaged her child was by her cancer. She had once been a vibrant, joyous kid. She loved music, dancing and, much to Christine's constant surprise, WWE wrestling.

But what had started as an achy back that they had both put down to a camping trip with friends, turned out to be something much more sinister and invidious.

Shauna's breathing was shallow, raspy but regular. The 11-year-old was asleep in a chemically-enhanced haze. Machines gently monitored and beeped, keeping track of the decline that Christine knew was accelerating.

It was in these quiet moments, that CC's mind wandered to thoughts of what was right and wrong, what seemed fair and unjust. How did you measure a life? And how could it be endangered when it had only really just begun? To Christine, her daughter's slow and undoubtedly painful trek to this point in life, where a cancer called Ewing Sarcoma had closed its fist around her spine and clenched, seemed a fate that should only be reserved for the worst of mankind, not a child.

And when those thoughts and feelings crept up on her, it was then that she felt the worst pangs of guilt, hurt, and the anticipation of loss. But she also realised that what she really felt was anger.

Angry with her daughter, angry with the world, angry with nature, angry with God.

This girl, her little girl was now being toyed with by cancer, making her dance to a tune of pain.

At first she had prayed that it would be all okay. God's good, it'll all be fine, the doctors will find a way. And Christine had needed to believe it. Needed to know that by being a good person, daughter, mother, copper you made a difference.

But as time and the cancer marched on, she felt foolish for hoping. And that led her to anger.

And what could she do about it? What could anyone do about it?

Nothing.

Deal with that, CC girl, she thought to herself.

And while she tried to reason with herself, Christine sat there and listened. Every beep, each ragged breath, soon realising that she was holding her own until the next vital intake, however weak.

Movement in the bed, a flutter of papery eyelids.

Shauna was awake.

"Mum, is that you?"

"Hiya, sweetheart. Here at some crazy hour as usual."

"I don't mind, Mum."

"Want to move up the bed? I can get those pillows a little higher?"

They did it together; Christine feeling how little there was left of her now as she helped Shauna into a sitting position.

"What's the latest? Catch any bad men today?"

It never failed to surprise Christine at just how much Shauna loved to chat about her police work. Most girls her age wanted to talk about celebrity gossip, the male nurses, or pop stars. But Shauna never seemed to tire of her Mum's latest news.

And Christine obliged with a child friendly version of the days events. And Christine felt better for it, they both did. Certainly easier than conversations about chemo or surgical options (of which they were running out or simply there were none) and newfangled drugs that no-one could afford (there were tons).

When the day's news had been talked out, Shauna motioned to the drawer of her dresser.

"That male nurse, the tall one. He gave me something today, look in the top drawer."

Christine reached over and into the drawer, pulling out a newspaper.

It was folded to a double page spread with a big photo of Shauna's favourite boy band at its centre.

"That was nice of him, love. A whole page dedicated to your favourites, and their shirts seemed to have disappeared! I'm not sure this is suitable for a young mind like yours!"

"Mum! Stop being a weirdo! And look at the other page; I spotted it ages after Keith the nurse gave it to me."

Christine flipped the page to another double spread story. There was a huge photo leading the editorial line.

The shot had been taken from a long way off, so it was grainy but clear enough to make out the shape of several men prone on the ground with a lot of other people around them. The peaked caps with black and white chequers on them singled out the police easily enough. The men on the ground were, logically, the baddies, prone on the ground and in the papers under a headline that declared:

GROUNDED! Heathrow Haul Record As Cops Foil Huge Drug Deal

Looking closely at the shot, Christine realised, with a little surprise, that she could see herself in the foreground. Not that anyone could have instantly recognised her, but she knew her own time and place, and she had definitely been there.

She looked at Shauna

"I thought that was you up front, but I couldn't be sure."

"Well, it is me but this stuff is supposed to just happen and fly under the radar."

"I knew I was right...but anyway, back to the nurse. He was asking all about you...I think he thinks you're sexy!"

"Shauna Chance!"

The exclamation full of mock indignation prompting a fit of giggles from both of them.

"Well just, you know, saying. He has nice eyes."

"Enough, you, you'll be getting both of us into trouble. And anyway, what would I want with a man, they're just hassle."

"Yeah, but fit hassle and anyway, they love me in here, I can get away with loads."

Christine immediately felt sad when her daughter said this. And Shauna fleetingly felt it too, so no need to go there. Not tonight. Being a cancer ward's best customer was never a title to be aspired to.

Tiredness finally hit Christine like a heavyweight in the third round. Trying to stifle her yawn, Shauna knew instantly what was happening, and before CC could protest her kid was starting to tell her goodnight.

"Go on, get some sleep Mum, we can talk more in the morning."

CC nodded. "I'll be in tomorrow, we need to talk doctors and stuff, find out the latest."

Shauna dropped her eyes to her chest, and agreed softly, before adding: "Will you get another gold star, commendation thingy? For the airport job?"

"There's talk."

"And you still won't go along…"

"Who needs gold stars, eh?"

"I like them. I get to keep them in my shoebox, with the others and old teddies and stuff."

"G'night Shauna. Love you". A kiss on the forehead

"G'night Mum, love you too…I'll tell Keith the tall nurse you said hello."

CC waved her comment off, and walked away from the bed, feeling like she was on the end of a string, like a yo-yo, spinning away as far as possible, only to shoot back on herself again as fast as the pull of the string allows.

Danny looked into her eyes. Green-flecked with hazel, they radiated so much emotion, more, he thought, than any other he had known. Belonging as they did to one of the few people he trusted, these eyes gave him a sense of calm, as though nothing could rock or blow him off whatever course he might be set upon. The irony of this was not lost on Danny seeing as he knew Celeste rarely approved of any of his courses, and now was no exception.

Mind you, what would you expect from your big sister?

"Bloody hell, Danny, I hate it when you do that!" slapping him on the chest as she said it.

Danny did like appearing in her kitchen when she least expected him to, standing there enjoying the aroma of fresh coffee and toast, the table bearing the aftermath of a breakfast enjoyed by two kids and a husband who had already left for school and whatever it was he did in the big city firm.

As he silently let himself in through the back door, his sister had been stood with her back to him, staring intently at her Blackberry, her thumbs a blur over the small keyboard.

Growing up, people were always mistaking them as twins, when in fact Celeste had three years on him. She was tall and dark haired like Danny. She moved with the same gamine fluidity he did. Now an executive mum with a high powered job and high maintenance kids, Danny thought she was amazing, while she thought he was still a kid like her own two.

Except this big kid had a taste for trouble.

Celeste was just about the only remnant of his family Danny cared about. When Danny was with her, he was glad to be there, even if she was judging him, lecturing him or both at the same time.

"Danny, I hate it when you creep up on me…and where have you been? You look like shit." Then a manicured finger in the air. "Don't answer that, I don't want to know…"

"I had some unexpected visitors."

Her eyes instantly widened.

"Were you arrested? What are you in to now, for Christ's sake?"

Danny only shook his head in reply, and pointed his finger in the direction of the coffee pot.

She took the hint, grabbing a mug and pouring.

"I haven't got long, I have to be at the office for nine. What is going on?"

"I have made some new friends, and I am not sure I like them. I just came to pick something up."

Celeste was now puzzled, her eyebrow arched.

"What? From your old things you left in the garage about two years ago?"

Celeste had often marvelled at Danny's habit of moving flat about once every year, sometimes helping with interim storage, sometimes not, if she was in one of her "I don't approve of your life choices" moods.

"Who are these people, Danny? What kind of a fuck up are you setting up for yourself?"

The pitch of her voice rose in tandem with her sense of alarm.

"I do just fine Celeste, my life is my own...I am not like you, I was not built for all...of this"

Danny gestured to the room, house...the family home.

"I do just fine, don't measure me by your standards, sis."

They both knew they were spiralling towards a very familiar argument, one which neither liked, but felt strongly enough to dig their heels in over. Danny tried to head it off.

"I just need to get into your garage."

"It's not locked, but you already know that, let yourself in, you do most other places..."

"Come on, sis...don't be like that."

A pause fattened between them, both circling their love for one another as well as their frustrations. Celeste broke first.

"Dad was asking for you..."

"Really? I'll write the date down. I don't know how you can even talk to that old man."

"DANNY!"

The tensions threatened to build again so he turned on his heel, making for the utility room door that led to the garage.

Once in there, he didn't need the assistance of the overhead lights to locate what he was looking for, lifting up his sister's beloved treadmill from the front end, reaching underneath.

His fingers soon located the black leather pouch he had sequestered there nearly 18 months previously.

He unzipped it and checked its contents, satisfied and turned on to go, only to bump straight into his sister, who, it seemed could be as quiet on her feet as he was.

She reached up instinctively to cushion the impact of their collision, her hand pressing the black leather pouch flat against Danny's midriff. What she felt there caused her eyes to widen, shock flash across her face, replaced by fury in the very next instant.

"DANNY, IS THAT WHAT I FUCKING THINK IT IS!?"

"I have to go, sis, it's just a tool of the trade and a little money. They cleaned me out...I'm sorry."

He was brushing past her now, trying to get out before the storm of her ire really hit, and God did she know how to get angry.

Mind you, who could blame her? How many sisters with small kids would be that happy about a Glock 19 handgun holding 17 rounds and a spare clip being stored in the garage?

5

✧ Due Dilligence ✧

A few, unsettling days had passed since Danny had walked away from Harkness. Unsettling was the right word, in fact the only word, simply because everything else around him seemed so unchanged and normal.

Danny had a lot of thinking to do as he made his way through a Central London evening.

Harkness had left him to find his own way back home from the building site - The Big Cop and his mates seemed to instantly lose interest in him and just drove away.

Once back at his small flat, Danny was amazed to find that while all the walls had been stripped back and the money gone, the flat had actually been left tidy.

Life seemed to trundle on. No strange cars in the street, no catching half glimpses of a face, a shadow sent to keep an eye on Harkness' newest acolyte...you know, just to make sure that a disappearing act was not imminent.

No, Danny was not being followed. Nor was there any sign in the papers or the broadcast news about his recently, dearly departed collaborators, Frank and Janusz.

Life was unnervingly quiet in Danny's opinion. Of the three basic, instinctual human reactions to trauma: fight, flight or freeze…he couldn't find any great enthusiasm for any of them. He reckoned if he tried flight, Harkness would somehow know where to look. He seemed a resourceful type. As for freeze, well Danny Felix would never allow himself to be much of a panicker.

God knows he had been in enough high stress situations to know his own heart and mind, and they had never thus strayed to flapping or fluster.

As for fight? Well, now that was the trickiest of options.

Danny was not a traditionally violent man. He felt that sometimes force could be a useful tool; more precisely he knew that the threat of implied or impending violence could be just as good and way more efficient as the act itself. But then again on some occasions a fist, a flash of blade or at the worst the bang flash wallop of a discharged sawn-off was the only way left to go.

Not that he was against killing someone if they got in the way. Danny didn't much like people. They had an unerring way of letting you down in almost any situation. But equally he felt that if you resorted to killing, it must be a sign that you were not fully prepared in the first place, or you were trying to steal something so big, that the lives lost outweighed the pay off.

Fighting unknown quantities was simply nothing short of stupid, Danny thought. Know who it is you are about to slap. Know how they like to slap back. Know where they least want and expect to be slapped. Due diligence, see? Preparation was, as with every job, crucial. What was that irritating phrase that boring people who did boring jobs used? Fail to prepare… prepare to fail. That was it. Now if someone ever used that phrase to your face, then you'd just go ahead and slap them straight away. What would a man who used handy phrases like that ever have in his locker to hurt you with?

Danny preferred his wisdom a little more elegiac. Like Connery in *The Untouchables*, with his Scottish growl proclaiming "The Chicago Way". "They come at you with a fist, you go after them with a bat. They pull out a knife, you pull a gun," or something like that anyway. Connery, stealing every scene he's in, despite his Scottish/Irish brogue mash up, putting a much younger Costner to shame.

Well, Danny Felix had developed his own Chicago Way, the Felix Way and it all starts with due diligence. Ask a few questions, the right queries put to the right people and you had something to conjure with.

Not that Danny was preparing for all out war with Inspector Harkness.

Not right out the gate anyway.

If he was honest, Harkness was intriguing. Danny didn't think he'd ever heard of this copper. That made him an interesting quantity straight away. But, he had to admit, Harkness had burst upon the scene in the most colourful of ways. He had made sure his agenda was set out with some panache. Danny had liked Frank. Janusz he tolerated because of his skill set, but he wasn't married to them, so when they turned up all glassy eyed and limp at the building site, he hadn't been heartbroken…more surprised. No mean feat for one member of the criminal fraternity to surprise another, even if this member was a gamekeeper with aspirations of poaching.

So the mystery had to be unravelled a little, the unknown quantity had to become a known one. Questions asked and hopefully answered. Which meant a trip to see Dexy.

In London, the saying goes that you are never more than 50 feet from a rat. In some parts of the city though, Danny figured you could probably revise that estimate down to about ten feet. Especially in the centre of the city, where tourists, trannies, showbiz agents, media luvvies, prossies, actors, pickpockets, pimps, publishers, drug dealers and even the odd copper all rub shoulders: Soho. Danny loved it.

Clubs and coffee shops now festooned what used to be the most luridly colourful section of the bustling, busy West End. Peep shows and strip bars had been marginalised, but the underbelly still existed...just in a much more stylishly acceptable way. Soho had gentrified. But not completely.

And Dexy's place was a perfect case in point.

From the outside Dexy's is just a door. An anonymous looking door, but one that leads to a place where people gather. They talk, eat, drink, carouse and complete all manner of transactions, some financial, some sexual and even some political. Whatever your trade, if you can afford the membership or have a special arrangement with the owner, then Dexy's will open its door to your knock. A private members club where the management are as discreet as the clientele are varied.

Danny Felix approached the door, pushing the button on the security system and hearing the buzz and click as the entrance to this furtive wonderland opened for him.

Inside the décor was just the first of many talking points. The walls were plain coloured but finished with velvet. The art was like a greatest hits collection of the bright new young things on the market, with the paintings, etchings and hangings refreshed regularly due to the never ending sway of fashion.

The bar and restaurant were dotted with battered old leather sofas that still manage to take the weight of even the most indulgent of members.

Dexy's had an air of informal opulence. Despite their proximity, the seating areas all managed to dull the confidential chatter. The velvet walls absorbed the sound of even the most delicate of conversations.

Even the toilets prove a bohemian surprise, with the velvet walls replaced with a collage of nudes, both male and female, engaging in everyday activities, just without the aid of clothing. Danny had only clocked what made the pattern on his umpteenth visit and when he did he had laughed out loud, drawing an askance look from the city gent next to him.

But the real surprise about Dexy's was that it had been created and maintained by filthy, rotten drug money.

Dexy, the owner, was not really called Dexy of course. It was a nickname from back in the day when money was to be made by delivering the intoxicant of choice to the rich, famous or just plain fabulous. After a very early brush with the law in daylight hours Dexy had sworn to only ever to deliver after midnight... hence the nickname was born, after the eighties pop band: Dexy's Midnight Runners.

And Dexy's business had boomed, investments were made until enough cash had been generated and, in turn, laundered to buy some respectability and fulfil a vision. A vision of a members club where the customer could come and get just about anything they wanted or achieve whatever they needed to whether legal or not. And all in an air of polite sophistication away from the prying eyes and ears of the outside world.

"Monsieur Felix, what a pleasure to see you again."

Francois, the maitre d', had long eyelashes, snake hips and an appetite for young men of questionable virtue. He liked Danny. And he endlessly impressed by knowing every member by name.

"Will you be dining with us? The Sea Bass is exquisite this evening."

"Not tonight, Francois. But I would like a quiet word with you know who..."

This was greeted with the arch of an exquisitely manicured eyebrow. "Let me see..."

Francois flicked through a leather bound diary he produced from small drawer in front of him.

"Hmmm...company. Let me slip a note through. You might be lucky. Have a drink at the bar and I will let you know."

Danny moved through to his favourite room in the club. He loved the fact that the bar was like a celebration of every type of alcoholic endeavour man had ever applied himself to creating. Aged whiskeys rubbed shoulders with speciality bourbons, the relative young contenders on the hard liquor block. Absinthe, gin, designer vodkas and brandies that were as rare as they were expensive, all draped in soft lighting that allowed their myriad, shimmering hues to splash the walls and ceiling in the kind of light that makes you want to drink whether you need to or not. Danny had always thought that if you arranged the lighting and atmosphere right in a bar then it would be as effective as a siren song, beckoning you onto the rocks of boozy ruin. This was one call he found easy to indulge.

Making his way between sofas draped with a Member of Parliament, several models and an aging movie star Danny had once quite liked, he approached the bar. The MP was in conversation with a particularly notorious entrepreneur who had managed to be linked to a huge counterfeit money scam. While damning evidence had never materialised, the whiff of suspicion had never quite dissipated either.

"Sir?"

"High West Whiskey please, a double..."

"And one ice cube as usual?"

Danny nodded, impressed that the Croatian bar tender had remembered correctly. Mind you, Danny remembered her too, especially the thick dark hair, and the grey eyes.

His reverie was cut short by a polite cough just behind him. A waitress.

"Monsieur Felix, Francois would like to invite you to go upstairs in exactly five minutes."

A few sips and exactly five minutes later, Danny was climbing the stairs leading to a dark red door at the very top of the townhouse. This, he knew, led to a private apartment set into what had once been the attic of the building. Now, it was a very private space, one that only a few could get into, and he was one of them.

The door opened and a young, lean bodied man exited, all dark eyes and designer shirt and jeans, looking a little flushed of face.

"Danny Felix..." was the soft call from beyond the door. Danny stepped through to see Dexy.

"Danny, Danny, Danny...if I had known you were coming I would have changed my plans...but, as you may have noticed, I have just put one out...as it were."

Danny couldn't help but smile at Dexy. Here she was in her ultra smart private apartment sat on top of the mini empire built on the strength of London's predilection for white powder, whacky backy and pill-popping.

Dexy was the kind of woman you noticed. Just turned 50, six feet tall, red haired and Amazonian with a temper to match. She had as much street savvy as you could ever wish to pack into one human being. Danny found her bewitching, but then just about every man who ever entered Dexy's orbit could not fail but be entranced. You would never describe her as beautiful, but her face was one that had character in every pore. High cheekbones down to a chin that was a little too long. Some light acne scarring on her cheeks, with eyes that were just a little too far apart. But for some reason she fascinated Danny, always had done, like the actress Cate Blanchett. Not beautiful, no, but undeniably attractive.

"Now, Dexy, behave. We haven't 'seen' each other for a long time, and anyway, I know you like them younger and prettier than me nowadays."

Dexy tilted her head back and closed her eyes, smiling softly at a memory. "Yes, but you know me Danny, I like rarities and you as I recall would be a most welcome return fixture. A bit like a grand vintage car...polished, smooth...a beautiful ride."

"Hey hey...less of the vintage, I'm only in my late twenties." Mock outrage on his face, Danny moved to her, kissing her on both cheeks, trying not to let his gaze fall to the gape in her silk dressing gown, loosely tied around her waist.

A laugh from her, caused Danny to have his own flashback. He had always found her cut glass English accent with it's huskiness at the edges one of the most alluring things about her.

"And so, Mr Felix, why have you beaten a path to my door this evening?"

Without his asking she had started to pour Bourbon for him, sliding a single ice cube into the crystal tumbler as she waited for him to answer.

"I need to do a little digging, and I know you are always an excellent place to start."

Dexy was lifting a television remote control, flicking a wall mounted LCD into life. Images from her members club below appeared on the screen.

"Isn't that a Minister from Her Majesty's Treasury talking to Fake Freddie? I knew things were bad on the economic front, but really?"

Danny smiled, knowing that she was waiting for him to tell her why he was here.

"Dexy, I seem to have picked up a new friend, maybe an unwarranted friend, and the thing is, I have never come across him before."

"Are we talking a colourful character or a serious man in a blue uniform, darling?"

"Well that's just it, a bit of both. The name is Detective Inspector Harkness."

Dexy's face clouded for a spilt second, before recovering. Danny clocked it, but said nothing, waiting for this woman who knew just about all that you needed to know about London's trickier side of life to share her own thoughts.

Her eyes met his over the rim of her champagne glass.

"Ahhh, Detective Inspector James Harkness…a relatively new addition to the ranks of ambitious boys in blue. Now, how have you managed to catch his eye, Danny? Let me wrack my brain for a second."

She stared off into the plush curtains that decorated her window onto Soho life, a smile playing at the corners of her lips.

"A cash replenishment van, about two weeks ago. You poured petrol over the guard as he came out of the van, and stepped back while you levelled a gun at him in one hand and smoked a cigar in the other until he handed the bag over."

Danny spread his hands wide, sitting down on a chaise longue as he did so.

"I couldn't possibly comment, madam."

"Harkness really is fresh meat, but I hear his star is rising at a phenomenal rate. He is, well, let's say... enthusiastic."

"He knew a lot about me, which I never like."

"Oh, darling, someone been chatting? Not like you. I don't know an awful lot about your new admirer, but that is easily rectified. What I do know is that some of his colleagues think he is a little...unorthodox?"

"What? They suspect he is dirty?"

"No, I don't think it's that, rather they consider him to be an individualist. He likes to accelerate the game plan whether anyone else is strapped in or not."

Danny flashed back to London buildings whizzing passed the car window with Harkness howling his feral cry.

"That I can believe. So, can you help me with my due diligence Dexy? You know me, I never like surprises unless they come packaged with red hair holding a glass of Tattinger."

Dexy liked the compliment, he knew, and she would help him, but first:

"Of course I will take a closer look at Harkness for you. But maybe, in return, you can do a small favour for me."

Danny sipped his drink, feeling the dark brown heat in his throat.

"We have a member here, she is about to enter a new phase of her life; Music deal, high profile TV presence, probably a candidate for the 'Nation's Next Sweetheart' etc, etc. Problem is, and it is a particularly twenty first century problem, she was a little cavalier in her private life before this new found success."

"I dread to think...has someone got a little souvenir of their time with this starlet?"

"Exactly, a moving picture type souvenir, and he

seems to be intent on grabbing his opportunity for mischief. You can imagine the kind of upset this might cause our friend here. She has the chance of a fabulous period in her life. Do you think you could find a way to acquire this mini movie for us, if I were to point you to its director?"

"It would be impolite to refuse, Dexy, especially as you have asked so graciously and you know I love the movies."

"Excellent. The subject of the film is a young talent called Honey Sister, her real name is…"

Danny cut her off "Sarah Grimes. I read the papers Dexy, I couldn't have not seen her picture in the last month or so."

"Yes and her former flame is one Barry Blount, a reality TV star whose '15 minutes' was more like three and they are very definitely up. The footage is about two years old, but can still pack a heavy punch for our Honey."

"A reality TV muppet? It will be a pleasure to make his acquaintance."

"Thank you Danny. Francois will slip you his where-abouts as you leave. And now, I must get dressed and ready myself to press the flesh in my humble little club here. It has been a pleasure to see you again."

And with that Dexy slid her arms around Danny's neck, whispered good night in his ear and kissed him slowly, fully on the lips.

Danny could still taste the sweet, heady mix of lipstick and champagne as he descended the stairs back into main part of the townhouse.

6

✧ A Day's Work ✧

"I shouldn't even be talking to you! I mean really, who wears a yellow tie with a pink shirt!?"

The policeman in charge of the interview blushed as he looked down at his tie.

It wasn't every day that CC's colleagues interrogated a grown man wearing an electric blue lycra catsuit festooned with diamante. The shiny fake diamonds cascading down the front in supposed random order until they gathered near the waistline to form a shimmering arrow pointing at the owners' groin.

But then this was no everyday snitch.

His name was Fisty, a surprisingly talkative drug dealer enjoying some enforced Metropolitan Police hospitality. But the panic his invitation to the police station had generated lead to a tip off that set CC and her Old Bill colleagues onto a job that had now been running for four days.

Fisty had been eager to ease some of his own troubles, through a little chat about other people's, especially as his friendly, arresting officer had told him that they had proof one of his pills had caused the death of 16-year-old schoolgirl. Her face had laughed hauntingly from the front of the newspapers for a whole week. She had been found dead in the bathroom of her best friend's house after a party to celebrate the end of exams. What should have been the start of her future turned out to be a full stop.

The part about proof of a link to the girl's sad exit was all a huge dollop of make-believe suggested by Christine Chance. Fisty fell for the hook, the line and the sinker. CC had suspected that Fisty liked his own product as much as some of his customers did, and so might have just enough of that paranoid edge to panic at the first sound of a jailer's set of keys. And panic he had.

The interview with Fisty had been like a Shakespearean soliloquy, a babbling litany of "he said this", "he did that", "she knew him" and "that's stashed there". Enough leads for an entire division of Old Bill to work on for a month. But one scrap of info had leapt out at the interviewing officers, simply because it featured the name of what officialdom liked to call 'a person of particular interest'.

Ignatius Adesina, a Nigerian, a giant of a man.

He was a suspect in 15 separate reported incidents and, Christ, did these incidents read like a Quentin Tarantino script.

The worst, a robbery and aggravated assault with a deadly weapon had made CC's stomach turn when she read the witness accounts: suspect enters a Chinese restaurant with a machete and threatens the staff until he is able to access a back room where about 20 Chinese nationals are in the middle of a high stakes poker match. All highly illegal of course, but a lucrative takeaway if you can manage to exit the building in one piece. The robber had 'convinced' the players to let him leave by casually lopping off one of their hands with one fell swoop of his butcher sharpened blade and then scalping a second when he tried to raise out of his chair.

The robber had been fully ski-masked-up, but had forgotten his hands. Specifically he had forgotten to cover a tattoo of a snake coiling around his middle finger, the head seemingly poised to bite the finger-nail. Ignatius had been arrested, along with a few other local stars of a similar nature, about 24 hours later and questioned at length. Once in the nick the arresting officer noted that Iggy's right hand was bandaged up. It soon revealed a burn that could only have been attributed to lowering a finger into sulphuric acid and as the police had no photos of Iggy's hands prior to this unfortunate accident, there was nothing to connect the six foot ten inch berserker to the crime. Plus his sister gave him a cast iron alibi; he was at home with her and her two sons watching the Eurovision Song Contest at the time of the job. Iggy, a fan of Europop? Yeah, as if. Still it gave CC a buzz to think they might get behind such a dangerous player so soon after he'd figuratively given them the finger…

Fisty was telling tales like a penitent sinner on speed, saying that Iggy had been to see him. He had wanted a reference for a muscle man who had looked out for Fisty during a testing time of his life. Could the muscle be trusted? Could he handle himself? Was he any good when tooled up? Because, for the job Iggy had in mind, he would have to be, and soon-ish too because this opportunity was coming up fast.

And so now Christine and the rest of her team were out and about bouncing around different parts of north London at 5am on a June morning, with London traffic beginning to think about gearing up.

They'd been on the follow for about an hour, behind a white Ford Transit van driven by Adesina. CC was growing increasingly frustrated because Iggy seemed to be leading them on a merry dance and she needed to pee...like really badly.

Apart from stopping early in their journey to pick up some faces, the white Transit van had proceeded to do nothing but "dry clean" as the coppers called it. This entailed driving in a series of squares, backtracking on a route several times over to make sure that there was no following vehicle or faces that popped up repeatedly too many times in traffic.

None of this was new to the team but, still, avoiding being caught was a pain in the arse and meant everyone having to be on their toes for every second of the follow, making it weary work.

"I don't think this lot are going to go for it today, Freethy. Traffic will be too heavy for them soon."

Christine was on her mobile to her best friend and colleague, Detective Constable Mark Freeth. She knew better than to have informal chat over her two-way, since radio scanners were easy to come by and so it was deemed best to only use radio for formal operational chatter. Freethy was in one of her other follow cars.

"Agreed. I feel like a bleeding cabbie here, except fuck all chance of a tip at the end of it. I'll text the others."

"What are you up to, Iggy? What is it this time, my old china?" CC asking the question out loud to the emptiness of her car.

CC was definitely puzzled, a state of mind she didn't like. She retraced the morning's route over again in her mind looking for a pattern, a reason behind the zigzagging across the leafy suburbs. She became distracted, glancing at the map on the passenger seat beside her.

Christine looked up just in time. She had to slam on the brakes to avoid rear ending a van that had pulled out in front of her. A black van sitting low on its suspension and driving bang on the speed limit.

She took a breath; lucky no-one had been in the car with her to see the near accident, which would have been an office fine and a serious dose of banter from the others when they finally arrived back to base.

The van pulled off to the right into another street, when Christine's radio squawked.

"Seven seven seven, if you are still on Percy Avenue, heads up, suspect vehicle is turning into your road now."

'Seven seven seven' was Christine's call sign.

As indicated, Iggy was at the wheel of the white van pulling into the road ahead of her car, but travelling towards her on the opposite side. CC instantly signalled to turn left, feeling lucky there was a street into which to do so. Once she had turned, she knew she was in trouble, because she had entered a cul-de-sac. No matter, she was in it now and there were the other team cars slowly triangulating, handing the white van from one to the other, keeping it in visual contact.

CC pulled over to the kerb, spotting an alleyway between two houses that looked just about the perfect spot for a long needed pee.

Christine peed...and peed. God, it felt good, comfort at last returning to her insides, and a chance for a quick leg stretch too. It was one of the knacks of the job, knowing when and where to break off for a pee. It might sound odd, but she prided herself on her capacity to hold it and the knack of knowing just when to dive behind a bush and get it done. She had peed in the most incredible of places during her time on the job, once even using the rubbish chute in a block of flats when she just couldn't hold on any longer.

Heading back to the car she could hear the radio

chatter softly progressing, the white van had travelled in a big square and was heading back on itself yet again, repeating the route it had taken just as CC had to pull into this road. Jumping into her car, she executed a swift, but controlled 'J turn' and began to creep towards the mouth of the street. Just then, the black van she had nearly pranged just minutes earlier passed in front of the junction.

Killing her engine, Christine sat still for a moment. Her instincts were jangling, thoughts playing at the edge of her brain. There was a pattern. No, not a pattern, but a reason maybe?

What the fuck is going on?

"Alpha, Bravo…tighten to lead car now, please."

Alpha and Bravo were Christine's gunships, armed response officers who were close by but not fully involved in the direct follow. She would only call upon them to engage directly if events went from puzzling to action packed.

"Received."

Instinct told her it might be time to call the gunships closer to her radius. Why had she done that? Her experience told her she was on to something.

"Four oh five position?"

"Sutherland Avenue, westbound. About 100 yards off target."

"Five one five, position?"

"Parallel on Percy Avenue, westbound."

"Five one five, what other vehicles have you got visual on?"

"Seven seven seven, I have one milk float, a red Mercedes estate and a black Transit van."

"Ok received…"

"Seven seven seven, four oh five here, target turning left onto Casper Vale."

"Five one five, what can you see now?"

"The Merc is breaking every traffic law and swearing as he tries to pass the milk float..."

"The van?"

"Turning left onto...Casper Vale, what's on your mind here, guv?"

"Four oh five, target vehicle turning into a dead end street. Think it's a mews, can't see the street name. He's stopping I think."

Christine snatched up one of her maps...mews, mews, off Casper...

"There, Casper Villas Mews."

"Five one five here...turning onto Casper Vale...are you thinking what I'm thinking here?"

That's when she called it: "THEY ARE GOING TO GO GUYS...HEADS UP, HEADS UP."

Christine had just got it. There was no job site, but there was a job target. It was the black van. They had been following the van. Whatever the fuck it was doing, they were tracking it.

"Seven seven seven!! Seven seven seven!! Four oh five, ROBBERY! ROBBERY! ROBBERY!"

The Black van had pulled into the mews, and as it did Iggy's white van reversed sealing off the mouth of the small, closed off street. Instantly the side doors of both vans were pushed open, spilling three men from each, all of them carrying enough firepower to take out the entire street.

There were shouts now, expletives, barked orders, counter orders. Iggy crashed out of the driver's seat of the white Merc van, sprinting at full tilt to the cab of the black van.

The first cop cars sealed off Casper Vale blocking the main road, stopping unsuspecting early morning traffic from finding themselves in the middle of the O-fuckin-K Corral.

As CC arrived upon the scene so too did the

gunships, six armed officers. Five with sighted rifles scrambled to take cover behind their own vehicle, other members of the team doing the same. The sixth armed cop used a loud hailer to command the adrenalin-hyped robbers to cease and desist.

Bullets, shotgun pellets and foul language joined the calls for law and order, as the trigger happy outlaws began to realise just what a calamitous cluster fuck they now found themselves in. Christine knew that as soon as the armed response officers' amplified orders were noticed the bullets would start to fly in this direction.

Somewhere a dog was howling and sirens were screaming as more ordnance was dispatched between the two vans. What the hell had they stumbled onto here? The confusion quota was rocketing with the arrival of several local police cars, spilling greenhorn local yokels out onto the street, all of them eager to help out in what seemed to them a set piece from a Lethal Weapon film. And in the middle of it Christine could see the big Nigerian, Iggy, hammering at the front windscreen of the black van with the butt of a full-size shotgun, trying to convince the driver, who was not to be seen but was presumably playing dead under the front seat, that he should open up.

And at that moment one of Iggy's boys did a very strange thing - a full pirouette, falling to the ground at the rear of the white van. When CC saw a vibrant red flower blossom onto the front of the would-be robber's chest, she realised that the firearms boys had finally decided to settle to their dark work. They had nailed him just as he had sighted his automatic rifle on one of his rivals.

Another two shots rang out, and suddenly the clatter of metal on the ground could be heard, as the latter day gunslingers began to realise not only were they outmanoeuvred here, but they probably stood no chance against the Met's marksmen. In securing the mews as the perfect bag trap for their prey, Iggy's boys had also created a no win situation for themselves. They literally had nowhere to run to...except straight in to the London-blue cordon that now 'bottlecorked' the street.

And just as an eerie silence began to settle on the scene, Iggy came roaring, bellowing like a rutting stag, trying to cajole his cohorts back into action.

"COWARDS!! YOU FUCKING CHICKENS! COME ON!! WE CAN TAKE THESE POLEEECE BASTARDS."

Iggy had his shotgun pointed skyward, but as soon as he began to lower it, the gun cop with his loud hailer began ordering him to drop it and himself to the floor or else...

Iggy kept coming like a bull through a red cape. Then he made his mistake. He loosed off both barrels of his shotgun in rage, aiming at nothing in particular, and just as he popped the barrel in order to re-load, the local plod boys made their move. In what looked like the best bit of American Football action you are ever likely to see, three burly, pissed off cops were on Iggy like flies on dogshit.

To say that he batted them off in the same way as you might flick some fluff off your trousers would not be an exaggeration. All Christine could think was how the fuck are we going to bag this monster up?

More coppers flung themselves at the huge Nigerian like demons possessed.

The other gunmen who had dropped their weapons assumed the position on the ground. The older more experienced officers who recognised an arse kicking when they saw one, had held back from a tilt at Iggy to break out their handcuffs; the wisdom of age made CC smile.

Iggy finally succumbed when a resourceful young female officer clanged him full pelt with her telescopic baton across the backs of his knees. It did the trick, Iggy went down. The might of his bulk blunted.

And then it was over. More sirens joined the cause as the people wagons arrived to take away the suspects. Scientific investigations officers rolled up and crime scene tape began to be unravelled.

And finally Christine was able to satisfy her curiosity. She approached the back of the black Transit van, setting eyes on what Iggy had been so crazed to blag.

The back doors of the utility van were both wide open, and what a sight it was, prompting a slow exhalation of air from Christine Chance as she surveyed the interior. Black plastic bags, at least 30 of them, some spilling their contents onto the floor of the van.

Money. Lots and lots of it...

"It's a collection van..."

CC turned. It was her four oh five, Detective Constable Mark Freeth...Freethy to his mates.

"Iggy was being a naughty boy! He was thieving another naughty boy's stash...can only be drugs or prostitute money."

For the second time in as many weeks CC and her team had helped to deprive London's criminal underbelly of a record amount of what it loved most dearly.

Filthy lucre.

Letting out a low whistle, Christine turned to survey the remarkable scene, and in doing so was just in time to see Iggy being bundled into a custody transport. This thankless task was requiring the efforts of six uniformed locals.

CC laughed out loud for what must have been the first time in a very long time.

7

✧ Light-fingered,
Warm-hearted ✧

It was an exercise that Danny had begun when he was much younger and at first he had despised the task. Now he found it therapeutic. A sharpener that aided his thinking and brought him an almost zen-like presence of mind. What had begun as necessary self-education was now a cherished form of meditation.

Ranged in front of him on his kitchen table was a selection of newly bought locks. Two for doors, two padlocks, two window locks and one heavy duty D Ring lock for motorbikes. Danny was picking them one at a time, aiming for each one to surrender in under a minute.

All the while he was mulling over thoughts about his sister.

Danny always felt out of sorts after crossing swords with her.

Their perceptions differed; Celeste could never see what he could.

Danny felt the first tumbler inside the door lock he was working on shift to one side.

He knew instinctively when something didn't ring true. While others had their noses pressed against their own personal glass, Danny could always see the bigger picture. Mapping the consequences and outcomes was like breathing for him. He saw patterns in everything. Locks, families, society...everything.

And he knew that was why he and his siste clashed. Not simply because he had an unconventional lifestyle, he could admit that much, but because from his teenage years he had been able to divine that their family system was not all it could or should have been.

She couldn't distil the reality of her home life from her acceptance of it as normal. But Danny knew it was not. He could see it was a system built on control, not love.

Angling his second slim pick tool under the first he felt the second tumbler start to give.

The problem was his father.

Growing up, it was all Danny could do to be in the same house as him, never mind the same room. It wasn't that he was openly cruel to Danny or to his sister (although he was cruel and violent to them in private) but simply that he was supremely boring. Also, their home life was modelled in the image of the main man of the house.

Danny endured endless hours of just living; a mantelpiece-clock-tick of an existence. Routine ran everything. They ate at the same time every day. His parents watched the same shit TV every night. His father read the same newspaper. They all attended the same church and spent the same Sunday after-noons with the same relatives, talking in the same banal tones about the same shit...ALL THE FUCKING TIME.

Tumbler three and four now gave in to his pick's probing.

His Father was a bank manager. The purity of numbers and an unshakeable belief in Jesus Christ set the tone for how he approached everything in life, even fatherhood. Everything was ruled by order, symmetry, scripture and compliance. Emotion was frowned upon. To say home life was sterile would have been kind.

Danny's fingers slipped, the lock ejecting his two picks instantly. Bollocks.

Within this stifling atmosphere, Danny had grown up to be a model son: achieving the right test results, getting the right secondary school, and simply being an all round goody frigging two-shoes. And even now, after all these years, the memory of his early self made him angry.

Then his teenage years hit.

Danny felt a glint grow in his eye just about the same time he discovered a spot on his chin and a stray hair growing where none had appeared before.

Tumblers one, two and three gave way again.

The tipping point for his teenage self was seemingly innocuous. A trip to the cinema...but it was the film he saw that proved revelatory.

A film he and his mates were too young to be watching. Growing up in a religious household he had been fed the usual diet of Disney and *Ben-Hur*, never getting the chance to see anything even remotely challenging. Until one wet Saturday afternoon, on an illicit trip to Central London, they finished up at The Prince Charles Cinema off Leicester Square. He remembered being cold and as the ticket prices were cheaper than the big cinemas, in they all went.

The film changed Danny's life.

Sean Penn and Gary Oldman in their wilder days were in a totally absorbing and believable crime thriller called *State of Grace*. Penn was a man who leaves behind his not-so-healthy roots in New York's Hells Kitchen, then returns. Only this time he's an undercover cop, tasked with infiltrating the very criminals he left to get away from in the first place.

The story went off like a bell in Danny's head, a chime so clear he couldn't ignore it. Here was a man caught in a web that was constructed solely by his background and circumstance. Penn's inexorable journey to his tragic fate enthralled Danny...and informed him. The pattern of how past constructs present and tees up the future was screaming at Danny from the screen.

He would have to make the break in his own life.

The lock in his fingers sprang open. A glance at his stopwatch showed a minute and 28 seconds. He immediately snapped the lock closed and started again.

Looking back on it now, Danny could see that the film re-wired his brain. He began to look at the world, his world, in a very different way. Seeking out the patterns, systems, trails of emotional bread crumbs that could lead you back the way you came and help you to recognise where you might have turned left instead of right.

And because of his youthful outlook, Danny believed that if the system didn't serve you, then you should and could just change it. Most systems couldn't handle such simple subversion.

Danny's fingers were flowing now. In his head he could see a mental picture of the innards of the lock. It gave more easily. Time: one minute five seconds. He snapped it closed and started again.

His thoughts drifted again to his family. Young Danny resolved that he had to jolt his family system, give it cause to sit up and take notice. If he could jolt his father, light a little fire under the all consuming routine, he might help the whole family shift.

He hadn't just rebelled in one fell swoop. It was gradual, he remembered. A failed exam here, a homework left undone there. All the time trying to push for some sort of a reaction.

Nothing.

The most he got back was a shake of the head and a silence in return. Sometimes there would be a physical reaction, usually a beating carried out to the refrain of some hymn or bible passage. At that time Celeste began to take up the gauntlet of chastising him, just like she did now. But that was not the change he was after.

The stopwatch was reaching 40 seconds when the lock gave way. He repeated this process three more times, getting the lock finally to submit in less than 30 seconds.

Danny paused for a second, stretching his fingers out, feeling the sinews flex, the muscles relax.

The next lock.

Celeste had never forgiven him for how far he had taken things, never mind the fact that he was still going. The point she was missing was that their father's unmoveable spirit had led Danny to the very life he was now leading. No comeback had simply made the teenage Danny more determined. If he could buck the system it might be shown a better version of itself...a version that turned his father into Dad.

The willingness to challenge the status quo had blossomed in his brain like weeds in an untended summer lawn. The urge to rebel coincided with his other adolescent urges presenting an opportunity to really shake shit up. An opportunity in a very attractive form.

Angela Phillips was the hottest girl at Danny's ever--so-boring school.

She was known as 'The Untouchable Babe'.

She was the headmaster's daughter. That could put a dent in any boy's plans especially if the plans involved skipping school for a day of romance, fish and chips and a fumble in your front room. Angela travelled to and from school in the passenger seat of her Dad's Ford Sierra. It might as well have been an armoured transport for the amount of step-away-from-the teenage-girl menace that fact alone generated.

Plus, she had a boyfriend. An older boyfriend. From another school. An older boyfriend who no doubt carried an older boy's pair of fists. Neither Danny or his mates had ever laid eyes on him, but they all believed he existed and somehow this communicated to them that "older boyfriend" equalled "older minded activities". Ipso facto, Angela most definitely gave out on a serious scale. Hence...Angela was mysterious and dirty...the perfect combination.

And finally, the third and most important reason as to why Angela Phillips was the 'untouchable babe' was the fact that she was beautiful. Intimidatingly, drop dead, stop the traffic beautiful. Long hair, blue eyes and a laugh that lit up her face, the room and every teenage boy's loins for miles in every direction. All you had to do was to look at Angela to know...untouchable.

Except to Danny Felix. The new, fuck-every-convention Danny Felix.

He was laughing to himself. The locks were melting under his examination now, all of them in under a minute each. To push himself that extra mile he wanted to pick them one after another in under two minutes.

He had been pushed back then too, egged on by his friends and his own boundary breaking momentum. He knew he had to take a run at Angela Phillips.

And like that, his future had been sealed.

He just didn't know it.

"You are full of shit, Felix."

Not the most promising start to a flirtation. Nevertheless, Danny felt the fact that Angela Phillips was talking to him meant something.

"I'm telling you I can. I know the bouncers on the door."

"Hollywood's is an over-18 club, except for those stupid Sunday afternoon gigs for little kids."

"Listen, if you want to go to Hollywood's on a Saturday night with me, I can get us in this Saturday night. Simple and sweet as. I even have a fake ID."

"What's in it for me? Why should I go anywhere with you?"

"Cos...I'm fit...and no-one else round here can get you in to Hollywood's on a full-on Saturday night. And as far as I can see, no-one else round here is asking you. They all think you're untouchable. Up your own arse."

It was a gamble, saying that she had a reputation for thinking she was above everyone else but he figured he had nothing to lose.

"Hollywood's? On a Saturday? I don't believe you can get us in."

"I can get into anywhere I like, girl."

"Big words come cheap, mate. I tell you what, prove it to me. On Monday bring me something from somewhere impossible, proper proof of something and if you do, you can take me to Hollywood's next Saturday."

The course was set.

Danny remembered it all like it was yesterday, and

at the same time it felt like a lifetime ago. His stopwatch showed he was still over two minutes as he decided to take a final run at all of the locks in a row. Who was he kidding? He would keep going until it was easily under two minutes. He couldn't let a challenge lie, now or even way back then. Which is why he had gone as far as he had to try and impress Angela, and if he succeeded he might just kill the second bird with one stone.

Danny had thought about an ashtray from Hollywood's, but there was a problem. Every Sunday afternoon the nightclub was transformed into a throbbing youth club. Under-18 discos without a hint of alcohol or even dark corners. Reasonably, Angela could claim that he had simply attended with all the other loser kids and stolen the ashtray then.

Danny needed a game winner. And he thought he knew where he would find it.

At four in the morning.

Fourteen-year-olds are lithe.

Danny was living proof of it.

The kitchen window had been the way in. Old-fashioned fan lights topped the longer windows in the kitchen. And one fan light was open.

With the assistance of a gas bottle meant for the barbecue, Danny was able to mount the window sill, reach down through the open fan and, just about, reach the handle of the larger window underneath.

Dropping lightly to the kitchen floor, Danny began his search, looking gently but promptly, behind closed cupboards for his intended target. No joy.

Fuck.

He remembered his initial nerves as he registered he was still over two minutes in his current lock challenge. He was still slightly in awe of his own brass balls back then, just suddenly deciding that burglary was the logical way forward.

He had made his way through the downstairs, his confidence was growing by the second until he became aware of a low sound. A snore.

Sweeping his eyes across the gloom of the living room.

Second fuck.

A dog. A big one. Of some kind. Hard to make out exactly what.

The journey to the hallway had seemed to take forever. Every rustle of his clothes was freaking him out. He had been sure that any second now the dog would erupt in a show of barking and lights would go on all over this house and he would be left with crap in his pants and a tricky story to tell.

What Danny didn't know, was that the dog was called Napoleon and was 14-years-old. He was most certainly no longer lithe and to complete the set, he was as deaf as a post. Danny could have played the bagpipes at full pelt and Napoleon wouldn't have batted as much as an eyelid.

In the hallway Danny used a trick he had seen in an old black and white film. He couldn't recall exactly which one, but there had been a burglar and he had mastered the art of scaling stairs in absolute silence.

Placing his left foot into the left corner of the first stair, where the carpet meets the banister, he tentatively put his weight on that foot, making sure the weight was transferred to the outer edge of his trainer. He then did the same thing with his right foot into the right corner of the same stair. Effectively he was going to climb the stairs on the edges of his feet. Rolling his weight into the smallest possible surface area of each foot to make his pressure point on each stair as small as possible, and in the corners where the wooden stair boards had most support. According to the big screen thief, this was the way to eliminate stairs creaking.

Third fuck.

Except a good one this time. It worked.

He rested at the top of the stairs where it opened out to a landing, peering again through more gloom.

A laundry basket. And it had stuff spilling out of it.

FOURTH FUCK!!!

The laundry basket had been just that, a basket, made from whatever vegetation they made baskets from, just like the one in Danny's house. And from experience he knew that if you lifted the hinged lid it would make that dry, raspy squeal.

Kneeling before the basket, Danny prayed to the patron saint of teenage housebreakers for assistance.

He rummaged through the contents which were spilling out of the top. Underpants the size of a small house...urgggh.

A night dress made from obviously flammable material and then finally, exactly what he was looking for.

It had taken another five minutes for Danny to silently exit the house, this time with the help of a dining room window. No point risking the wrath of the 'living room wolf' a second time. As he sprinted home at 4.35 in the morning, Danny Felix's face held the thrill of his first real theft.

And with the memory bright in his mind, he was also pleased to see the last lock give way to him now, with the stopwatch reading one minute and 55 seconds.

The next morning Danny had lain in bed visualising how it would go down. His whole being was still racing with the adrenalin of his night's work...

UNFUCKINGBELIVABLE!

The pure RUSH!

RUUUUUSSSSSSSSSHHHHHHH.

Then school.

Break time.

Angela Phillips' locker.

"So, you came back?"

"Well, Miss Untouchable, I like a challenge. Not that you set me much of one."

"What have you got me, a pressie? Let me guess? You spent your Sunday afternoon trying to nick something from Hollywood's that would convince me you can get us in there?"

Danny had smiled. He flipped his school bag open and handed Miss Untouchable Angela an item of clothing.

A grey, sports bra.

Inside out, so that it showed what Danny had seen on the inside of his own P.E Kit. A pen written name on the label.

Blue Pen. Big Letters. Spelling out the name 'A. PHILLIPS'.

"What the fuck?" was all she could manage.

"By the way, Angela, what is your dog called?"

Danny's labours had been rewarded with another close up experience of how systems worked. This time his school system. He had been expelled two days later, and only narrowly avoided a police interview after the pleas from his oh-so-respectable parents. It turned out that Angela's dad was an active and respected member of the local Conservative Party, just like Danny's father.

The day after that an older boy called Rufus kicked the living shit out of Danny in front of the local leisure centre. Telling him, as he did so, to leave his girlfriend alone and then writing the word 'PERV' in marker pen across Danny's face once the fracas had ceased to be a contest.

But that was not Danny's biggest disappointment.

That came in the evening when his father came home from work to find Danny battered and bruised but still defiant. Even now, it stung Danny to his core and it twisted in his gut to admit it.

His father had simply looked him up and down.

"What is the matter with you, boy?"

And at that it had all came out. Danny screaming, hurling abuse, pouring out his every frustration. It ended with the 14-year-old Danny marching out of the front door.

He had hoped, about 50 yards down his old street, to feel a tug back on his shoulder.

That tug never came.

As he cleared away the locks and his picks from the small table, as he tried to put aside his frustration with his sister Celeste, Danny admitted to himself that it all still had a strong pull on him. The one system he had been desperate to affect had remained unmoved.

And Celeste wondered why he looked at the world and still tried to see how he could upend it, jolt it into a better version of itself? Alright, his methods may be unconventional but the most obvious thing that the Angela Philips blag had taught him was that he was good at something.

That night of supposedly romantic derring-do had given Danny the taste. He had been bitten by a bug. The undeniable rush.

He was now a thief.

8

✧ Dirty Dishes: Dirty Deeds ✧

The wash up. The debrief. The post-match bish bash.

Christine loved this. It was one of the best parts of the job, standing around in a favoured pub, pints in hand, retracing, retelling, reliving a piece of work well done.

And here they were now, CC, Freethy and the team all standing in the Shakespeare's Head walking each other through their personal angle on the events. The blow-by-blow accounts of who saw what, who said what and who nicked who.

It felt good to CC; it was, to her, one of the fundamental parts of being Old Bill. It was in these moments that they all stood together, having fought together. They could all revel in being part of what was known as The Blue Wall. An old dog of a beat constable had once described it as such to her when she was a young probationer.

The Blue Wall...the reason why order won out over chaos.

And the members of that wall loved to rip the piss out of each other and now was the perfect time to do it.

Banter.

The release valve that allowed all of them to deal with the violence, the tragedy and disappointment they faced in the job. A good laugh at your teammates expense, all in the name of being able to deal with their ferocity and consign experiences to memory. In moments of extreme pressure, the touch of humour could make their task bearable.

And Christine was in full flow, enjoying the moment, blossoming amidst the camaraderie.

"So the Black Mariah's pulled up and our lovely Custody Sergeant Donnelly..."

"DIGGER!"

The group toasted the cell sergeant sarcastically.

"...lovely Digger is at the rear doors trying to act all respectful, telling all six-foot-something of Iggy Adesina that it is "up to him". Impeccable manners, our lovely Digger."

CC adopted a deeper tone.

"We can do this the hard way or we can do it the easy way, sir". Nothing in reply, even if lovely Digger was being charming! So Donnelly, helped by five other Old Bill, of course, goes ahead and opens the door. Well, Jesus, if Adesina doesn't come out of the cage like a lion screaming "The fucking hard way!" And all hell broke loose!"

The laughter lifted up to the ceiling in the pub, decorating the moment.

Freethy raised his pint glass:

"Here's to a fucking great month! I mean, what a haul, first Heathrow, now this lot in north London. It is a bad time to be a face in London."

But at this, Freethy saw something fleeting pass across Christine's face, enough to know that something had irked her even if it was just for a nanosecond.

The rounds kept piling up and the day went from late afternoon to evening until CC and Freethy found themselves in front of one of their favourite places in the city.

The Pasty Shop on the concourse of Marylebone Train Station, with an Eastern European girl struggling to understand their slurred requests for two pasties...each.

"Every time I go on the beer with you, Freethy, I wake up the next morning with a mouth full of burns from these

71

fucking pasties you love so much. Do they have to come out thermonuclear? We are so shitfaced and hungry we don't notice we are roasting the roof of our mouths off."

Freethy, giggling now, his eyes taking just a moment too long to shift from her face to the money in his hand, counting it out for the piping hot pies.

"You love them just as much as me! Now, shut up, eat up, and then you can tell me what's troubling you, Detective Chance."

CC was looking at him now, trying to chew and cool the food in her mouth at the same time.

After a third degree burn of a swallow...

"I dunno...it's nothing."

Freethy answered her with a slightly tipsy, arched eyebrow.

" I'm just...it's just...it all feels a bit too...easy."

"What you fucking talking about?" Freethy, incredulous now, as well as drunk.

"The Heathrow thing that made the papers, then this morning. They kind of just fell into our laps."

"You never look a gift horse in the mouth, and you think way too much. They were good police work. The intel, the job, the pavement: all good solid stuff."

"Yeah, yeah, I get that. But still, not saying we were lucky, or we weren't good today, but it just feels like it was on a plate. I mean, how long from the snout stuff to the actual job?"

Freethy was looking at her, trying not to scar his tongue with the heat of the food while also not telling his best mate that she was full of shit.

"I know, I know. I am full of it."

"That's not the half of it, CC. Next, you'll be telling me your Spidey sense is tingling and you've consulted a medium who's told you where we can find all the diamonds from that Hatton Garden job."

Freethy cupped his hand on the back of his mates' neck,

playfully pushing her aside.

"Let me guess. You gonna go see her now?"

Christine was just nodding back, pointing at a plastic bag she had been carrying now resting on the ground at her feet while she ate the pasty.

"Give her a hug from me. Tell her that she has a crazy mum, but she's still lovely."

"Shauna knows that already...see you tomorrow, Mr Freeth."

Unsurprisingly the lock took Danny less than a minute to spring open. The real difficulty was keeping his body out of the infra-red sensor, which if triggered, bathed the entire walled back garden in white light.

This made his approach to the lock awkward. He couldn't be sure that the house was empty and the lack of security light activity back here would preserve his element of surprise should he find some company in the west London garden flat.

He had spotted the sensor while he watched the back of the property before making his move. He was in the shadows in an alley that ran along the back of the Notting Hill houses when he clocked the languid slink of a Siamese cat that would help his cause. Strutting though the back garden, the cat's swagger triggered the telltale red dot that heralded the sudden wash of light meant to deter people like him, and equally make the occupants aware that someone or something was making their away across their manicured lawn.

Danny had thanked the cat, and got on with his B & E.

After feeling the last tumbler on the lock slip under his pressure and persuasion, the door handle began to relent. Then he had heard a rustle to his left. There making its way through the bedding plants was the Siamese cat, retracing its steps.

Danny was discovering the full truth of the Siamese breed at exactly the wrong time. Crouched as he was, holding onto the now fully co-operative door handle and preparing to make his entrance to the flat, the Siamese made a beeline for him, meowing like it was greeting a best friend on the way to a mouse hunt. If the cat made it to him, it would break the infra-red beam en route and set that white light wash off again. Never mind all the racket the mewling made which accompanied the feline's approach.

Danny hissed low and long through his teeth at the cat, trying to sound menacing. This only seemed to embolden the cat further. It sauntered closer, weaving its tail in the air in a way that made Danny think of Dexy in her silk dressing gown with a glass of champagne in her hand and a knowing glint in her eye.

Danny looked around for something to toss at the cat, but then realised that might set the light off anyway.

Just then a huge white moth flittered its way across the garden, attracted by a street light just beyond the garden's wall, and the cat was distracted long enough to change course, following the erratic path of the big insect.

Seeing his chance, Danny whirled through the doorway, still in a crouch and closed the door behind him as gently as he could.

A dimly-lit kitchen.

Alarm? There were no indoor sensors blinking at him, so that was a good start.

The object of this evening's sport was to locate and acquire a laptop. It belonged to Barry Blount, formerly of 22 Unknown Road, Obscurity Town, but now a minor league celebrity after appearing as a contestant in one of those wretched, overblown pieces of shit TV that was dressed up like a social experiment. Danny didn't mind breaking into a Z-grade celeb's home, they deserved it as far he was concerned, given that usually they would climb over a pile of their dead relatives to achieve 15 minutes of fame.

Mind you, 15 minutes was more like 15 seconds these days, such had the fickle finger of fame become fast forwarded by the internet, tabloids and general lack of attention span amongst the target audience of such degrading shows.

Still, Danny thought, Blount had obviously made the most of his flash in the pan, because this flat was in a great part of London and would hold its value handsomely as Barry's notoriety flushed itself down the publicity toilet. A process which had already begun.

Blount had gained a 'cheeky chappie' reputation on his reality show, calling a spade a spade and talking like he was working class hero with 'salt of the earth' tattooed on his backside at birth. In fact, he literally did have 'salt of the earth' tattooed on his backside, but that had only been done the day he found out he had made the show.

Turned out Barry was not really a working class hero. He was not even working class. He was an out of work, and increasingly desperate, wannabe actor who came from a very moneyed family and actually spoke naturally with a cut-glass Surrey accent. Barry had flung himself into the 'role' of 'cockney sparrow' because he had heard that the producers of *Trial By TV* were short of that kind of personality for their project.

Having got himself picked, he knew he would be seen buck-naked in the showers of the communal house that was the setting for *Trial By TV*. The tattoo, therefore, was a tool, by which Barry could convince the audience that he was a working-class diamond geezer, not a failed actor desperate for a fix of the crack cocaine that is a bit of fame.

The tabloids loved Barry, especially after a spirited debate one night with some of the girls on set about personal hygiene and in particular the merits of intimate waxing. Barry couldn't see the contradiction in expecting women to be fully waxed and buffed to within an inch of their lives while men could sport hair for hairs sake in every orifice.

What happened next gave Barry his 15 seconds; four of the girls held him down, waxing him live on national television in a place where the sun don't shine. For the remainder of his time on the show, as his hair steadily grew back all Barry could be heard to intone regularly was, "Me nuts, me nuts". A catchphrase bereft of wit or guile was born. Back in the real world, after the show had finished, Barry became the face of a brand of salted peanuts sold all over Europe in pubs and bars. That alone had paid for the flat that Danny Felix was now stood in.

Danny was here to nick Barry Blount's laptop. It contained an MPEG file, a mini movie that could jeopardise the future success of pop star and national sweetheart-in-waiting, Honey Sister. This was the price Danny owed Dexy for due diligence on his new friend Inspector Harkness. Honey Sister was one of Dexy's newest, and obviously prized, members.

Barry must be threatening to talk tabloid with his home movie, and as Honey Sister was at a tipping point in her career Dexy had been implored to help out. That desperate prayer had found its way to Danny who found his way here.

Blount was obviously more than familiar with how the gutter press worked their worthless magic given that it was their indulgence which created his fame in the first place. And when they had tired of him they also set about revealing his actual roots. His upper class background now relegated him to the small stories used to fill up celebrity pages each time he turned up in a West End nightclub with a horsey set girl on his arm.

Danny figured his footage of Honey Sister doing something she ought not to was Barry's latest attempt to climb back up the tabloid news agenda.

Dexy, and now Danny, were going to stop that.

Moving through the silent flat, Danny was all eyes about, looking for the flat outline of a laptop, or its telltale pulsing light if it was still plugged in. No joy, until he found himself in a hallway in front of what was undoubtedly the lounge door.

Danny kept light on the balls of his feet, moving silently. He cracked open the door.

He didn't go all the way in because there was a low light on in the room, and he could smell something familiar.

Whiskey.

Being drunk.

Through the crack he could see two big L shaped sofas dividing the room up, the closest one with its back to the door.

MIAOWWW. Meow, MIAOOOWWW.

The fucking cat.

Fucking useless-cupboard-loving-aloof-until-you-feed-it—cannot-even-take—them-for-a-fucking-walk-cat.

From the other side of the sofa: a grunt.

"Do shut up, Teasie!"

The cat pushed past him, through the partially open door.

So Danny had a live one here after all...persons unknown at home, but probably Mr Nuts himself, Barry Blount.

Checking that the door was not about to catch on the carpet that ran all the way through the flat, Danny slowly and quietly pushed the door of the lounge open pulling a balaclava over his head as he did so.

That's the thing about rubicons, Danny thought, if they weren't for crossing, what the hell were they for?

In he went and Danny could now see over the back of the sofa. On the long bit of the L, lay the underpants and nothing else-clad body of Mr Barry Blount holding a bottle of Johnny W, the top off. On the short part of the L shaped sofa was a laptop computer. It was on. The internet browser was open at a page of Google Searches.

Barry Blount was home alone, chugging down whiskey and Googling himself.

Danny was weighing up the next move, when...

"You might as well come in. Teasie has already alerted me of your presence, haven't you darling?"

The cat was now doing a figure-of-eight in front of the sofa, using the overhanging cushions as a scent marking post. Barry didn't get up.

"Come on, show yourself. I'm too squiffy to put up a fight and I have no money in the flat, but I do have some primo marijuana, and if you want a compromise we can light that up. I'm depressed anyway, nothing new about me on Google for a fortnight. A facking fortnight!" It was a moan that only the 21st century could have produced.

Danny rounded the sofa and looked down at Barry Blount, pale and wan in the glow from the Google page that was evidence of the fickle finger of fame.

Barry was, to use common parlance, hammered. If the Johnny Walker had been new when he cracked it, it was now down to the last quarter.

On seeing Danny's balaclava-ed head, Barry seemed to decide there might be more jeopardy to the scenario than he had first considered. Still, it took a good twenty seconds and a lot of effort and heavy breathing for him to get to a sitting position on the sofa. He almost lost the Johnny on the way, but somehow managed to rescue it before the good whiskey went to waste.

Danny had only one thought. Get this over quick.

"Give me the laptop and your mobile phone and your wallet and I am out of here. No-one has to get hurt." Danny wasn't ready for the reply he got.

"You must be jolly well kidding...my laptop is my blood life...I mean life-blood. I can't do without. I have a lovely Tag watch. Maybe that instead, hmm?"

Danny couldn't believe his ears. Barry was negotiating.

With a burglar.

"My stash is in the armoire against the wall over there. Come on, let's have a toke and a chat..."

Barry made to get up towards the cupboard against the opposite wall, only for Danny to do the unthinkable. He grabbed the waste band of his underpants resulting in a painful wedgie.

"Owww, owww, owww, come on! That's a bit much, isn't it? Owww."

Barry Blount began to sob.

Big, heaving, can't catch your breath sobs. His naked shoulders quivering in time to the sad noise.

"Look, I...I...SOB."

"I have nothing here of value to...SOB...you...I have nothing to give...SOB...anyone. Can't we just have a quick... SOB...puff and then you can hit me or do whatever you like, but don't...SOB...take my Mac Air. I'm a celebrity!!"

The last bit accompanied by the biggest sob.

But Danny now just bent down and grabbed the laptop. He'd seen enough...a grown man, crying, over an Apple Mac and a miserable Google result.

Barry went to stand up but then thought better of it when he saw Danny draw back his arm ready to lash out.

"iPhone. Now. Where?"

"On the top of the armoire, you...SOB...bastard."

Danny could see it. He grabbed it, and as a second thought he opened the drawers of the dresser until he found the plastic bag with the hash in. There were three joints rolled already along with a sizeable cube of resin.

"Ooo now...COME ON! Not my doobies too!"

Barry you need to look to your priorities, Danny thought, but returned to stand in front of the hapless has-been.

"Here...light up and take a big old hit."

Barry, confused now, as Danny handed him one of the pre-rolleds and the lighter from the stash bag. He did as he was told, lighting then pulling in on the joint like a man coming up for air.

Danny watched Barry's eyes go glassy.

"Again...deep drag again."

Barry did as he was told.

"Now, more smoke. And take your pants down."

"WHAT? Are you some kind of bumbandit bandit?"

Danny almost laughed, but held back, feigning another punch in Barry's direction.

"Now toke again and play with yourself"

The now naked and unsteady Barry started to listlessly touch himself. "Well, you are a strange one..."

What Barry hadn't noticed was that Danny had been filming him with his iPhone from the first moment he had lit up the joint.

When he reckoned he had enough and that he'd had enough, Danny planted a foot in Barry's chest knocking him back onto the sofa.

The hash and booze combo was fully kicking in now; Barry was incapable of stringing too many words together.

Danny reckoned it was time to do one out the door.

"Barry, listen to a voice of reason. Don't call the police mate. I have kept your stash bag and if they come looking it has your fingerprints all over it, okay? Just put this down to bad luck, mate."

"You...you...know me?" Barry slurring, off his tits, circling the airport.

"You..." Big pause. Barry trying to grasp the words out of his addled brain...

"You...recognise me!!"

And Barry Blount started to laugh and clap, suddenly happy in the drug-addled knowledge that he still had it... he was still a celeb.

Danny just rolled his eyes, scooped up the laptop, placed it in his black rucksack with the newly acquired mobile phone and said goodbye to Teasie the traitorous cat, pulling his balaclava off as he went.

Walking back towards Notting Hill Gate, Danny couldn't quite shake off the pitiful sight of Barry, sat in his underpants, confronting an intruder and being more concerned about the death of his public profile rather than death itself.

Just as he was about to enter the Tube station, Danny caught sight of someone in his peripheral vision. Big guy. A really BIG GUY, steaming towards him, right up to him, grabbing Danny now by the elbow, something sharp and hard pressed into his ribs.

In order to avoid that sharpness going between those ribs, Danny relented, moving towards a car pulled up to the kerb. An Audi, back door swinging open. A face Danny didn't recognise framed within. But Danny knew he had to do what that face was telling him, especially as it uttered only one word:

Harkness!

Danny ducked into the back of the Audi, now sandwiched between the stranger and the guy with the knife.

"Harkness," was all Danny said in return to his new travel companions, nodding his head gently as he did so, and the car took off into the night.

9

✧ Visiting Time ✧

It was all in the timing. It was a ritual that over the last few weeks had quickly become a favourite.

Shauna opened the bag of Haribo gummy sweets to match her mum's faked coughing fit. That way the nurses wouldn't hear the rustle as the plastic bag gave way and she would be able to taste her favourite sweets for the first time in a week. Shauna didn't care what the doctors had told her mum. How could a mini-coke bottle kill you?

They could if you ate a mountain of them, but Christine had invented the ban in order to give Shauna a secret treat, an indulgence to compensate for some of the others that had been denied her. It felt like an overly simplistic conspiracy, but the way in which Shauna had dedicated herself to the subterfuge once CC had planted its seed in her head proved that it was fun and sufficiently naughty to make it feel like defiance in the face of her illness. A defiant sense of fight that Christine found it hard to summon up sometimes.

"Awww, Mum, you are a legend! Sooo much tastier when they are not allowed."

She looked tired, though Christine didn't mention it. Tired in a weary to the very bone way, like she had just had enough of everything.

CC produced a copy of the *Evening Standard*, London's main daily newspaper, placing it the right way round so

Shauna could see the cover. It was a full-page story on the arrest of Iggy Adesina and the gun battle. Once again, she was struck at how good fortune had lumped a stack of illicitly-gained cash into the laps of the Met Police.

"Uh oh, Mum. Were you in this? Heavy shit!"

"Shauna Chance! Language."

"Seriously, Mum. If you keep going like this you'll put yourself out of a job, no baddies left to catch." This last sentence was slightly garbled through a mouth full of jelly sweets.

Shauna pushed herself up onto a Matterhorn's worth of hospital pillows.

"That's just it, sweetie...there's something not right about it." Christine sank into the chair beside the bed, alcohol and work fatigue claiming her all at once.

"Wah? Since when did taking out the baddies on the pavement make for bad news?"

"Listen to you trying to talk like a copper. It just feels a little weird, like it was meant to happen. We were in the right place at the right time twice in a few weeks, and I'm beginning to ask why?"

Shauna's eyes were now closed, the click of her drying throat as she swallowed a jelly ring and a little bear.

"D'you remember last year, in the summer holidays, that girl Bethany told us all she could get us backstage to meet *The Wanted*?"

CC was a little thrown by the conversational change of direction.

"Umm, I think so. The concert in Shepherd's Bush or somewhere...?"

"Yes, and you didn't let me go because you thought it might be too much for me. Plus you said not to believe all Bethany used to say?"

"Unhuh..."

"Well it was just like you said, Mum. If it looks too good to be true, then it usually is. The girls ended up waiting outside the Empire until midnight without even so much as a signed photo to show for it."

CC didn't know whether to smile or feel sad. Was it her passing a cynical police sense of fate that made her daughter question everything, or was it the hand that fate had dealt her with regard to her health? She couldn't be sure, but she certainly had a point to go with the wisdom of beyond her years.

"Well, 'Detective Inspector Know It All', you might just be right there." Christine stood to kiss Shauna on the top of her head, careful to manoeuvre past the drip that was providing her with pain-killing morphine.

"I could go on, Mum. You also told me you make your own luck and you always say, if something is wrong go back and look at the details. You even told the doctors that before they got my diagnosis right."

"...Details." Christine repeated her own mantra. It was a line she had heard a million times from her own dad. Except sometimes she wished it wasn't such good advice. She remembered when she had to force her doctor to look at Shauna's symptoms again, and now when she should be cheering job success and her gut was saying something else.

CC sighed, longer than she meant to. Her daughter read her thoughts without saying a word. The subject needed changing.

"Mum, did you bring any ice cream?"

A smile now, reaching into the plastic bag.

"Why'd you think the gummies feel cold?"

"Ahhh, the clues are in the details, Mum."

"Yeah...except it's probably melted by now..."

The car journey took Danny all the way from the west side of London to the West End, the bright lights of the theatres and restaurants splashing colour before his eyes as he watched out the window. Then out the other side of the kaleidoscope of tourist traps and into the real power-house of London...The City.

They finally came to a stop outside a venue that looked like a rundown church, sitting uncomfortably cheek by jowl with shiny skyscraper offices and a smattering of high-end restaurants.

It wasn't a part of London Danny ever felt comfortable in. During the daytime office workers scurried around like insects, barely able to look each other in the eye. Then at night it became a kind of ghost town. The place felt abandoned as though people were frightened to be caught there after dark lest they be shackled to their desks forever.

Danny was bundled out of the Audi. His backpack was searched but returned to him. After all, what harm could a laptop and a mobile phone do to someone? Little did they know, thought Danny, as he was pointed towards a pathway that led down the right hand side of the old church.

His escorts were taking no chances. The big guy behind him, the driver and his other passenger lead the way. As they rounded the front end of the building the noises of a crowd could be heard. A lot of voices. Excitement. He could see an entrance ahead, right in the middle of the building, a wide sets of steps leading under the main wall. A banner proclaimed some kind of charity function and the letters M.M.A. As they drew level with the steps the noise increased. And then Danny realised. They were entering the crypt. A space that ran the entire length of the building. Tables arranged in circles out from the centre, festooned with men in city gent suits, cigar smoke hanging low in the air despite smoking indoors having been banned years ago. And in the very centre of this large underground space was a huge cage. And Danny got it...

M.M.A. Mixed Martial Arts. He had been brought to a cage fight.

He was shown to a table at 'cage-side' just as a slight Japanese lad took a roundhouse kick to the head from a heavily-tattooed opponent. Danny could hear the thud of the impact despite the baying crowd around him. The boy collapsed like a slinky toy on a flight of stairs, going down onto the canvas in stages, a little stagger, then knees first, then a full face plant, out for a count that even the referee knew was unnecessary.

The crowd went wild.

Torn betting slips were launched into the air. Men who would look like pillars of society in any other context leapt out of their seats, sending drinks and plates flying, baying like rabid dogs at the scent of blood. The victorious fighter strutted, inked arms aloft in the cage as though some great moral justice had been delivered instead of a flying foot.

A number of greying men were around his table, two standing now applauding the end of the bout, another chugging on a cigar that was roughly the length and girth of a baby's arm. None of the men acknowledged Danny, but he did note that there was still one free chair left in the round. The strong arms who had led him here backed off, content to watch him from a distance.

In the centre of the table was a sweating ice bucket, filled with decent looking champagne. Three bottles were already turned upside down to show they had been decommissioned, but another three proudly pointed at the ceiling. Danny thought, well if you can't beat them?

As he poured himself a glass the hubbub began to settle. The stricken fighter was being helped out of the ring and replaced by a dinner-jacketed 'master of ceremonies'. His voice was like every local radio DJ Danny had ever heard, all oil and rounded vowels.

"Gentlemen...I hope you are all enjoying our entertainment. I think you'll agree we have witnessed some great sport this evening. We have just one bout left to rock your world. The young ladies will pass among you to collect the betting papers for our final bout, and don't forget this is all for a fabulous cause, The Freemasons Grand Trust. Doing good for our people in the community when they most need our help. Bet generously gentlemen, and remember this worthy cause gets to keep all the forfeited bets plus ten per cent of any winnings."

At this, a gaggle of girls began to pass between the tables. Danny realised they were the only women in the subterranean venue. Using champagne buckets they were collecting betting slips and wads of cash from the tables.

So far, so posh boys big night out. But where was his host? When would Danny's new boss show his face?

"Gentlemen, tonight as always we have reserved the very best to last. A heavyweight contest in every sense of the word. Three five minutes rounds. I think you'll all agree it is a fitting bout to complete the finale of this evening's sport. So without further ado it's mayhem time! Let me introduce our final pair of gladiators. First, the challenger to last year's champion, a veteran of both Afghanistan and Iraq, at a height of six foot five and weighing in at 200 pounds even, Grant Corky Corkhill."

The crowd erupted again, as a skin-headed ex-squaddie entered the basement hall. All swagger and arms aloft, tattoos covering his upper chest and arms in the manner of an ex-convict, the blue and red ink depicting a lion standing over a fresh kill, blood dripping from defiant jaws. A side door in the cage was opened to allow the fighter to enter, skipping around the canvas inside, jabbing at the air and rolling his shoulders, ducking and weaving.

"And now to the defending champion, all six foot eight inches of him, 230 pounds of machine-like muscle. The man with the flying fists, the legend that is the Darkness we call Harkness!"

Danny's surprise levels rocketed. Making his way through the tables towards the cage, bare-chested, long shorts wearing those little half-leather gloves that cage-fighter's love - was Harkness. His skin glistening in the lights. Men were patting him on the ass and arms as he passed them, and bellowed support as he progressed to the centre of the room. And as he made it to the entrance to the cage, Harkness looked straight at Danny and winked. Fucking winked.

Either you really are bat-shit crazy or you have balls of solid steel, Danny thought.

The referee brought both fighters into the middle of the cage, giving them cursory instructions and making them bump fists.

An air horn sounded and the two combatants made straight for each other. No sparring or dancing around to size each other up. Oh no. This had the feel of some kind of grudge match. Memories of Hagler/Hearns, Tyson/Holy-field, now Corky/Darkness Harkness. Both men were swing-ing big roundhouse punches at each other. Corky ducking now, dropping fists trying to work into Harkness' ribs, stepping back to then rejoin with another flurry of punches, this time aiming for the solar plexus. But Harkness was ready for him, meeting the squaddie square in the midriff with a lightning quick knee, rocking the man back on his heels. Then Harkness was on him, a rapid combination of jabs to his head and face, then a step back to deliver a high kick, his foot con-necting soundly to the side of Corkhill's head.

The crowd was up and screaming as Corky tried to get his head back in the game, trying his own forward lunging knee jerk, only for Harkness to catch the knee and flip his opponent onto his back like you might flick a beer mat in the air.

But the war hero wasn't to be so easily dealt with, athletically springing back to his feet from a horizontal start before Harkness could finish him, using his jumping momentum to meet his rival with a pile driver punch, evad-ing Harkness' guard-up fists, delivering a head-snapping, bone-crunching blow to the nose. Boom! Harkness' face was now covered in claret, his nose pushed over to one side. Danny was certain he was done for. But he should have known better.

Harkness started to laugh. While the rest of the room was literally going ballistic at the sight and smell of the blood all over his face, Harkness started to howl, the same feral noise he had used that first time he had driven Danny on that joy ride to see his ex-partners form foundations for a security hut.

And there it was. A twitch, just a twitch in Corky's eyes. He knew, Danny knew, the crowd knew and Harkness knew...Corky was shit-in-his-pants frightened.

The Big Copper made his move then, ducking under a flash of punches from the soldier, wrapping his big arms round his rival's waist and hoisting him up, high into the air, only then to double over and spring with his legs. Both men then took off, toppling in seeming slow motion until they hit the canvas. The cage shuddered with the force and weight of the impact, an audible whoosh was heard as all the air was slammed out of Corky's lungs, his head smacking into the canvas too, blood dripping all over his face from Harkness, now sitting astride him. The referee was hovering waiting for the coup de grace, but when it came even he was taken aback by its ferocity.

Harkness began what can only be described as a barrage of full-on punches and blows to Corky's head and face, fists literally a blur until splashes of crimson joined his gloved hands in the air.

The referee tried to intervene, grabbing Harkness by the shoulders to drag him off. He was thrust away for his trouble and Harkness returned to his stricken opponent, swinging down with more vicious blows. The ref made a second attempt, this time with help of the ringside trainers, and finally they managed to haul him off.

The room was a tumult of screams, cheers, howls and bedlam.

The whole fight had taken less than three minutes.

All Danny Felix could do was to watch, open-mouthed, as Harkness once again turned to look in his direction, a snarl of a grin on his face spitting out his mouth guard, a crazed look in his eyes, as he pointed at Danny and began to bellow:

"I AM ALIVE!!!"

Danny was escorted by his earlier captors upstairs through a series of corridors until they came to what must have been the original sacristy, the room where the priest would have prepared for service.

As he entered a doctor was just sticking two tubular bandages up Harkness' nostrils. Then, taking a tight grip on the bridge of his out-of-place nose, the doctor yanked. A crack and a roar from Harkness signified that they had jointly shifted it back into its rightful place in the middle of his face.

The first bloom of bruising was already forming under his eyes, which were streaming from the repositioned nose. He finally sat on the edge of a chair.

"Danny Boy, a delight to see you again. How did you find this evening's...ah, how shall we describe it...entertainment? Yes that fits...'entertainment'?"

Danny just held his stare.

"Ah, the silent treatment again. All steely eyed and quiet of mouth...I invited you here this evening for two reasons."

As he spoke, a trickle of blood began to run from his nose, the two tubular bandages were evidently to no avail.

"Firstly, I think you can tell from tonight that I will not tolerate any brinkmanship. If I enter an arena it is with single-minded determination. Secondly, I want to put you on notice. I have a job for you and it will be imminent. So be on your fucking mettle. No drugs, no excessive intake of alcohol, and no pointless games of hide and fucking seek."

Harkness paused to breathe through his mouth for a second, his tongue snaking out to mop up the single line of blood that had now breached the top of his lip. He stood up and started to pace the room, slowly rolling his head on his shoulders, flexing his neck muscles, trying to release some of the ache.

"At 7am and 9pm sharp everyday you will check in using the phone number that Skelly here will give you before you leave. Don't neglect this. It is not a request. If I need you in between times I will send either Skelly or Denzil to fetch you. You will drop everything and come, no matter what. Is that understood?"

Danny watched for a second and then gently cleared his throat.

"I am not your pet dog. You do not own me," said Danny evenly, without emotion, just stating the fact.

A smile raked across Harkness' face.

"Let me ask you a question? What do you want from this life, Danny? What do you want to remember when your last breathe is ready to rattle from your chest?"

Harkness was now moving towards Danny, looking down to meet his eyes solidly, without blinking.

"When opportunity comes calling, do you want to be able to say that you were all ears, ready to reach out and grasp tightly onto the thrill of a lifetime? Do you want to write your own bit of history, Danny, and see it mean something? To you? To this city? To those like me and you?

"Men like you and me, Danny, we need to be seen, we need to leave a mark, we need to be like Churchill, mate. He said: "History will be kind to me, for I intend to write it." That's our kind of life, Danny. If you step out on this journey with me, I promise you we will make history. And you will be handsomely rewarded for it. If you don't...? Then I will just have to swat you like a pointless fly."

"Jesus, Harkness, you do love a speech," countered

Danny calmly. "Listen, I don't know you, so I don't trust you. I only work when I want to and with whom I want to. Why should I help someone who is supposed to be a cop? And while you're at it...how about this, didn't Henry Ford say that all history is more or less bunk?"

Harkness began to laugh, reached out and placed two hands on Danny's shoulders.

"You sound like a man with a choice in the room. Ford did say that, but all Ford ever did was make very dull family cars. You, Danny, want to have a life. I know the likes of you: you don't just steal to put money in your pocket. You like thieving. That's what makes you so good at it. And that is why you are here, to help me steal something. Something fucking spectacular. Do me the honour...stay in touch Danny, just like I have told you to. Don't make me come looking, it won't go well for you. But I will make it worth your while, sunshine. I promise you that. Take him home, boys."

The three muscle men shifted in their positions. Skelly, the driver, and Denzel stepped out of the doorway, which left the enforcer who had held a knife in Danny's ribs earlier that evening to shepherd him out of the room.

Sidestepping them, making as if to take a run at Harkness, Danny caused the big bodyguard to move between them, his right arm coming up in anticipation of a blow, which is exactly what the thief wanted.

At lightning speed Danny grabbed the enforcer's arm, throwing his weight in the opposite direction and up, twisting. The bodyguard doubled over to stop his arm getting wrenched out of its socket.

But Danny then shifted his weight immediately again, a satisfying crunch as he drove his victim face first into the door jamb, his own size and heft doing most of the work against him. Wood and bone both splintered in the impact.

The other two were unable to come to their colleague's aid because their joint surprise and haste meant they blocked each other from actually getting back through the doorway.

Danny now had the big guy on the floor at his feet. Meeting Harkness' gaze full on, Danny calmly raised his foot knee high. Then brought it down. Hard.

He stomped on the man's collar bone. The sickening snap was loud and soon followed by the victim's scream of pain.

"I'm not going anywhere, Harkness. You're not the only one in the room who can fight. And let me be clear, I'll meet with you one more time, later this week. And when I see you, do me the honour: Reveal your hand or fuck off out of my life. I can't bear grandstanding. Come and get me when you are ready to talk business instead of just filling the room with bullshit. I'll make my own way home gentlemen. You'll be busy taking your friend to casualty."

As he walked out of the re-purposed church, all Danny could hear in his ears was the echo of Harkness laughing.

10

✦ New Crew, Old Habits ✦

As Christine parked her car she was idly marvelling at how so few of the local residents realised that their neighbours were one of London's most effective anti-crime squads. The west London base for the Barnes Flying Squad was a pretty anonymous looking building. It was a scruffy 1970s red brick affair, boxy, unremarkable.

For such a well-to-do area, this team handled gritty cases across the whole of the south east of England and sometimes beyond. Criminals didn't tend to think about jurisdiction when they were identifying their targets, but if they came from the London area, chances were that no matter where their job was going to be pulled, the Barnes team would be the ones on the hunt for them.

The sun on her face, as she walked from her parking bay into the office, gave her cause to sigh out loud. This was something she knew she was doing frequently these days. Christine had come straight here from Shauna's bedside at the hospice. It had been another night of fitful, shallow sleep, punctuated by random beeping, imagined and real, from the equipment, which was telling the story of her daughters' slow decline.

On such sunny mornings it felt cruel to her that a world was still going about its natural business despite Shauna clinging on to what little life she had left. Christine felt that she wanted everything to stop and have an almighty pause of breath while she and her little girl dealt with whatever fate God meted out. But then wasn't she equally scared of stopping to face the eventuality that lay ahead?

When she reached her desk a yellow post-it note summoned her to a meeting with her Detective Chief Inspector, "as soon as you get your arse in".

Entering the 'guv'nors' cramped little office, Christine had to pretend that she couldn't smell the smoke from the crafty cigarette her boss had lit up before anyone else had come in for the day's work.

D.C.I Collinson was round, and becoming rounder. He was a copper from the old school. An ex-beat bobby, who rose through the ranks when experience mattered more than politics, and was now close to retiring out. He had a month left in the job. The expanding waistline, a severe smoking habit, commendations coming out his ears and a regular pension on its way. He was plain speaking, politically incorrect in private and a cracking policeman. CC respected her D.C.I almost as much as she had loved her own father. She would miss this man whom many underestimated when they first met him...and all went on to regret it.

"Alright, Chance, come in, have a seat. Who's on coffee run this morning? I'm parched." Collinson's voice was craggy and gruff, with a cockney accent carved out by a lifetime of Embassy Regals.

"Freethy, Sir...late as usual."

"For his own funeral, mate, his own funeral. I better open the windows, bit stuffy in here."

CC looked down to hide the smile she couldn't stifle.

"We've had an excellent few weeks, haven't we? Good numbers, good results, lot of faces taken off the streets. And, I have another job that looks like it might pop sooner rather than later. Another chance to tick some boxes without too much overtime."

"Another? We have had a lot of luck of late, guv."

"Yes, but good intel is our oxygen, young lady. Don't knock it."

He threw a buff-coloured folder across the desk at her.

"It looks like we have a bead on a team of Russkies. They've been running a load of high class Toms in the West End for the last 18 months or so. Now before you say it, yes, I do know that we aren't the vice, but get this - it's a cash industry, as you know..."

Christine frowned mock indignation at this suggestion.

"Well, you know CC, get it where you can...haha. Anyway, these Russkies and their dirty money have caught someone's attention. In the folder you will find details, some useful, some not, for a gentleman called Abasin Yusufzai. He is of Pakistani origin, but was brought up in Bradford. He moved to the bright lights of our fair city three years ago. He is either the founder or, at least, a major player in a group of Radical Muslims called Mohammed's Way. Usual thing, death to the west...virgins await in heaven...all that good stuff. Anyway, he's had a team of lads on the sniff around this Russian outfit for six weeks. Seems they want a slice of the cash business, without having to sully themselves with the mucky business of trafficking girls and all that untidiness. We have confidential informant intel that says the job is imminent. Especially as this week sees London playing host to that big football conference... *UEFA*, *FIFA* all in town. Our Allah-loving-friends figure that it could be a cash-rich few days for the likes of the vodka drinkers. The girls will be working their arses off."

CC winced inwardly at the unintentional pun, but there was logic in the rest of it, for all its insensitivity. She had started to leaf through the contents of the folder as her boss talked, noticing that many of the evidence sheets had been severely redacted.

"Sir, there are a lot of blacked out passages here. Is this from anti-terrorist by any chance?"

"On the money, sunshine. Names, paragraphs, details

removed all over the place, but I have been told the rest is all reliable. The full bill of the race."

"Well, sir, excuse me for saying, I don't like doing dirty work for SO15. They usually drip feed us and sit back and watch as we chase our tails."

Collinson sat back, taking Christine in for a second. She thought she was about to get a bollocking.

"Listen, young Chance, I dislike those MI5 wannabe wankers as much as you do, but this looks credible. We can take a few players off the board and everyone gets to sleep soundly in their beds. You'll find that this file is not as drip drip as they usually are. Quite a bit of detail once you read through it which, frankly, surprised me. They've even given last known addresses for the entire crew. We're on a roll at the minute, so why don't we just get our heads round this and see if we can't keep that going. Any old nonsense with the detail or any interference from the Yard, just let me know. I'll kill it dead. Okay?"

At that moment Freethy knocked on the door carrying several takeaway coffee cups.

"Freeth! You're late! A man could have died of fucking thirst before you'd get the water to him! Ten quid fine!"

"Aww, guv. It was packed in there. Yummy mummies and all that..."

"Fine stands!"

CC started to chuckle. Office fines were handed out regularly. The money was split between an office beer fund and a donation to charity once every few months. Fines could be for anything deemed untoward by the guv or on a majority of opinion of the team. This could be anything from referring to an Irish national as a "Paddy" right through to the crashing of service vehicles while in pursuit of a suspect.

Once Freethy had left the coffees in their rightful places and exited mumbling about the "bleeding coffee run" Christine looked to her D.C.I for the rest of the briefing.

"You'll have to have armed support on this once you've established contact. Not only are the ragheads tooled up but we are sure the Commies are too."

The guv'nor had just racked up about fifty quid in fines in that one sentence.

He continued with a bellow.

"Bleedin' hell, Freeth, where'd you get these drinks? One inch of coffee and seven of fucking foam!"

When she finished laughing, Christine asked what she knew to be a crucial question.

"So SO15 have a man inside? Any chance they will let us know who? Is he one of the crew? Is there someone we will be scooping but then letting go...anyone to avoid?"

"Not that they have directly shared, but that may come later. No such thing as a free lunch. They will want us to manipulate someone most likely. The key to this is to get behind them and make sure that we know where the counting house is, and get the stopper on it before you have another wild-fucking-west style shoot-out in a leafy suburb."

"The counting house isn't in the file?"

"Not as yet. Might be another drip to come. Now why are you pulling a face?"

"Nothing guv'. It just seems this run of luck is all very convenient."

"Read the fucking file and clean up their radical jihad bullshit before anyone gets their balls blown off. I hope that's not beyond you. Now out of my sight. My one inch of coffee is getting fucking cold."

11

✧ Should've Would've Could've ✧

The first thing Danny noticed as he ducked his head into the back seat of the silver, chauffeur driven Lexus was the black designer business suit she was wearing. It was cut like a man's, but you couldn't get any more feminine than the way Dexy wore it. Danny had to focus in order to brush aside the hot, intense flashback it gave him, his memory being backed up by the keen smell of her scent in the car.

It was early and the pick up was in Regent's Park, just as arranged. Danny had Barry Blount's laptop with him.

"Good morning, young man. How are we?"

"Always pleased to see you, Dexy. I think you wanted this?" he said, passing the computer across.

"I saw your girl on breakfast TV this morning. Looks like she really is flavour of the month. Mind you, the interview was so sickly sweet it could have given me diabetes."

Dexy was already busy powering up the machine, the chime of a windows operating system greeted her efforts.

"The nation's sweetheart should be exactly that, Danny! She has a chance to make it. Recovering this should certainly prolong her window of opportunity, so thank you. She doesn't know you but she does owe you."

Danny waved a hand gently in the air, knowing it was Dexy who would honour the debt.

A log on screen now presented itself. Dexy looked quizzically to Danny once the machine prompted them for a password for access.

"Barry's not the sharpest spoon in the drawer...is he?"

Danny smiled and nodded agreement. So Dexy typed "password" into the password box, and sure enough the desktop came to life in front of them. Danny gave a short laugh. His next guess would have been 'misternuts', all lower case.

It didn't take them long to locate the Quicktime video file that was so precious to Honey Sister. Barry Blount, once again, proved not to be a candidate for MI5. He had saved it to the desktop itself, unencrypted and filed as 'Honey Movie'.

"Before I double-click, darling," purred Dexy, "please remember I am an innocent soul, so you may have to explain what is going on..."

"Ever the convent girl, Dexy..."

This earned Danny an elbow in the ribs, which hurt more than it should because of Harkness' henchman and his bladed enforcer from the previous night.

Dexy double-clicked and a video box filled about a quarter of the computer screen. After taking a few moments to load the data, the frame jumped into life. It was a beach on a sunny day.

"Oh, a little al fresco romance," purred Dexy, leaning into Danny a little as the video began to play.

It wasn't what either of them was expecting.

Waves lapping gently, Barry Blount's voice was clear from behind the camera or camera phone. He was directing, asking Sarah Grimes, or Honey Sister as she would become more widely known, to stop being shy and perform. After a few minutes of back and forth, the budding starlet relents.

She finally walks into view, looking younger, a little more fresh-faced, a little less manufactured. It was unmistakeably the same girl who had been giggling on Danny's TV earlier that morning. The only difference being, on the computer screen she was carrying a little girl. A little girl with sunny blonde hair and grey-specked eyes. She had a cute button nose dappled with freckles. All just like the woman who was carrying her. For the avoidance of doubt, about 15 seconds into her appearance on screen, the little girl tightens the grip of her arms around Honey's neck and says, clear as day, "Mummy...ice cream...ice cream."

Dexy hit pause.

"Well, that's an unexpected development. She really does want her fame."

Danny sighed: "I'm out of my comfort zone here, Dexy. I am capable of doing a lot of things, but denying a child..."

"Danny, darling, you can wipe that look off your face. You and I are capable of everything if put in the right position. Holier than thou is not becoming of you. "

"I don't like manipulation, Dexy."

"Then don't play the game, my love."

Before their version of the moral maze could escalate, the driver of the car cleared his throat.

"Ma'am, apologies, but I think we have someone following us."

Their route had taken them north out of London's centre and they were now circling the estate that contained the national football ground - Wembley.

"Go through the stadium complex. Plenty of blind turns in there," Danny barked, as he shifted in his seat to see who or what was behind them.

A Ford Transit van. A black one, Danny recognised instantly.

Harkness and his team.

Instinctively Danny felt under his arm. The gun he retrieved from his sister's place would have been there, had he deemed it appropriate to bring it this morning. The gap his hand found made his heart sink.

"Pick up the pace," said Danny, the Lexus now speeding through various industrial units, swerving to avoid a tipper truck full of masonry in attempt to put distance between them and the black van.

"What the fuck is going on, darling?" Dexy was looking a little less composed than usual.

"It's Harkness, the guy I was asking you to sound out."

"From what I was able to discover he is quite the action man," said Dexy. "Three tours in the Gulf for the first war, another three in the sequel and just three years ago he was in Afghanistan. Trouble is no-one seems to be able to pinpoint exactly which regiment he served with."

"Flying under a black flag?"

"Maybe, but not so covert. I was able to find out he was there and the number of times. No, the real mystery about your Harkness is how he has risen so quickly at the Met. Did you know he is Anti-Terrorist Squad?"

"I assumed Flying Squad..."

"I thought you might, but no, he is definitely SO15. It fits, given his recent military experience. Anyway, his colleagues all seem to like him. No whiff of anything corrupt or dirty. No wife or kids, an elderly father, also ex-service, originally from Aldershot. Aside from that, I really couldn't find anything of great value."

They were interrupted by the Lexus lurching sharply to the left as their driver took a corner too tightly. The rear wheel bounced off the curb, the clang of the alloy audible even inside the vehicle.

His urgency was clear. The black Transit had now been joined by a motorbike with two riders, the driver brandishing a ballpeen hammer while the pillion gripped a sawn-off shotgun.

"Brace yourselves" was all the driver could say, as Dexy turned to look at Danny, urgency now in her voice.

"How have you ticked these chaps off, Danny? Don't answer that. One last thing: Harkness was given a dishonourable discharge from the Military. He slit his Afghan translator's throat. The motive was never explained. He's all business, your new friend!"

There was an explosion of glass as the driver's window gave way to the hammer and the double-barrels replaced it.

"Ma'am?"

The driver did the sensible thing. He pulled to a halt before he lost the left side of his face to buckshot.

Instantly, the van pulled tight to the rear of them. Figures jumped out, yanking the rear doors of the car open.

"Get the fuck out. NOW!"

"You do keep very charming company, Danny."

"Careful Dexy...that list includes you."

And with that Dexy was being dragged by her red hair out of the car.

Danny knew he should have brought the gun. But if he had, would he have used it?

Almost certainly.

The hands now reaching for him received a fine reception. Danny wrapped his arm around the wrist and pulled with all his body strength, enjoying the ping as his assailant's head was smacked against the door frame. Danny shuffled over to Dexy's side, the door still hanging open. He pushed himself out with both hands. His body began to straighten as the pillion rider on the bike reached him.

Knocking the shotgun to the side with lightning speed he used his upward momentum and right arm to smash into the soft flesh of the biker's throat, crushing his windpipe all the way back, mashing it against his spine.

Leaving him to collapse on the curb, Danny whirled around, trying to get a fix on where the first set of hands had dragged Dexy. Setting off towards the black van he saw the last flash of her red hair as she was bundled in the side door.

In his haste, Danny got too close to the front end of the van. As he drew level with it, the passenger door was flung open with full force, cracking into his knees, his momentum allowing his nose and head to join the party.

Down he went.

Eyes swimming, head clanging and woozy, gravel forcing up under fingernails as he scrabbled to stand up. Only for a heavy foot in the chest to smash him back down.

Danny didn't need his vision to clear to know who was standing over him.

"Danny, my son. A good man knows when his race is run."

Harkness surveyed the scene around him briefly. He then turned to his remaining men.

"Get rid of the driver and get Spikey back in the van and get out of here. Leave me the keys of the Lexus."

Spikey was choking. He was doubled in two at the side of the road, coughing up blood, fighting for air.

Danny slowly sat up. Harkness was now hunkered down beside him.

"I couldn't let you think your insubordination last night was even the smallest of triumphs, Danny. So here we are, letting you know the lie of the land...again. And just to hammer home the fact, I have your friend now too. Maybe now, you will start to listen to me."

Danny just stared at him, taking on board the magnitude of what The Tall Man had told him.

Harkness grabbed him. He pulled him to his feet taking him towards the rear of the Lexus. Harkness pressed the button on the key he'd just been handed. The boot popped open.

"In you go."

Danny now began to resist, pulling back on Harkness with as much energy as he had left.

"If you think I'm getting in there..."

His words broke off as Harkness swept his legs from

under him using his own left leg. He hefted his upper body weight into Danny's waist simultaneously, folding him into the boot of the big executive car.

"Get in and shut the fuck up. I don't want you to see where we're going. Once there, all will be revealed."

As the boot sank, the daylight shrank. Danny had the second flashback of the day, this one a lot less pleasurable than the one Dexy had inspired.

In his mind's eye he saw a man standing over him, closing a door tight, blocking out the light on a equally small space. Danny began to shiver, both at his enclosed space and the sight of who was shutting him in to this black hole. In that instant he was back, a small boy...and the man standing over him was his father.

12

✧ Culture Clash ✧

When Katerina knocked on the door of room 520 of The Grosvenor House Hotel, she was, although she said so herself, looking particularly stunning. A chic Banana Republic business suit, sitting immaculately over Agent Provocateur lingerie. She felt confident and ready. The persona she had created in her own imagination allowed her to screen the real her from these moments of exploitation. She waited for the door to be answered.

It was opened by a Middle Eastern man. He had a smile on his bearded face, his eyes not able to help but look her up and down as she stepped over the threshold. She recognised the naked desire in his eyes; she had seen it many times as she stepped in to rooms like this one. To Katerina, hotel refinement always seemed to belie the animal purpose that this room was about to accommodate.

"Good afternoon, handsome, sir."

Despite flashing her best smile at him, Katerina's thoughts were full of nothing but contempt towards the latest pathetic imbecile to rent her body. What was it today? Three hours? A cool £5,000 for the privilege, she believed, even though she wasn't supposed to know her own price point.

Her next thought was disappointment. He was Arab, so she wouldn't even have a glass of champagne or wine to break the ice with, to help take the edge off the first exchanges.

"Excuse me, darling. I need to prepare," Katerina said, her high heels clicking on the tiled bathroom floor as she closed the door behind her.

She took her time. Not because she wanted to be just right, but because she wanted to delay the inevitable. Her instinct was flaring. There was something about this one she didn't like. She hoped he wasn't going to be one of the rough ones who felt that once they'd paid, they could do whatever they fucking liked.

When she finally emerged into the bedroom he was sat on the edge of the bed, his hands spread out on either side of him on the quilt. He took an involuntary gasp at the sight of her in her high heels and expensive underwear.

She walked towards him. She stood over him letting him smell her perfume. Her smile was rictus, plastered across her face by the force of her own will.

He stood up. Meeting her eyes now he kissed her full on the lips. Something swished in her peripheral vision, a reflection in the mirror that hung on the wall facing the end of the king size bed.

And then he was holding whatever it was in front of her face; a black silk scarf which he gently draped across her wrists once he had pulled them in front of her. This was what she had been sensing then.

A kink.

Was he someone who could only get it up by having the woman completely under his control?

He tied the scarf in a tight knot, and then produced a second, identical scarf. Katerina waited to see if this one was for her eyes or to tie her to the bed. But he had a surprise again for her. The scarf came up over her head, down round her neck and then, suddenly, viciously, he pulled across her mouth, swiftly tying a large, tight double knot, which pushed its way into her mouth as well as held it in place.

And then he reached behind him, under the pillow

nearest to them on the bed. She waited to see another scarf, except this time it was a brute-ugly handgun.

And now Katerina was scared. Scared enough to start to weep.

The 'intel' had been spot on. CC's team had been following the Mohammed's Way acolytes for 48 hours, and today it was clear they were gearing up for action.

CC's team were trailing them in West End traffic, the edge of expectation building as they all sensed imminent action. But there was a problem.

They had lost the main man, Yusufzai. He had separated off in the afternoon. Despite her team having split in order to stick with him, he had slipped the net via the London Underground. The follow had lost him in the labyrinth that was the new Kings Cross network, too many interchanges and people in the way.

At least they were still behind the rest of the team in their battered Renault van.

CC was driving a short distance back from the van, following as it snaked its way round Marble Arch and down onto Park Lane. The radio chatter gave all of them a constant commentary on their movements. The van started to signal a left-hand turn. Christine looked at Freethy in the passenger seat next to her.

"Let me jump out here, CC. If they turn up and head back towards Oxford Street I can intercept them on foot. You won't see where they go if you make the turn behind them now, we are just a touch too far back."

Stopping at the kerb, Freethy leapt out straight away, checking he had his radio covered as he began to sprint down the blocked off street.

CC gunned her BMW back into the traffic, a few blared horns greeting her for the apparent aggression.

She made the turn around the front of The Grosvenor House Hotel about 25 seconds behind the Renault, and just at that her radio came alive. Freethy.

"I'm by the taxi entrance of The Grosvenor. Two have switched into the back of the van. Good news is we have our main man again. Abasin Yusufzai just got into the front. But he's not alone. Can't say for definite if it was a woman, but it is someone dressed in a burka."

He had forced Katerina into the burka. Cleverly the black silk scarf blending in with the full black of the burka. She was still gagged, but of course behind the burka's hood, no-one could see that she was tied at the mouth.

Katerina fought her rising fear, pushing the bile back down into her throat, as panic kept forcing her to gag. As she walked next to this man, particularly through the hotel lobby, she had fought with herself. Should she try to pull away from him? Scream?

The hard pressure of the gun just to the left of her spine was enough to keep her compliant, hidden in the folds of his sleeve and the cloth of her new outfit.

As she had put the outfit on, he had started to babble at her in heavily-accented English. It was a few minutes before she could comprehend that he was taking her some-where, somewhere to meet some men she might know. Still, as she was none the wiser, Katerina's panic and fear fluttered like a captured bird in her chest. This all felt to her like the last straw, the latest indignity that might just break her resolve, leave her bereft of self respect, robbing her of her carefully constructed façade. She felt like a piece of meat, robbed of the one thing that she clung to; hope.

Was this man taking her somewhere to be forced into something completely debased and debauched at the hands of several people? Would she live? Could she bear to live if that was to be her fate now? Katerina may have thought she had developed a tough outer shell over these last months of abuse, but now she knew just how fragile she really was, just how little her life was worth in this world, just how disposable she was.

CC had seen the burka-clad figure get into the van milliseconds after she had turned the corner into Park Street. What the fuck was this now? A woman? On a job? An Islamic woman? Unless it was no woman under the get up?

The Renault van started off again, heading north towards Oxford Street, as Freethy had predicted. CC slowed to a partial stop at the Grosvenor to allow him back in the car.

She had a choice to make. Keep the follow going, or if. anything, tighten it up. But then what? With a woman aboard, was the job really on? At what point could she call it? When should she call on the gun ships if the job was a live one?

"Any signs of coercion? Do you think it's actually a woman under that outfit?"

Freethy was already shaking his head, a rueful expression across his face.

"To be honest, I'm not sure. I wasn't paying them much mind, not expecting to see a man and woman even approach our target vehicle. It was only as they reached it I realised it was our main man. As for whether that's a female? Could be, slight enough build to be female, but can't swear to it."

"Fuck." Was all she could manage as she picked her way behind the Renault, which was now turning left again, back towards Marble Arch once again.

Katerina was in the middle seat in the front cab of some kind of van now, sandwiched between her supposed client and another man. He had a scarf on and a baseball cap, but it couldn't hide his beard, dark eyes and swarthy complexion. Both men were babbling to each other in a language she neither knew nor could identify.

Her captor spoke to her again in poor English, prodding her ribs with his gun,

"Look up, keep head still, no look down, until I say, whore."

She did as she was told, only to feel him bring her tethered hands up and in front of her. Something round, cold and metallic was forced between her fingers, then the sticky pressure of heavy duty tape being wound around her hands, whatever it was now wedged between them. Finally, there was some fiddling with the end of the metallic object, where it protruded from both her fingers and the tightly-wound tape.

"Fuck," was all Katerina could think. "What the fuck?"

The Renault van meandered through west London down into Knightsbridge then deeper into Kensington, until eventually it pulled into a dead-end street.

CC had to cruise past it, instructing one of the other cars to deposit a man on foot to see if he could get a closer look at the van and see why they've stopped.

But before they could get someone in position, the van was back on its way again. Pulling back onto the road it had turned off and once again start to retrace its route, back into the streets of Knightsbridge, towards the rear of the world-famous Harrods department store. It wasn't a long journey.

Christine concentrated on her gut for twenty seconds,

and then reached for the radio. She called the gunships in closer.

The short stop was a simple one. It allowed the Islamic team to pull on masks and distribute weapons from the rear of the van to the whole team. Katerina was still sat up front, still being forced to look up, her neck now beginning to ache from the prolonged pose.

She could sense that the atmosphere in the van had now changed. There was an added tension to the foreign babble amongst the men. The van began to travel again and after what seemed like hours, she was given instructions, once more in strained English.

"When we stop, we get out, you no fight, whore. No fight, you will live. Understood?"

She nodded affirmation.

"When we get to door, you move when I say."

The van came to a halt. She was pulled out of the door roughly, onto a plush west London street. They pushed her up the steps of one of the large terrace houses on the street. From the looks of it the building had seen better days. She was placed front and centre before the door of the house, and her supposed client banged his fist on the door rapidly. As he did so, he whipped the hood of the burka off her head.

And now, as she waited for a response, she had the presence of mind to look down for the first time at her bound hands. There, sticking out from the tape was some sort of metal egg, with a ring on the top of it. From the ring what looked like clear wire, attached and leading all the way to her left, where her supposed client stood holding his gun pointed at her with one hand and the end of this wire in the other. And then it struck her, like a horse kick to her chest.

She was holding a hand grenade.

It was a fucking nightmare. The street they had stopped in was wide and fairly clear of traffic but there was nowhere to hide. CC daren't pull into it, she hurriedly dispatched Freethy on foot to get a fix on what was happening.

Then her mobile phone started to ring, Freethy on the other end.

"We're fucked."

Panic was blooming in her chest. Katerina was whipping her head from side to side wildly, looking from her captor on one side of the portico, to the rest of his team on the other side. And then the sound of a peephole being opened on the door itself. A puzzled shout come from behind it.

In Russian.

The Bouncer's mistake was his instinct to open the door once he recognised one of the boss' girls on the doorstep. But why was she was wearing a gag?

Suddenly there were masked men in his face, guns pointing, one of them babbling in crazy English something about "boss" and "a grenade". The talker thrust the girl's hands under his nose. Now he understood the bit about a hand grenade. The explosive and a gun under his chin forced him to lead them down a long hallway. They finally turned into a big room on the ground floor. It was a kitchen. At a table in the middle of the room sat five men, all eating a meal that a sixth man was still dishing out to them. Dinner was about to be ruined.

"They've gone in, armed, with the girl. It is definitely a girl, they seemed to force their way in. But unless we hear shots we can't go in. If we roll up too early this has fucking 'siege' written all over it."

Freethy was right. All they could do was to block the street away from the house and hope they didn't force the issue. But that might be too loose. There could be back alleys or cut -throughs between the houses that would give them passage out.

Christine started doling out instructions on the radio, getting the gunships to close off both ends of this street, but not too close. The next thing she did was hit the panic button on her mobile, calling in the big boys. If this was going 'siege', she wasn't going to be able to hold on to the scene on her own for very long, and nor did she want to.

The Bouncer was pistol-whipped from behind as soon as he crossed the kitchen threshold, and Katerina was shoved through the door straight after him.

Despite her terror, because that is what it was now, out and out terror, she was not so panicked that when she looked round the room at the men eating that she couldn't help but recognise one or two faces.

Sat at the table was Losif. The man who had laid the ground rules for her new life when she had been first brought to London. He had become her "boss".

The other face, however, was far more shocking to her. Like a knife twisting in her chest, the final indignity delivering a 'coup de grace' in this nightmare of hers.

It was the man who had courted her back home in her native Russia. It was the one who had whispered sweet nothings to her on the night he had first met her, waitressing in a Moscow nightclub. He had wooed her, romanced her over many months. He had taken her heart as easily as you might pick up an apple and take a bite. When he had suggested a trip to London for a romantic weekend, she was convinced he was going to propose. On arrival, they hadn't checked into a beautiful hotel, or booked a lavish restaurant for dinner. He had simply handed her over to this Losif and her descent into exploitation had begun. Kirill had been his name, or so he had told her and now here he was, in front of her.

Sitting there. Eating. Here, in this London house. The first time she had seen him since he coldly walked away from the speeding car that had abducted her.

Her fake client spoke directly to Losif.

"Everyone still, please. Look to her hands. See? Grenade."

He jangled the ring on the grenade by gently tugging on the catgut he had tied to it earlier.

"Anyone moves, I pull. Anyone not answer my questions, I pull. Anyone try trick me, I pull. Yes?"

Losif, slowly nodded, coolly wiping his mouth with a paper napkin as he did so.

Her captor spoke again. "More men?"

Losif shaking his head slowly. "No."

"Money. Where is money? Show my men."

Losif nodded to the pistol-whipped but still conscious doorman and said, in Russian, "Show them."

Katerina was simply too terrified to move, taking it all in. She didn't turn to watch as the men left the room with the door guard. She could not take her eyes off Kirill.

She had loved this man. She had dreamed of a life with him. She had put her faith in him. And now look. She was here, a grenade in her tethered hands. Her body defiled and disrespected. Over and over again by so many strangers. Her dignity stripped from her. All because of this man, Kirill, who had once held her face in his hands and told her she was an angel, a gift to him from God. And yet all she had been was a product to be traded. A business transaction.

Katerina felt sick.

The team of radicals were now ferrying money in large canvas bags out to their van.

CC now had the street blocked at both ends, a gunship just around a slight bend, about 100 yards from the target house, but far enough away so as not to be visible to the men who were now piling bags into the back of the battered Renault van. The other armed response team was close enough that once they started to try and make their exit, the hit could be put into place easily.

One of her team was now trying to edge along the opposite pavement, using parked cars for cover, trying to get some photographic evidence of the theft going down. When the phantom woman had been added to the mix, CC had radioed that she hoped the photographer on the team had managed to "smudge" her, to photograph her, not just for evidential purposes but for identification should they need to let her slip while in pursuit of the main suspects. CC was yet to get a response to her hopeful question; this was an answer in itself.

Freethy was also trying to get a better angle on proceedings. He was trying to get to a vantage point behind some bushes at a property diagonally opposite the target house. All the while he was on both the radio and the mobile phone to Christine, one conversation clipped and professional for the radio records, the mobile phone chatter much more informal and useful.

Mobile: "Looks like they are loading up, no sign of the bird. Maybe she is a hostage, but can't tell at this point."

Radio: "Standby all Assets, suspects loading cargo."

Mobile: "They are pointing to the west end of the street, so make sure the pistol packers at your end are ready to move their arses this way."

"They are itching, don't worry about that, Freethy. They love this kind of shit…"

But CC hoped she wouldn't be sniffing gunpowder in the air this evening…

Katerina had started to shake. She knew how these men thought. She would be blamed for this, even though she neither knew the Arabs nor knew of what their original intent had been. They would suspect her; they would want to dispose of her. Robberies attracted unwanted attention. Loose ends needed to be tidied up.

Yet all she could do now was stare at Kirill. The man she had loved. The man who would probably be given the job of killing her after this.

Five very long minutes passed until the gang's bag carriers returned to the kitchen, telling their boss, Abasin, that they had all the money.

Abasin nodded gently, his eyes never leaving Losif's face. His stare had been fixed on him from the moment he had walked in.

"We leave. No one follows to door, the grenade stays safe."

"I will find you. This is a very bad day for you," There was no threat in Losif's voice. He was simply stating a fact.

"Allah is great," was the reply. Abasin slowly backed towards the door, his cohorts aiming their guns, doing the same. Katerina was being drawn backwards by Abasin's gun hand.

And then it changed.

She felt an outpouring. Every hand, every mouth, every touch, every degradation, every fear, every tearful sleepless night, every self-recrimination, every humiliation, every faked smile and orgasm.

Every. Single. Misery.

They all boiled up in Katerina's head, her heart was fit to explode.

Whipping her bound hands from left to right in front of her, Katerina pulled the catgut taut from where it was attached to the grenade all the way back to Abasin's hands, and then with a brutal flick of her forearms, she felt and heard the ping as the metal pin and round handle across the top of the explosive was suddenly spinning wildly in mid air.

She leapt forward for all she was worth, her head burying into Kirill's chest. He rose out of his chair to try and escape this woman who had launched herself at him. But he was too slow. They were all too slow. Her bodyweight pinning him back against the cooker that was flush against the wall behind them.

Abasin suddenly knew what was possible here. Turning to run, screaming in his native language to his men.

"Get out, get out, get out, get out, get out."

But they weren't quick enough either.

The grenade fulfilled its deadly purpose. It exploded. Right next to the gas hob that had just cooked the last meal for these Russian criminals.

There was a crack. Freethy heard it first, CC a split second later. Puzzlement struck each of them at the same time, but the roar that followed took both of them into complete surprise and shock.

The gas explosion triggered by the grenade literally took the whole of the front of the house out. Bricks, plaster and debris were flung high in the air. The Renault van was rocked from side-to-side by the force of the blast. The driver was at first wide-eyed and unsure of what to do at the noise, and then the burden of choice was removed from him. A large slab of portico slammed into the bonnet of the van, pushing the engine free of its mooring and onto the road beneath it.

And now CC was screaming into her radio: "Go! Go! Go!" The gunships hurtled in, along with the rest of the team, crowding round the van hauling the driver out of the door. Christine was standing looking at the front of the ruined house once she got there, whispering out loud: "Fuck, Fuck, Fuck."

13

✧ The Wrong Foot ✧

Dark, enclosed spaces held a terrible fear for Danny. It had been a long time since he found himself in such an unwelcome position. Now that he was here he was struggling.

Encased in the boot of the car, he tried to focus his mind in order to wipe away the images from his past assailing him. But even concentrating on his battered body and the throbbing cramp in his knees didn't help. Memories of his father were a stubborn spectre. Flashes kept poking through his attempts at slow breathing calm...his dad forcing a five-year-old Danny into the cupboard under the stairs, reading from a bible as he did so. Dark and cramped the hours passed, until light flooded all around him, only for his father's form to block it out as his raised arm brought a belt down with a vicious swish. A shrill rendition of the Lord's Prayer was always the refrain to these beatings.

His sister, Celeste would sometimes try and sneak food or drink to him, but Danny had always refused to take them, his young mind knowing instinctively that if caught his sister might pay the price.

The slowing of the car helped him finally push the memories down, instinct now kicking in as he listened to the sound of tyres on the road. Then he heard a change, a ramp of some kind as the angle of the car shifted and forced him to slip back against the end of the car. And then a stop. The door of the car opened. The balance of the vehicle shifted as he felt Harkness leave the car.

The boot lid opened, causing Danny to blink and hold his hands out in front of his face, squinting in an attempt to adjust his vision.

"Ah, Danny. I think we got off on the wrong foot."

This bloke is fucking nuts, was all Danny could think in return.

They were in a multi-storey car park. Theirs was the only car on this particular level. Danny bent over, trying to stretch off the ache of having been curled up in the boot.

He straightened up and looked at Harkness wiping dried blood from his face.

"Danny, we will not harm her. She's just a little insurance policy is all. A keepsake to keep you on the straight and narrow."

"What are we doing here, wherever here is, and why?"

"I like your attitude, young man. All business. Cutting to the chase. You don't need to know exactly where we are, but I have a little mission for you. Think of this as a sort of job interview. I have heard from all sorts that you are good, Danny. But I want to see it myself. A little Doubting Thomas, I am... need to put my fingers in the wounds."

Danny just stared at him, his level gaze never wavering.

"What do you notice about this car park, Danny?"

Danny took his time before breaking his gaze away from Harkness' face.

"It's brand new. No tyre marks or debris. The dust is still settling."

Harkness clapped his hands together.

"Correct! And as it is brand new, it is empty...except for the lower levels, the basement. Where just about now, an illegal event is happening. All very naughty! And we are about to make it even naughtier, you and I. A little thievery to brighten our day."

"Why the fuck would I want to rob somewhere without even the chance of a recce, or planning of any kind? Getting fucking killed is no measure of how good I am at anything other than dying."

"Where is all that positivity gone? It was here a second ago. Danny, I have thought of everything. You don't need a recce. One of my boys is doing one for you right now. Take a look."

Harkness produced an iPad mini from his inside pocket, activated the screen and tapped an icon to open an app. Handing the device to Danny, it came to life with a black and white image of the basement several levels below.

The screen showed a crowd of men, all huddled round each other. Try as he might, he couldn't fathom what they were doing. Plus he was still busy trying to work out just how he might get the hell out of Harkness' crazy scenario intact.

"My boy is down there now, wearing a pair of glasses that also happen to have a camera in them right here," explained Harkness, touching the bridge of his nose by way of illustration.

"Genius, isn't it...have you worked out what they are doing yet? It's a dogfight. Easy money, a load of gypsies, all flashing cash. Now there is probably only about 20 grand changing hands, give or take. I don't really need the money, but I want to see you in action, Danny, and I wanna see the fabled Felix magic."

Danny was about to protest, taking a step towards Harkness, only to see him reach inside his coat pocket, the hand emerging with a gun in it.

"Play the fucking game, Danny. It is what we do. I'll even show you a little trust."

Harkness flipped the gun around in his hand proffering it butt-first to Danny.

"This is insane. We could get torn apart down there.

They must have security of their own. They must be tooled up already."

"Yes they do, but the beauty is that I provided them with the heavies. They are all my boys, undercover. So once you make your move the bouncers won't interfere. Of course, I can't vouch for the pikeys and their customers, but I am sure you will think of something."

Instinctively, Danny checked the gun, slipping the cartridge out of the butt, surprised by the sight of live bullets in it.

He looked again at the iPad. Harkness' man swept his eyes around the site in a slow pan, travelling to and fro so that Danny could start to form a layout of the place in his own mind.

"Exit strategy? How do we get out once we have the money?"

"There will be a car waiting at the top of the basement ramp, driver aboard, ready to whisk us away. How we get there is your challenge, my son."

"We'll need to distract them somehow."

"Again, I am sure you will think of something..."

Danny blew his cheeks out, knowing in that moment he was going to do this. He knew he was going to do the one thing he never thought he would: wing it on a job. But apart from trepidation, there was another emotion at play in Danny's heart.

Excitement.

He wanted to have a go. It was just too delicious to resist. He would never want Harkness to see that in him, but he couldn't deny it to himself.

"C'mon Danny, think of it as a game. It'll be fun!"

"Alright, let's be reckless then, Harkness, but here's the deal. The money, it's all mine. No split. You've already said you don't need it."

"Cheeky bugger."

And again he was clapping, gales of laughter and mirth

dancing in his eyes. A lightness that scared the living shit out of Danny, but thrilled him just a little too.

There was about a hundred men, of all shapes, sizes, age and creeds. The air was thick with feral excitement, expectation of the brutal entertainment in front of them. As Danny and Harkness approached the rear of the throng one man was spreading sawdust onto the concrete floor, soaking up blood from a fight just finished. Another man was loading a limp-looking Staffordshire bull terrier into the back of a blacked-out van, actual tears in his eyes and tenderness in his movements.

Nearby, another two vans were parked up, one of them rocking from side to side, from the force of the dogs inside. They were eager to get going, to fight. Bloodlust.

Danny set to what he did best.

His eyes were 'all about', processing all of the information around him at lightning speed. As he stood at the back of the throng, he assimilated the images he had watched on the iPad, correlating them with what he could now see for real. In moments like these, Danny seemed to go inward on himself. It was as if he could float above the room. The set-up was clear in his mind, like a snapshot of his immediate surroundings. He now had a clear understanding of the size and shape of the room and crowd. Next he scanned the faces, taking each individual in, making instant judgements as to whether each presented a threat, a hindrance, or were just another bystander. A combination of experience and gut instinct provided him with all of this data at lightning speed.

His next move was to take in the physical evidence around him. First, he was keenly aware of the smell of the body odour of the man next to him at the back of the crowd. He was sweating profusely, and Danny knew instantly he had either a lot to lose or had lost already.

He scanned the gathering again, this time isolating in his mind the big men. He scouted for bulges in their waistbands or underarms revealing who was tooled up and who wasn't. He assumed that those who were belonged to Harkness. At the same time he was also taking in snatches of conversation, picking out little titbits of information. There was a Seamus here, a fuck off there, a David calling odds for the next fight. All a jumble that Danny was filtering for anything useful as he moved through the crowd.

Then back to their faces. Danny swept a look around the people assembled, deliberately making direct eye contact, using the split second engagements to measure the reactions his eyes provoked. The shift in a face might sometimes barely be perceptible, but Danny never missed even a flicker or unconscious twitch. He had read an article about it once. They were known as 'microfacial movements'. A whole plethora of 'telling info' in literally the blink of an eye or less. He could spot a minute flinch from fifty paces and know whether the person who just gave themselves away was a 'lover' or a 'fighter'.

And last but not least, Danny looked at the floor, because in his experience feet never lie.

People subconsciously gave their intentions or feelings away by the way they positioned their feet. When the action kicked off, he knew that he could tell who was going to have a pop and who would make a bolt for it with a cursory glance down at their feet.

Danny had assessed the entire situation in just over one minute.

And once done he let his eyes settle on the man who was running the entire show. He knew this as soon as he had laid eyes on him.

Older, about 55, with reddish-brown hair turning silver at the edges. He had small, dark piggy eyes set beneath a forehead that was slightly too big for the rest of his face.

This was completed with a thin-lipped mouth that gave him an overall look of someone who could be cruel or kind in the same heartbeat.

The giveaway that it was his gig was the number of men standing unnaturally close to him. And the fact they were paying no mind to the action about to unfold on the concrete before them. They, like Danny, were too busy scanning. Their no-nonsense glares kept everyone just far enough away from the main man. One particularly tall bouncer leant in to whisper in his boss' ear every now and again, a small nod or shake of the head each time a question was asked.

No doubt Piggy-eyes was the guv'nor here.

"What you thinking, Felix? Talk me through it," said Harkness, doing some whispering of his own now.

Danny laid it out for him:

"We'll have to be quick, incisive. To our left, eight o'clock. Heavy set man, black, short, bald. He's tooled up, but not one of yours. He's not ex-military so keep an eye. Dead ahead. Small guy. Leather jacket. He's a fighter, meets a look full-on. I'll have to take him out of the game straight away. The one we need to talk to is over at three o'clock. Piggy-eyes. He's got plenty round him but it's his game. He's the one we have to convince we aren't joking."

Harkness was nodding gently, impressed that Danny had taken the scene in so quickly.

"Leave the convincing to me, Danny. Just nod when you are ready to kickstart the fun."

Danny stepped away, not liking the sound of the last comment. Convincing? Apart from winging a job, the only other thing Danny had never liked in a plan was a team-mate who was as unpredictable as Harkness.

Two men were now in the centre, each holding a dog. Danny was surprised to see two Jack Russells, both snarling, snapping, pulling at their leads, the smell of the blood from the previous fight firing them up. The flaring of their nostrils and curling of their lips adding to the anticipation of the spectators. The men were goading them, edging the dogs towards each other close enough to provoke a bite then hauling them back at the last possible second before contact was made.

Money was furiously changing hands, with wagers being placed and side bets multiplied before the start of the bout. Finally, Mr Piggy-eyes raised his voice. He had a thick, rough cockney accent.

"Let's get on with it. Get ready to release."

Danny was now stood just behind the short man in the leather jacket, the one he had told Harkness was up for a fight.

It was showtime.

Danny tapped him on the shoulder, and as he turned to react Danny calmly reached up and bounced the butt of his gun on the bridge of the guy's nose. Blood shot everywhere as he fell to his knees, and the blow caused the crowd around them to divide like someone had just declared the plague. Danny then levelled his gun across the circle at Mr Piggy-eyes, and at the top of his lungs shouted: "DON'T FUCKING MOVE AN INCH!"

At the same instant two of the bigger men Danny had clocked earlier, one wearing glasses, each put a hand on the shoulders of two of Mr Piggy-eyes' closest associates, their expressions enough to discourage any reaction.

At Danny's feet the short guy was struggling to stand up, ready to strike back (even through a blood-soaked face) when Danny calmly sideswiped him again with the gun, barrel first this time, opening a huge welt on his cheek. More claret joined the rest.

As the hubbub started to subside, Mr Piggy-eyes spoke up.

"Who the fuck do you think you are? Are you fucking mad?"

One of Harkness' men tossed a black holdall into the

middle of the fight ring, just in front of the dogs.

Danny: "All the Money. In the bag. Now. We have enough guns and men to make a right mess of this place. Don't be fucking stupid. Just get on with it. Nobody wants to try and be Mad Max here. Okay? No fucking heroics."

A movement to Danny's right caught his eye. The dog handler shifted his feet, pointing them this way.

"A dog as a weapon," thought Danny.

Pointing the snarling Jack Russell at Danny, he released the lead. At almost the same instant a gunshot rang out. The fierce little dog's head exploded across the feet of the crowd.

Harkness was holding his gun level on the other side of the circle, just behind Mr Piggy-eyes, who was now clasping his hands over his obviously ringing ears.

"See? The man means business. The money, gentlemen. FUCKING NOW," said Harkness, looking very pleased with himself at this point. He turned his gun now towards Piggy-eyes, whose face showed both rage and resignation.

Danny picked the holdall up and started to move around the room, using his gun every now and then to encourage someone to hand over the wad of money they might be holding. It didn't take long for the bag to start bulging.

In a matter of minutes, Danny had gathered what he thought was enough, nodding to Harkness that he was ready to make an exit.

Then turning to the throng, making sure his gun was cocked and visible to all, he declared: "Gentlemen, a pleasure doing business with you. We will now take our leave. Don't try to come after us. It's easier to pick out a target from above on this ramp than to dodge a bullet from below."

Danny was backing towards the incline. Harkness and his men joined him, dragging Piggy-eyes with them as they did so, a gun at the back of the boss man's head.

As they reached the bottom of the ramp, Danny saw it.

The 'tell' he had been expecting. The one that proved to him that Piggy was too stupid or too proud to just roll with the punch. Again it was slight, but it was as clear as day to Danny.

Piggy had tensed his core muscles in anticipation of launching himself at Harkness. The element of surprise was meant to deflect the gun away from the back of his head while he swiped at The Tall Man. But Danny was ready. As Piggy shifted his weight and started his pirouette, he calmly shot him in the thigh, the smell of gunpowder, burnt cloth and blood suddenly all around them.

Harkness was incredulous. Staring now at his new-found friend, he realised he had saved him a lot of grief, perhaps even more.

"Now, Gentlemen, see what I mean. No foolishness," said Danny, instructing the crowd again.

And then he put in his insurance policy, the one thing that would guarantee them a little time to get the fuck out of there.

Looking at the guy who had been calling the odds, he shouted "Hey, David, thanks for the tip-off…"

The bloke was gobsmacked and then suddenly horrified as he realised what would happen next, as the rest of the men all turned to look at him.

Danny didn't want to look back as they sprinted up the concrete slope.

14

✧ Kiss And Tell ✧

Fisty was enjoying the spotlight.

To describe him as flamboyant would be like saying Lady Gaga wore sensible clothes.

He was renowned as being London's campest man alive. Given to wearing outrageous outfits to big club nights in the heart of London's Soho, Fisty could always be relied upon to turn the eccentric level up to max. Papparazzi loved catching sight of him at some of London's hottest venues. His outfits were so outrageous they had inspired a weekly column in one influential fashion blog dedicted to nothing else.

And this evening was no different. In the Parrot Feathers Club, a basement venue on Old Compton Street, the music was loud, the dance floor heaving and in the middle of it was Fisty, holding court like a 21st century Liberace.

He was having to shout at the top of his voice.

"I just knew that a summer's evening of naughtiness called for my green mankini with matching tutu ensemble. It enhances my eyes."

Fisty dipped his matching fluorescent green sunglasses that looked like they were designed for a child and then made three sizes too big. The young, muscled man wearing the tightest 'Keep Calm and Carry On Cruising' T-shirt could only laugh.

"But Fisty, babe, aren't those platform high heels more

suited to strippers?"

"I can dance in anything, darling. And as for stripping, what would make you think I was that type of cheap queen?!"

In this room, Christine Chance stuck out like a sore thumb.

As she made her way down the stairs into the throbbing nightclub, she was half amazed and half uncomfortable. Some of the young men looked like Michelangelo statues, their physiques cut like stone, their tight clothes leaving nothing to the imagination. She wondered if she might be a little jealous of what fun you might have being gay in these days of tolerance, cheap gym membership and social networking. But she was also greeted by some of the clientele with openly aggressive glances and the odd, "Dyke night is on Tuesdays, love" as she scanned the room in front of her, looking for the snout who had tipped them the wink about big Iggy Adesina.

When she spotted him dancing, she couldn't stop herself from laughing out loud. One of her copper mates had told her where to look for Fisty, saying that really, you won't be able to miss him once you are in there. Well Jesus, he wasn't wrong.

CC had never liked Kylie Minogue, and she liked her even less now. The music was loud enough to make CC feel almost dizzy. As she pushed her way through the crowd she was reminded of a school of sharks circling a shoal of fish, just waiting for the moment to swoop and feed.

When she finally reached where Fisty was, he was whirling like a dust devil. His arms were flailing in time to the incessant beat that was giving CC a headache. When he finally spun to face her, she grabbed him, stopping him dead in his tracks.

"Fisty, I need you to come with me for a little chat. Now. "

He said something back, but as Kylie was being shocked by the power, CC couldn't hear it. The bloke next to him tried to pull Fisty away. CC simply grabbed the guy's wrist twisting and using the straightened arm, pushed Fisty's mate to the floor, face first.

She had Fisty's full attention now.

Looking down horrified at his protector's new angle on life, Fisty did what any chemically enhanced diva would... he became mad. But in a bitchy, queenie way. Coming at CC with a blur of fake nails, fake tan, sweaty mankini and a high pitched scream. She reckoned that if she was going to avoid having her eyes scratched out, there was only one thing to do. She sidestepped calmly and grabbed Fisty by the balls and twisted.

This was followed by a squeal. His face drained to white and a tumble of legs was completed by an unfortunate realignment of the mankini.

"Yuck," was all CC could manage.

Suddenly a pair of powerful arms wrapped around her waist picking her up, turning her away from the stricken informant. However, she was quick enough to pull her Met Police brief up before the eyes of the second bouncer who was just arriving on the scene. A little late, it had to be said.

The flash of the badge was enough for her to be set back down and the big lads to back off.

She turned, grabbing hold of Fisty who was now whimpering. Fisty's right hand man was now less inclined to interfere, not wanting another chance to kiss the dance-floor with his face. Plus he had seen the badge.

CC pushed through the crowd, with the informant first, up out of the venue, into the bustle of Soho and finally into the back of the waiting car. A car being driven by Freethy.

Once they were under way, Christine gave Fisty a wedge of tissues pulled from a box stuck in the door compartment of the car. Fisty wiped away the tears that had started to stream down his face, his eyes still fully dilated which told Freethy and CC that their passenger had been sampling a little of his own product this summer evening.

Between sobs, he managed: "You frigging bitch, why'd you have to grab me like that?"

CC just looked at him.

"I mean, I just asked Craig to take you outside so he could find out what you wanted, you didn't have to go all frigging Lara Croft. I should be calling the Old Bill and my solicitor, you fucking breeder."

"He didn't see my badge. That might be useful," CC thought.

"Okay, enough now, Fisty. I'll tell you why you are sat here once you stop whining. Understand?"

Fisty shifted in the seat, adjusting his ridiculous mankini. CC daren't look down to see if the dealer had been success-ful.

"Talk to me about Iggy Adesina," she instructed.

This prompted a look from Fisty. One of camp irritation. She had to admit she liked this guy's chutzpah.

"I don't know who or what you are talking about, darling, do I look like I know anyone called Iggy?"

"You were arrested in Soho and detained at Finchley Road nick on the 11th of this month. What did you tell them?"

Fisty squirmed ever so slightly at the mention of Finch-ley Road.

"Listen, Tinkerbelle, you can kiss my arse! You should know when you do what we do for a living, getting nicked is simply all part of the musical. I wasn't asked about anyone called Piggy, or Iggy or 'getting Jiggy with it'. I was being quizzed about matters I know nothing about. Hence, why I am a free walking bitch."

"Fisty. Look at me."

He did. Now staring directly into CC's Met Police badge.

"Awww, fuck. You buggers don't play fair. And I've chipped a nail!"

"Fisty, cut the crap and just tell me what you told them

about Iggy Adesina."

"I didn't know too much. My interest in him was purely personal, you know. Everyone likes a challenge, a nice big black man like that. I figured I could turn him. I dreamt I could, anyway."

"I'm not asking you if you fancied him, Fisty. Freethy, if he dodges another question, I'm gonna roll him out the back door. Okay? So just give me a little room, I don't want to ding the paintwork on the car."

Fisty looked wide-eyed now.

"You wouldn't! You can't! You bitch!"

"Iggy Adesina."

"I don't know that much!" The whine was 100 per cent back into his voice.

"He was sent to me. He wanted some muscle. And if there is one thing I know…it's muscle. He wanted some boys to help with some heavy lifting. I just passed on the fact that he was asking to one of your friends in blue. They put two-and-two together. I'm just a free-spirited entrepreneur."

"You are drug-peddling degenerate, Fisty. Don't try and dress it up. If it deals in shit, takes shit and looks like shit, it's generally shitty. So you put Iggy next to some heavy-lifters then? And what did you get out of it?"

"I want my phone call!"

"You fucking idiot. I'm not arresting you. I just want the information. This is not official, just a little fishing. Hence why I can throw you out the car if I want."

Fisty was panicking now. The look on CC's face was just about believable, especially if your last line of cocaine was still fully motoring in your veins.

"I…I put him in touch with some boys. I'm like Craigslist, just trying to be helpful. I didn't get anything from it, nor would I have. I just liked the look of him…you know, that skin…it's almost blue it's so black. And he's so big. You have to believe me. He was just a crush!"

Christine reached across Fisty, hooking her fingers into

the door-pull on the rear passenger door, ready to lever it open, perfectly positioned to shift her weight and dump Fisty onto Tottenham Court Road.

Fisty let out a girly scream!

"I'm telling you the truth, the truth! Stop frigging scaring me! You lot are all the same, fucking crazy bastards!"

Christine thought she might actually have got some honesty after all, but decided to push for one last question.

"Who sent Iggy to you? Who was the connection? Don't tell me you met on Grinder!"

Her fingers were still curled around the door release.

Fisty just looked, a new, deeper terror creeping across his face now, something CC didn't expect.

"Nobody! No, nobody important. Just some fuckwit. I have told you everything."

Freethy pulled the car to the side of the road. Christine met his eyes in the rearview mirror. The message between the two of them was clear.

That was to be their lot. If they held Fisty any longer and under more duress, there was nothing more but trouble in it for them. There were plenty of people about who saw CC flash her badge. There would be CCTV and if Fisty wanted to make a real complaint it would be pretty straightforward to do so.

She opened the door on the other side of Fisty. She just looked at the man in the ridiculously garish outfit, make up drying on his chin and chest.

"Get out."

Fisty didn't need a second invitation. He was gone like the wind, the sound of whimpering tears trailing behind him just like the scent of his overpowering cologne.

CC closed the door and Freethy pulled out into the traffic.

"I think we need to sit down with Iggy."

Christine nodded her agreement, a troubled look on her face.

"Did Fisty seem genuinely scared to you?"

"You had your psycho face on, Mrs. I don't blame him."

"No, over and above that. When I asked him about the connection. That was when he looked really spooked."

"Maybe. But you're right. Iggy might tell us a bit more than Fisty. He looks to like the type who doesn't panic too easily."

"Hmmm. Let's have a chat with our Nigerian friend, then."

"Tomorrow?"

"Well, yeah, not now. It's getting late."

"Yeah, you'd have to change your clothes if we were going now anyway."

"What you on about?"

"Take a look at yourself," grinned Freethy, beginning a chuckle that would soon develop into a full belly laugh.

CC looked down at herself, only now realising that where she had been manhandling Fisty, she was covered in glitter. The snitch had obviously been wearing some kind of body paint or make up...and now she was too...pretty as a picture, all covered in sparkles...

And before she could do anything about it, Freethy was snapping a picture of her with his iPhone. The flash, she was sure, was bringing all that glitter to life in a photo that was certain to end up on the office notice board.

"You cheeky bastard!"

15

✧ Immediate Futures ✧

It was the driver who released Danny, blinking, from the boot of the car.

Stretching slowly while eyeing the six foot lump who had freed him, Danny had two questions.

Where was Harkness? Where was the bag of money they had just liberated?

He didn't bother asking. He wouldn't reply, and anyway the lump was already climbing back into the car, driving off without so much as a "cheerio", leaving Danny outside his flat.

As he went through his front door the smell hit him instantly.

Aftershave. A scent he recognised but was not surprised by.

He walked into the small kitchen. The little two-seater table was pushed up against one wall. On it a bottle of Gentleman Jack Single Barrel, two shot glasses and two cold bottles of beer.

On the other side of the table sat Harkness, relaxed, smiling. He gave a little wave of hello.

"You could have knocked..."

"Well, where would the surprise be in that Danny, eh?"

Danny shucked off his jacket, pulled the remaining chair towards him and sat down, an unexpected weariness settling upon him. When'd he become so tired?

"Danny, first of all. Let me apologise. I have not shown you proper professional courtesy or respect."

Here we go, Danny thought.

"Here is the deal, young man."

Harkness paused, long enough to pour the Jack Daniels into the two shot glasses in front of him, gesturing to them as he sat back. Danny waited silently.

"Oh...I get it." Harkness leant forward again and took the glass nearest Danny, sank the shot in one and chased it with a mouthful of the beer next to it, condensation sliding down the side of the cold bottle as he tipped it to his lips. He then took a second, smaller swig from the other beer bottle and set it down, pushing it towards Danny.

"Okay? Now that you can see that, you won't keel over, have a drink, Danny. Chill out a little and hear me out."

Danny reached across and shot the bourbon, then chased it with the beer. It tasted great.

"When we first met Danny, I told you we would make history in London Town. I was not lying. You caught my attention because you are, not to put too fine a point on it...fucking good. I saw that for myself tonight. Oh, and I almost forgot."

Harkness shifted in his seat, uncrossed his legs and slid a canvas bag full of money across the floor, leaving it at Danny's feet.

"You have pulled at least 35 jobs. Never been arrested. Been looked at a couple of times, but nothing to stick you with. By my estimation you have probably socked away a cool three or four million in the last five years or so.

What I want to offer you is a chance to do twice, maybe three times that in one hit...your share."

Danny had been waiting to know what was on Harkness' mind. And now here they were, shooting Jackie D and Coors and finally getting down to it. "Good numbers too," Danny had to admit. He was interested but was he interested in playing with Harkness?

"You can plan an armoured car job better than anyone. The job in Willesden Green, the petrol, the cigar…classy. You gave yourself maximum impact in minimum time and used the chaos that is Cricklewood to make good your escape. How did you get away so quick, by the way? The car was dumped, where? The bottom of Walm Lane? What is that, a mile from the job site?"

"Bike," Danny stated simply.

"Motorbike? Hmm, that'll work."

"No, bike…bicycles. Three of them. I divided the money into back packs and we went our separate ways. Old Bill weren't looking for cyclists panting their way down into Kilburn. They went up into Cricklewood looking for fast cars and some *Need for Speed* action."

Harkness started to laugh. Chuckling, he reached for the JD again, pouring and shooting straight away.

"See…fucking great. What about the Rickmansworth gig? Used a stolen bus to pin the replenishment van to the wall of the bank while you got the delivery boy to cough up."

"Now, that was motorbikes. Straight out and up onto the M25. It was like a car park, roadworks everywhere, and we sailed through. They closed the exits in both directions but we ditched before then. Had a car waiting in Denham to spirit us away."

"That's why you've turned my head, sunshine. That's what I need, right there. And I have the fucking mother of all jobs for you. But it will need your imagination mate, I won't lie to you."

"Well, stop knocking my best men off and I might be interested."

Harkness pulled a face, as though offended.

"Forgive me, Danny, you would not have even had a conversation with me if I had not applied a little…persuasive pressure. And anyway I wanted the organ grinder. The monkeys mean nothing to me…or you. They knew the game they were playing. The game just caught up with them."

Nothing from Danny. He let the casual dismissal of two lives hang in the air.

Harkness took another pull of his beer, and finally added: "Over the last few days, a substantial pile of cash has become a little bit more enticing. You may or may not have been reading the papers, but the Old Bill have been enjoying a tiny bit of a purple patch."

"Heathrow. The drugs shipments and money involved. north London, with a money pick-up van."

"That's right, Danny. Yesterday, another little job came off. A bit messy from what I hear but a substantial wad of cash has been liberated from undesirable hands in Knights-bridge."

Danny thought about this for a second.

"Russian money?"

"They do love a bit of Knightsbridge, don't they? Our Eastern European friends. Thing is, those three hits all came out of the one office. And now, the evidence room is overflowing, not to mention being a bit of a security night-mare now."

Danny suddenly knew where this might be going. Fucking crazy.

"You are having a laugh, mate. I know what you are suggesting, but I am not going to rob a frigging cop shop."

"But, my dear Danny, that is the beauty of it. You won't have to. I will know when they are going to move the money, and where to as well. And let me tell you, because of the most perfect mix of arrogance and beautiful budget cuts, the Old Bill don't use a Brinks van, or a G4S. They move their cash in an unmarked van, sunshine. With only one or two escorting vehicles, because they assume that no-one knows what's in the van, and even if they did, nobody would have the balls..."

Harkness paused for effect, tilting his bottle, looking Danny in the eyes.

"But you and me, Danny? You and me son, we've got balls of steel!"

Danny was staring at the shot glass in front of him. He tipped some more Gentleman Jack into it, and before raising it to his lips he asked the main question.

"How much Harkness? In total?"

"Twenty million, Danny. Twenty million or maybe even a little more. The final total is still to be weighed in."

"Unmarked van? One or two escorts? Even for that amount? That is mental."

"The Metropolitan Police never knowingly overestimated. But I need the Felix magic, because the thieving will be easy...but the getting away will be fucking murder. Over to you, young man."

"Why do I only scoop around six million if there is twenty at least up for grabs?"

"And now you see why I had to show you how your old buddies ended up helping to support a building in White City? Because I said so."

Harkness stood to leave, picking the bottle of Gentleman Jack up from the table.

"Harkness...I'll think about it. But there will have to be a re-balance in our relationship. Starting now."

The Big Man stopped. Turning to look at Danny, he cocked his head to one side.

"I know you've left the money. Leave the Jack Daniels too..."

"I'm going to enjoy working with you, Danny. You've a brass neck to go with those steel balls..."

Harkness smiled, looking like a cat that had just caught a canary, savouring the fluttering of the delicate wings inside his mouth just before the first tightening of his jaws.

Christine was watching Shauna sleep. It was a moment

of calm after a vomiting bout, caused by her radiotherapy, greeting CC on her arrival at the bedside.

Shauna's face was serene. Her breath was regular. Her hair, what was left of it, bunched up behind her head on the pillow.

What are the odds? Christine grappled with this almost daily. A bone cancer that attacks mostly the limbs turning up in her child's spine.

CC felt raw. She was someone who spent her life assessing the odds, deciding when and where to engage. Yet here were odds that came from nowhere that didn't play fair. Like stepping on a needle in the deepest, softest carpet. A sharp, hot pain from the least likely source.

CC felt immobile. Caught in paralysis, just as her daughter would eventually be. She could not move past her fears. Her heartbreak, her agony, all were tumbling on top of her to the point that she couldn't even speak any of it out loud. She couldn't give form to the emotions.

At work, she could tidy it all away, but she knew this was only avoidance. The reality lurked for her as soon as a shift ended or a suspect was apprehended. When she downed tools, out came her own, very private, ghouls.

And Shauna's approach? She was head-on, matter of fact, no messing. Who was the child and who was the parent? In this situation, CC wasn't sure.

"Hi, Mum."

"Hey, sweetheart...how you feeling over there?"

"Rough. Can you pass me my drink?"

CC brought the orange squash to her. Sitting on the edge of the bed, she guided the straw in the glass towards Shauna's lips.

"Let's see how long this stays down..."

Silence settled between them. CC shifted onto the bed, lying parallel with Shauna, who nestled into the crook of her neck.

"What's it like, Mum? What is it like to fall in love?"

The question took Christine by surprise, so left field she didn't know how to even begin to answer.

"Open with an easy one why don't you...what's this about?"

"Just...I was reading earlier."

CC had known it was a mistake to buy her the *Twilight* books.

"It's not something you can sum up in a sentence, sweetie. It's more a...state of mind kind of thing. It's like you don't own yourself anymore. You belong to something...I don't know...greater?"

"That doesn't sound much like tummy flips and butterflies. They sound much more straightforward."

"You can get those without being in love. They can come just because that male nurse comes round!"

They both giggled.

"I knew you fancied him..."

"He is fit...and I'm a sucker for anyone who is nice to my girl..."

"What do you mean, something greater though?"

"Well, you feel like you've been seen, I suppose. You've been recognised, picked out and you have, a sort of secret. It's one that makes you different from everybody, because the person you love has chosen to love you back, really."

"That's a bit like how I feel about being ill."

Christine's breath caught as Shauna angled herself to look up at her mum.

"Not the being loved bit, but I do feel like I've been chosen. Picked out. And to begin with it was a secret. We didn't know that I was sick, did we? We just thought I'd hurt my back. But now I am part of something greater...it is something very big, isn't it?"

Christine's eyes were beginning to well up as she tried to regulate her breathing. She attempted not to dissolve into tears of helplessness. It took more than a moment.

"You're not special because you got sick, my little'un.

You were special from the minute I first felt you kick in my tummy. More so when I heard your first cry in the delivery room. You've been special every day of your life. And you don't need a boy or the bad luck of an illness to prove that. And never let anyone or any thing make you believe otherwise."

A pause. More quiet.

"It's a shame, though."

"What?"

"Just…I suppose I will never get to know. You know…feel it."

"Yes, perhaps. But we get to love each other right now. You have me, if that's okay?"

"You rock, Mum…how was your day or night or whatever?"

Smiling "Oh…you know, the usual. I grabbed one bloke by the nuts and threatened to throw him out of a moving car."

"Nice…how was he with that?"

"…frightened."

"We can show him frightened…"

"No…he was. Really. But actually not by me…by someone else, I think."

"Can you scratch my back? My sunburn is really going for it."

The 'sunburn' was where Shauna's skin was burnt by her radiation therapy, but they much preferred to dress it up as something from a day at the beach. Shauna shifted so CC could hit the right spot, the skin looking flushed and irritated.

"Looks angry. No wonder it's itching."

"That's good there…oh. Maybe that means it's doing some good. We can't really tell with the symptoms though, can we? It's the cause we need to kick in the butt. More to the left…"

She was right, the symptoms might be irritating, but the

sarcoma was the real bad guy, pulling the strings in the background.

The background...who was in Fisty's background? Someone who scared him obviously...

"How'd you know he was frightened? Did he start crying?"

"No, he told me he was scared." CC adopted Fisty's camp whine for the next bit, "Stop scaring me...you lot are all the same..."

And as Shauna laughed at her mum's voice, Christine's mind was off in a different direction. "You lot are all the same..." What had the snitch meant by that?

"Mum...you stopped scratching..."

16

✧ At The Pictures ✧

Danny needed to think.

So he went to the one place he knew he could do that to keep a clear head with no distractions.

He went to the cinema.

The Prince Charles Cinema just off London's Leicester Square had a late night showing of his favourite film *Blade Runner.*

Slouched down in his favourite seat, in his favourite row, watching his favourite movie, Danny let the spectacular images wash over him. At the same time he mulled over what Harkness had set out for him.

It felt too good to be true with too much of a golden pay day promise. Maybe it was a gift horse who really should be looked in the mouth. For him, though, the answers were always there, you just had to know where and, crucially, how to look. So he did just that.

Questions tumbled through his mind. Did he want the job? What about Dexy and her enforced detainment? Would Harkness really cut him in on the takings?

Danny began to trace the patterns, predicting how it could pan out, thinking through the logical next steps. How would the corrupt cop behave? What choices would he make? What counter moves could Danny then make? Consequences and outcomes, all clicking together in his mind as Ridley Scott's vision of a world filled to overflowing helping carry Danny's rumination.

On the big screen teeming civilisation made its way through 2019 Los Angeles, drenched in acid rain. Cities overrun with people, decay in some parts, lavish luxury in others. The film never failed to leave an impression.

Helter skelter. This vision of all our tomorrows was key to the film's message. 2019? Danny felt the Helter had been and gone and he was now well into the Skelter.

Harkness had talked to him of how cities were beacons of progress. How they never ceased, changing, morphing, rebranding and re-launching. But to Danny he was minded that in order for rebirth to occur there had to be a little death first. Sometimes not so little.

And there was the rub for Danny.

The possibility of 'death'.

For Harkness to achieve his own future in this never-ending city did Danny have to serve a purpose and then die to help Harkness reach that goal?

Was such a job, the robbing of a police transport laden with untraceable cash, simply an unachievable one? Even if they did intercept the cargo, how could they make their escape? With London and its own teeming civilisation blocking the arteries of the city, how could you spirit your ill-gotten gains away? Wouldn't every Old Bill be hunting you down in the same way that Harrison Ford had to hunt down the 'replicants' on the screen now? Chase you down until you felt a hot bullet in your back?

If only he could empty the city...just for one day, the very day that the Old Bill are moving their dosh. Now that would be a fine plan wouldn't it? Empty London out like you would pour away the water from your washing-up.

Or stop it from filling in the first place?

And now, up on the big screen, Rutger Hauer's murder-ous synthetic human was grasping redemption and glory from the jaws of defeat and damnation. Hauling his tormentor, Harrison Ford, up over the precipice of a

147

building, saving the life of the one man charged with ending his. Pulling off the impossible, confounding all expectation.

"I've...seen things you people wouldn't believe" Hauer tells Ford.

"Attack ships on fire off the shore of Orion. I watched Seabeams glitter in the dark near the Tannhauser Gate. All these moments will be lost...in time. Like tears in rain."

It was, for Danny, an electric moment of cinema. A brilliant set piece in which the supposed hero's life is saved by the most amazing u-turn, one version of fate being replaced by a completely improbable alternative. And now Danny was beginning to see it. A way for him to maybe, just maybe, do exactly the same thing.

17

✧ Forward Motion ✧

Iggy Adesina was still in custody, awaiting his first appearance at the magistrates' court after what the tabloid press had dubbed "Wild West London".

And he was in a foul mood.

Not that CC could give a damn except it would be better to have been the one who put him in a bad mood rather than being the one negotiating a way through it.

There was light at the end of the tunnel. Seemingly, Iggy didn't much care for the food that Her Majesty's catering had to offer a gentleman criminal like him. After almost an hour of talking to the big Nigerian without any sign of progress, Freethy had whispered a suggestion into Christine's ear that was met at first with a snort of derision but on reflection was actually a pretty decent idea.

Iggy wanted better food and while they didn't know of any Nigerian restaurants nearby, there was Jamaican Jerk House just around the corner from Paddington Green where they currently sat. Caribbean meat pasties were almost identical to Nigerian meat pies, so a peace offering might work wonders in a very dull, ill-tempered situation.

It took twenty minutes, but soon the interview room, and most of the corridor outside smelt of the savouries. In fact they had smelt and looked so good, Freethy had returned with enough for himself, CC and even one for Iggy's solicitor, who had sat quietly through the morning's proceedings. He was waiting to see if there was any angle he might work on behalf of his gun-toting client.

Not that Christine or Freethy had given much encouragement on that score. They had simply said that, given the nature of Adesina's recent exploits any information he might pass on now might make the court look favourably on him, but nobody could promise or indeed count on it.

They had talked for hours, back and forth, about how the African had known about where to recruit his team and about where the tip off came from, all they were getting back was "I cannot remember" and the sucking of teeth and shaking of heads.

But now, with a full belly, Adesina seemed to mellow a little, enough to let slip a smile when Freethy played out a little gamble.

"We know who tipped you off, Iggy. We know who pointed you in the direction of the collection van."

Freethy levelled his gaze at his suspect, who was now busy picking crumbs off his chest.

A suck of the teeth. A barely noticeable shrug.

"Now, we all know that we have you bang on for the gun bollocks. We have the gun. We have witnesses. Your clothes are covered in gunshot residue. Fuck me, we even have the mobile phone footage from three punters who happened to think *Sky News* rather than personal safety once you decided to go gun crazy."

CC's turn...

"So anything you give us now, Iggy, will help the judge see you are a right-thinking person of sound judgement. You help us...we will try and help you. Christ, you'd be helping yourself, Iggy."

The lawyer moved closer to the brink of his seat. He looked from Iggy to the coppers and back, seeing a gleam of a way out and a deal to be made.

But Iggy stayed quiet.

CC weighed in again.

"Iggy, we like a big fish, you know we do. Means we all come out looking like heroes. We can even make it sound like you were harassed into your actions, but we need you to point the finger first. Knowing is one thing, having a statement to back it up is way more valuable..."

The Nigerian shifted a little.

CC thought he wasn't going to go for the bluff.

"I know, Mrs poleecewoman."

CC held her breath.

"The ho-mo-sex-u-al. He tell you about me." Iggy dragged the word out, contempt in his voice. CC couldn't judge whether this was a comment on Fisty's sexuality or the fact that he had ratted on the job.

She spread her hands in a gesture of 'I don't know what you are talking about.'

"Feesty, he tell you what I am up to. He has no brain." Iggy tapping his head, as he says it.

"Man must know when to be strong. But also when to be a-frayed. If I were Feesty, I would be in fear now."

"Is that a threat, Iggy, against a third party?"

The lawyer started to clear his throat. About to jump in- between. He did not like how this formerly promising opportunity was starting to develop.

"What can I do from here? You shut me in and feed me sheeet. I cannot threat-en. But I can know."

"Iggy, whatever you know, if it prevents more harm, you can help us, others and ultimately yourself if you just speak up. Now."

Adesina let out a bellow of a laugh. His head arched back, the noise filling the custody suite.

"I help you and help me too? You think I am foolish."

Iggy was the one leaning forward in his seat now. The brief made to intervene, but Adesina's one free hand sharply on his arm shut him up.

"I tell you, I meet the devil. I know heem when I see heem. You say you know his name? You want me to say his name? In my country you say the devil's name three times and he will appear. This man, you do not want heem to appear."

Iggy's eyes were ablaze as he said all of this, looking directly at Christine, burning into her, telling her what he knew to be true. And CC believed him.

"Mrs Poleecewoman, the devil you say you know would have killed you by now if you really did have his name. He knows about your kind. He knows about me. He. Knows. Go find your help somewhere else, and do not spill my blood in the doing of it."

"I..uhm, I think this interview is over, officers." The Lawyer finding his voice at last, not really quite knowing what had just transpired here, but pushed his chair back, trying to bring it all to a halt with his own physicality.

But Christine had one last throw of the dice...

"Not all police are bad, Iggy. One bad policeman cannot stop the rest of us doing our work."

She had played out her hunch, hoping rather than expecting anything back. An act of desperation at the chance of a lead on her growing gut instinct, a firm chance to prove herself right...or at least that she was nosing in the right direction.

Iggy and the lawyer both stood. CC thought it had all slipped by, but as the Detention Officer was starting to unlock the door, the Nigerian let out a breath and turned to her.

"It is not that he is Poleece. It is that he is the only man ever to make Iggy Adesina feel a-frayed..."

Once the brief and the African had left the suite Christine and Freethy were left looking at each other. She finally broke the silence:

"Fuck me."

✧ ✧

The Tube train pulled in. The signature, low level whine-cum-hum of the Jubilee line train was a sound that Danny always associated with home. His home, his city, his manor.

Danny directed himself towards the very last carriage as it pulled into the Westminster Station. This late at night, there weren't too many passengers to jostle with for a seat. Heading north, the train took off on its predetermined path, sliding out of the uber-modern architecture of the station that always made Danny think of the silent film *Metropolis.*

Once at Green Park, the next stop, the doors opened and in came the tall figure of Harkness, looking city-smart in a linen suit. It was better for dealing with the humidity that swarmed through the tunnels of London's subway system in the summer months.

He took the spot next to Danny but waited for the train to exit the station before shifting sideways in his seat. They were alone in their half of the carriage. There was only a drunken man and an older lady at the opposite end, both absorbed in their own, individual existences to take any notice of two seemingly ordinary men who were about to discuss an extraordinary crime.

"So, Danny, are we about to make a little London history?"

Danny took a second before looking at Harkness. He knew that whatever he said next, he was crossing some kind of line, some blurred boundary that divided him from a fate that, no matter what his answer, was steeped in danger, treachery and risk.

But fuck it.

If you didn't take a risk in this life, thought Danny, you would never leave the house.

"I'm going to need money. Call it seed capital, grease for the wheel, whatever, but I'm going to need it. One hundred thousand in cash, untraceable of course, this week. I pick the team; you have no veto, say or influence.

Also, you will never know who they are. After our previous meetings, I can't trust you around good talent. And last but not least, this is a one off deal. We are not partners. We are not mates. We are not collaborators. I execute this job and this job only, then I am like a summer breeze...gone."

"And here was I thinking this was the start of a beautiful relationship. Proust once said that the bonds that unite another person to our self exist only in our mind. I think all of this skittishness is in your mind, Danny. The money is no problem. The job is yours to plan, but I will have no secrets here. You know how dirty little secrets can lead to doubt and doubt can lead to mistrust and misunderstanding. I don't want to end up misunderstanding you, Danny. You know where that kind of mindset leads me."

Danny stared straight at him, no discernible emotion on his face.

"Let's make a little mischief together, Danny. The evidence money gets shifted in nine days time. That is about as long a delay I can manage. Be ready. Work your magic, but keep me informed all the way. I will give you your seed capital myself tomorrow morning, 6am sharp. Be at the car park beneath the Olympic Way at Wembley Stadium. You'll see me coming."

Finally Danny nodded. His eyes never broke away from Harkness' face. Even as he stood to exit the train as it pulled into Baker Street.

As the door opened Harkness turned to look over his shoulder, blowing a kiss at Danny as he did so.

For his part, Danny didn't know if the decision he had just made was reckless, suicidal or, at best, foolhardy.

One thing he did know though; he was going to find out.

But first, Danny had a team to build.

18

✧ Big Man Boom ✧

The M25, like most of parts of London in general, is a contradiction. A fiendish gate to hell on one hand and a stroke of genius on the other. A huge road barrelling around the perimeter of the capital, designed to help manage the city and its clogged arteries of traffic. It funnelled people and their vehicles to the right points of entry into the city on routes that are set up like exit points on the face of a huge, lumbering, heaving clock. A bypass meant to put all others in the shade.

Except it grinds to a halt.

All the time.

A gentle shunt in a jam or a full-scale pile up, doesn't matter what it is, anything can, and often will, transform it into a huge car park.

At best the M25 was designed to make London accessible. At worst it makes it an infuriating destination out of reach because a 77-year-old old grandmother didn't mirror, signal, manoeuvre from the inside lane to the middle stream.

And today, to make matters worse, it was festooned with road works. An attempt to widen the road even further, so that more people can get stuck.

"Enda, why the fuck is the assessment not done yet for this stretch? Get your arse in gear, sunshine, will ya?"

Enda Crilley, was a huge tree trunk of an Irishman currently employed on the roadworks.

"I can't be fucking bothered, ya hooer," was the response he wanted to give to his section foreman but, for now, Enda didn't say it out loud.

He took a step over one of the impromptu rivers caused by yet another summer shower. The gush almost obscured where the new carriageway was supposed to be taking shape.

The avoidance of the water brought him unnaturally close to his superior, causing the engineer to swallow involuntarily as Enda towered over him.

"Now...now listen. You know the delay penalties we're working to, and I know the rain isn't helping but..."

Enda could make a sloth appear like a workaholic and, for him, being bollocked by this weaselly Englishman was a good excuse to stand still and work even less. As he tuned the supervisor's high-pitched whine out, Enda idly wondered if they gave him a set of 'bollix' along with the engineering diploma?

Enda was just about to vocalise his "fuck off" to the boss man, already anticipating the pint he could be having instead of being here when the sound of metal on metal interrupted. The crash and a handful of workmen shouting heralded a car leaving the main carriageway at speed.

"Holy Jesus on a bicycle," was what Enda ended up saying as the Ford Mondeo careered into one of the freshly dug road channels.

He whipped round, taking the opportunity to put his big meaty hand onto boss' face, pushing with all his might, sending his least favourite engineer sprawling about 15 feet away.

"Crilley...Crilley...you fucking wanker..."

Enda stifled a chuckle. "Ah, sorry sir, I was sure he might hit us, I was trying to save you, sir..."

The car would never have gotten to them, but why waste an opportunity was Enda's way of thinking.

He had turned back to where the Mondeo had ground

to a halt. Enda watched with a faint twinge of recognition as the driver's door creaked open and a short ginger-haired lad got out. Big Man Boom, as some knew Enda, started towards the car.

"Enda, don't be getting a hold of him. It looks like an accident," said one of his colleagues, suspecting that the shove on the boss was not the end of the action.

Enda waved him off, mumbling under his breath to himself. "I think I know you, lad."

A knot of other road workers began to form around the driver. They started bombarding him with a salty mix of questions about his health, both mental and physical, mixed with other entreaties as to whether he was a "fucking fuckwit?" But the redheaded driver was ignoring all of this.

He was now pushing his way out of the throng, striding to cut the distance between himself and Enda in sharp, purposeful steps. In no time at all they were stood facing each other. The ginger kid opened his mouth and spoke in a very thick Cork accent.

"You're Big Enda, ay?"

"What now?"

"Big Enda... Belfast Enda. I need to talk to you," he sing-songed through his freckled gingery nose.

"Well, Jesus Mary and Joseph, son, you might have used a mobile phone or something," said Enda, looking now at where the Mondeo was bleeding oil onto the freshly dug road.

"Sure, I have no credit on it," came the reply.

"Ay well, right enough," mumbled Enda to himself.

19

✧ Mr Right Now ✧

"Hello Fisty, darling...loving your leather hotpants!"

Fisty executed a beautiful pirouette for the topless body builder who served drinks at The Bearhug Arms in Soho.

"Jason, you either have it or you don't...but if you like I could give it to you!," came the response, accompanied by a lascivious wink.

"What an offer...but I think I'd rather take it from the Mr Straight who just walked in."

The waiter nodded over Fisty's shoulder with his chin, prompting another pirouette so that the fresh meat might be appraised.

"Oh, Jason...sadly you'll be too busy serving drinks, love. I'll have to take a run at him for you. I have a weakness for the part timers! You know how they are, love," Then adopting a deeper voice, Fisty added: "I have two-point-four-kids, drive a Volvo, like rugby, but I'm not averse to a little fumble in the dark room now and again."

He was tall, very straight-looking, with a shaven head but dressed like he'd come from a very stuffy office job.

This was one of Fisty's particular peccadilloes. The rush of seducing an outwardly straight man was truly thrilling sport for him. And when he knew they definitely had a wife at home, Fisty liked it even better.

And so the evening's entertainment began. Fisty flirting, making occasional eye contact, watching but not watching as the man drank from his beer bottle (subtle, my arse) and his eyes scanned the room taking in every tight little backside that passed him by.

Fisty was feeling supremely confident this evening, dressed as he was in a shimmering silk blouse and those leather hotpants. He had a feeling that tonight would be a wild night now that Mr Respectable was seemingly returning his stolen glances.

After about an hour of sipping Budweiser and tracking backsides, the straight-looking man made his way to the gents. This took him directly passed Fisty, who deliberately took a step back into his path as he drew alongside.

"Are you sure you should be in here, darling?" pouted Fisty, sipping on the straw of his mojito and cocking an eyebrow as he waited for an answer.

"I was just curious. You know. See how it works in a place like this."

"Oh, darling. Rule one is you don't come here to meet Mr Right, just Mr Right Now! A place like this is far too exotic for the likes of you...you may need a little training before taking a swim with the big boys."

"And who would you suggest shows me the ropes?"

Fisty cackled throatily at that.

"Oh love, I have more than ropes to show you."

And that was how it started. Double entendre, innuendo, and at least two more mojitos and a few bottles of beer.

Sometime around midnight, Fisty suggested that they switch from alcohol to something a little more medicinal and a little less likely to inhibit performance. A line each in the toilets, and a furious session of heavy petting and suddenly Mr Straight was telling Fisty to take him home with him.

Taxi!

And so they left for Fisty's little, one bedroom flat in Covent Garden.

The evening was progressing exactly as Fisty had hoped, and soon they were both naked and swallowing a dose of ketamine, letting the mellow high flow over them. Fisty allowed Mr Straight to avail of some of the more unusual bedroom accessories that adorned his king size bed.

"What should I call you, Mr Straight?"

"My name is Keith..."

Fisty greeted this with another throaty laugh. "Keith! How much more straight can you be?"

He pushed Keith down onto the mattress.

"Last Christmas I had these leather straps fitted to my bedstead. Santa knew I'd been a bad boy! I first tried them on a young Polish bike courier. Love him, he had more energy than sense!"

Keith giggled...a little nervous sound.

"Sometimes the straps are for me to use on others and sometimes I have a go myself. Tonight, I want to feel powerless and exploited, a shackled slut. Will you be a darling?"

It would be interesting, Fisty thought, to see how rough anyone called Keith could be?

Soon Fisty was hyper extended in all directions, aroused and ready to be toyed with by his supposedly hetero hunk.

But as he tightened the last strap, Keith surprised Fisty,

"Where's the stash of ket? I want another little hit, this one wasn't enough."

And so they both took another shot of ketamine, Fisty making sure that it was a half this time, no need to overdose tonight, not with all the fun he was having.

Not long after the room began to dance before his eyes, colours sliding around, Fisty noting how red and lush Keith's lips looked in the glow from the nightlights round his bed. Fisty felt warm, floaty and horny all at the same time.

But then Keith's face seemed to change. Or had it? Was Fisty tripping a little too hard?

Then it was Keith again, standing over him. But

something had changed. Fisty at first couldn't quite make it out, but then he noticed that Keith had...clothes on. And then he wasn't Keith again. He was someone else, someone Fisty knew and didn't like. Didn't feel safe around. Now Fisty didn't feel so dreamy, he felt cold. Very cold...and very aware that he was naked and tethered.

And then the glint.

Just a flash in the flickering of the night lights, a blink of a reflection off a transparent object.

And someone was singing, softly. Something Fisty recognised from his childhood. A song his mother used to sing to him, sing him to sleep with.

Hush, little baby, don't say a word, Mama's gonna buy you a mockingbird. And if that mockingbird don't sing, Mama's gonna buy you a diamond ring.

It was soothing, bringing Fisty back to the warmth again. Bringing Fisty back to feeling calm.

And if that diamond ring turns brass, Mama's gonna buy you a looking glass.

And if that looking glass gets broke, Mama's gonna buy you a billy goat.

So there was no need. No need to struggle when the man stood over Fisty and started to tap the inside of his forearm just below the crook of his elbow. No need to resist the cold sensation of sharpness penetrating the skin. No need to protest the rush of chemical into his bloodstream.

And as he spiralled off into a darkness Fisty thought he knew now. He recognised who Keith had become. Knew that the man shouldn't be there but there he was. There he was. There he...

And once he had loosened the leather straps and rolled Fisty onto his side and into a foetal position, tucking his legs up under his elbows, the man checked for a pulse, waiting a good minute and a half. And when he was convinced there was no pulse he stood up and set the syringe and the bag of heroin alongside the burnt spoon next to the night light he had used as a burner. Then it was time to go.

Harkness looked down at Fisty one last time and whispered to him gently: "Sleep well little Mockingbird. You have nothing to worry about anymore."

20

✧ Petty Cash ✧

The robbery was filling all of Danny's waking thoughts. At this point he always felt like he was entering a maze, mentally trying each blind alley in his nascent plan until he picked his way through every eventuality and found the best route to his goal.

Except this was no regular gig. The stakes were high, the rewards were higher and the unknowns were more complex than any he had faced before. Not least of which was Harkness himself.

Danny took a deep breath at that thought, as he stood in the shadow of England's home of football. He looked up.

Swallows were dancing in the cool June air above Wembley Stadium. Danny watched as they zipped and swooped in an aerial display of dazzling joie de vivre, decorating the morning with their patterns and sheer energy.

Despite all this concrete and steel, there was still room for nature to have some fun.

Fun?

That might be in short supply in the coming days, Danny thought.

He had been unable to shake the flash of his father's face when Harkness had been shutting him in the boot of the car a few days ago. The moment kept replaying itself in his head at night as he was drifting off to sleep. He knew what it was, of course. Harkness wanted to control him just as his father had.

What made it even more uncomfortable was that Harkness was in control. It was his job. He knew when and where the money would move. He had Danny 'bang to rights' once the size of the payday had been revealed and, let's face it, he had shown he was serious by knocking off Danny's now very ex partners and burying them under a west London tower block.

And last, but not at all least, Harkness had Dexy.

Danny looked to the sky again, at the swooping birds, one just behind the other, in perfect formation, the follower being led. Suddenly, the second bird flicked a wing, touching the surface of a huge puddle, taking off again instantly to eat whatever insect it had just caught.

Was Harkness such a problem? Was he entirely unpredictable? Or was he so busy playing the Billy big bollocks that he might miss Danny's own manoeuvring?

All his instincts screamed that as soon as the job was over, whether successful or not, he would be in a fight for his life. He would be the one lying glass-eyed in a trench somewhere, waiting for the liquid concrete to fill his mouth, his ears and his eyes.

And one other troubling conundrum. Why him? Who had talked? Dexy was sure the other night. Whose grubby little finger had picked out Danny?

Jesus, there was a lot to consider here.

Danny's reverie was cut short by a silver van bouncing its way across the car park towards him, bang on 6am.

Punctual, if nothing else.

The van pulled right up to Danny. It came close enough to make him want to involuntarily step back. Danny stood still, not wanting to show any nervousness.

Harkness was in the passenger seat. A fat skin-headed white guy was driving. How many were there in Harkness' private club? He had never seen the same muscle twice. It was quite something given the fact that, in the underworld at least, the more people that knew you were up to no good, the more vulnerable you became.

Harkness stepped out of the silver van, a leather satchel in his hand and a smile on his face. Aviator sunglasses were shading his eyes from the early morning light on a near perfect London day.

"My man, Danny Felix…"

Danny just nodded at the cop. No smile, no words, or barely visible acknowledgement of his presence.

"Here is your petty cash, Danny. I'll want a full spreadsheet of expenditure including VAT receipts for tax-efficient accounting purposes."

Harkness chuckled at his own joke. He placed the satchel in Danny's hands and took hold of him by the shoulders.

"There is £50,000 in there. I couldn't let you have it all your own way. I will stake you some more when you need it. Also, I want updates, including a full briefing of the plan. Along with the money you will find a mobile phone. When it rings you answer…it will only ever be me."

Danny was already shaking his head.

"No mobiles, no phones. Ever. You should know better. A mobile is basically a tracking device for the Old Bill. I don't use them. I don't have one. Never have, never will."

Danny fished into the satchel, and retrieved an iPhone. It was the latest model, probably capable of all sorts of technological wonders. It smashed very easily under the weight of his boot.

Harkness took a step back, taking Danny in. His face darkened. In a blink, Harkness stepped right up into his face.

"Listen boy, when my dog gets out of order I jerk his fucking leash. Don't make me jerk yours too many times. You hear me?"

Danny could feel spittle hitting his face as Harkness lent in to deliver his threat. The sudden ferocity and aggression would have caused most people to fold. But before he could say another word, Harkness was suddenly aware of something sharp finding purchase in the crotch of his trousers. He looked down to see the wicked glint of the stiletto flick knife that Danny was ever so accurately pressing against his balls.

"Now you listen to me, Harkness, you cunt. I told you before. I will pull the job, but only on my terms. I will keep you updated, but only when I see fit."

Danny now the one sounding fierce. He was telling Harkness what was going to be what.

"Keep your eyes on the *Craigslist* London website. If I want to see you, there will be a listing in the wanted section of the for sale ads. When you see an ad for a pair of "ruby slippers needed for the ball", I am ready to meet. We will rendezvous on the Tube at the same time and place as our last meet. Get it? You might have made this job too tempting for me to turn down, and no doubt I am one of the few in this city who could plan and pull it off, but that doesn't mean I am entirely...fucking...stupid."

With each of the last words Danny leant a little more pressure on the knife, making sure that Harkness could feel that he was in no mood.

"And I will need the rest of the fucking money."

With that Danny took a step back. Harkness now looked over his shoulder, wondering how in the fuck's name did fat skinhead boy miss what had just happened?

Then he started to applaud. A slow handclap rising in speed and volume until it was joined with that trademark throaty laugh.

"Bravo, Danny. Bra-fucking-vo. I like a little theatricality, a little dash of showbiz...that was cool. Like I said on the Tube, you are a skittish one, aren't you? And I also told you I do not want there to be any secrets or misunderstandings between us. You obviously aren't listening to me, so this might help you to pay some fucking attention."

Harkness reached behind him, tugging on the handle of a sliding side-door on the van. It opened up, revealing to Danny what was inside.

Sat, tied to a bench welded to the floor of the van was a figure, with a burlap sack over their head. The noise of the door opening caused the figure to start, thrashing against the ties that bound them to the spot.

And Danny felt an increasing sense of dread. Nausea started to creep into his gut like an ice-cold serpent. Twisting, turning, tightening.

Forget a switchblade to the balls, Danny was being shown that Harkness really was the boss here. He really was the man in charge.

With his own theatrical flourish, Harkness whipped the burlap sack off the head of the captive in the van. Long red hair tumbled down, impeded only by a blindfold wrapped around her head and a gag in her mouth.

It was Dexy.

"You are playing with the big boys now Danny Felix. This is to let you know she is still alive."

He slid the door shut again.

"Now, fucking do one. Get planning. We have money to steal. A fuck of a lot of it. Don't let me down. Don't let her down." Harkness flicked his head in the direction of the van. He turned to walk away, and then stopped.

"Oh, and by the way, Danny. How's your sister doing?" he said, without a smile. There was no mirth in his dead-pan face. And then he was off, into the van.

Danny was silent.

He knew that Harkness had just pulled a rabbit out of the hat.

21

✧ Digging Deep ✧

By the time Christine arrived at the scene in Covent Garden, the Scientific Investigation Division were just about done. Preparations were underway to move Fisty's body out of the small flat.

She quickly found the investigating officer, a new young detective called Ayoade. She'd never met him before.

CC strode up to the investigator. "Who found him?"

Ayoade was looking at CC and at her Metropolitan Police brief at the same time.

"Good morning, officer. I am Detective Inspector Ayoade of the Metropolitan Police. Why are you in my crime scene?"

She blew out her cheeks, realising how presumptuous she had just been.

"Sorry, Inspector. I'm Detective Inspector Chance. I have had a few dealings with your victim of late, most recently in relation to the gunfight in north London last week. He had provided certain information to us that is helping our investigation. I was just hoping to get a fix on what happened to him?"

Ayoade relaxed a bit.

"I should just tell you to piss off until such times as I've had a chance to do my work here."

CC gave him a steady look in return.

"I heard about the north London hooha. A lot of fireworks by the sound of it. A bit rock n'roll. All I usually get are the dead bodies. Most of them already cold, often homeless."

CC nodded recognition and Ayoade seemed to soften towards her.

"Your boy was a little over enthusiastic with his leisure activities. Track marks on his arm. Fixings left nearby. Alcohol in evidence as well as a recent and familiar visitor given the traces of sexual congress. SID reckon he overdosed. A full post will establish and most likely confirm it."

Sexual congress? Christ, this bloke was fresh into the job, CC thought.

"What about the visitor? Any leads? Any DNA?"

"The body was found by the cleaner. Not much of a cleaner, though, given the amount of fingerprints and other physical evidence in the vicinity. It looks like Mr Scott had a lot of visitors, if you catch my drift."

It took her a second to put Mr Scott and Fisty together in her head as the same person.

"Listen, none of this should come as a shock. The victim was a local drug dealer, wasn't he? Something of a Soho legend from what I can gather. A patron of Old Compton Street's finer establishments. It looks like he endured the end that most would have predicted for him."

"That's why I am curious, Inspector. Don't you think that a seasoned dealer like Fisty would know how to measure out his hits?"

"There are three empty bottles of mojito mix in the kitchenette and an empty bottle of rum to go with it. Now forgive me for making a leap here, but if I had that much cocktail in me I'm not sure I could unwrap a cough sweet correctly."

CC let out her breath, realising she had been shallow breathing from the moment she arrived.

The fear of culpability was giving her cause for concern. By bracing Fisty had they alerted whoever was behind this growing spider web of criminal intent that they were sniffing around? She hadn't exactly been subtle when she had pulled Fisty from the nightclub. Had she signed a death warrant for the drug dealer turned informant? Or had Fisty just been so off his tits that he had recklessly mismeasured?

"Any CCTV of the street outside? Is there a possible ID on who Fisty's visitor might have been?"

"Detective Inspector Chance, are you trying to tell me how to conduct my investigation here?"

She felt a buzz in her pocket. She pulled out her phone and glanced at it. Freethy's number was flashing up. But this was more important right now; she had one last chance with her fellow copper here. She was pushing her luck but she knew she would have to dig deep. So with a shrug she tried a different tack.

"Listen, Ayoade. I am sorry but Fisty is a loose end for me...for us. I don't like loose ends. Maybe if you could share the results of the post-mortem. Then I can either give you all the information we have on him, or we can both just put his demise down to over exuberance. Either way, we can help each other and I can stop being the arsehole who is annoying you right now."

Ayoade weighed it up. It was true that if the post mortem showed any kind of struggle or signs of coercion, then a fuller picture of Mr Scott's dealings with the Met would be invaluable. Maybe this wasn't going to be just another sad sack story. Maybe there would be a little rock n' roll too.

"Give me your number and I'll give you a call when I get the report from the Frankensteins."

Christine smiled at the slang for the medical examiner, scribbling down her mobile number on Ayoade's proffered notebook.

"Thanks. I appreciate it."

Leaving the scene, she felt her pocket throb again. Thinking Freethy, she pulled out the mobile phone, making a mental note to take the handset off silent now that she was out of the crime scene.

As she brought the phone up towards her face she spotted that it was a withheld number.

"Christine Chance."

"Ms. Chance, it's Sister Cavendish here from St. Michael's Hospice."

CC's breathing was immediately shallow. So fast it felt like her chest might burst. These were the kind of calls that made her heart leap.

"Is Shauna alright?"

"Yes, Ms Chance, but we felt you should know that she had a very poor night last night. She is stable at the moment but the doctor would like to see you when you come in next...and we would suggest that should be today at some stage."

"What are you saying? What does that mean?"

"Dr Shobnay would like to speak with you about your daughter's condition and the next steps. It would best be done sooner rather than later."

If you can hate a person without ever having met them, this was one of those moments. CC wanted to destroy the nurse on the other end of the phone, a nurse who was simply doing her job. But it was so much more. It felt like the phone call of reality. An acknowledgement of the truth. A truth she was trying with all her heart and soul to deny.

"Thank you, Sister. I will do my best to come in this afternoon."

"Thank you, Ms Chance...and my sympathy to you. These are never easy times for anyone in your position. We realise that at St Michaels. Goodbye."

"Bye..."

Christine stood stock still. Covent Garden crowds

swarmed passed her, but she just couldn't move. It was as if the reality of what was about to beset her and her daughter had finally settled on her. She felt pinned to this point of the earth.

She felt numbed, stricken and unable to move. Powerless, she was suddenly aware that she wasn't even able to cry. Shocked at herself, realising that with the exception of a few moments, she had yet to really allow her sadness to find expression in tears.

Her daughter was going to die. And she couldn't do a damn thing about it. Not even weep.

And then, from nowhere, a sound punched its way through to grab her attention. A siren, slicing into her frozen mind as a police car going who knows where, all lights flashing, whipped passed her in the street.

"I shouldn't even be dignifying you with my presence."

"Aw, sis, please. Can we just play nice together, even for just a half an hour?"

"Play nice...play fucking nice..."

"Celeste, you're hissing...you sound like you might have a puncture."

"Listen, Danny, what you did was no fucking joke. Keeping a gun...at my house. I have kids. And what have I told you about turning up at my work?"

"Sorry, I forgot to bring my bell...unclean...unclean..."

Celeste stopped dead in her tracks. She swung her handbag at him. This was the point at which he knew that his sister wasn't really angry. If Celeste had wanted to hit him, she would have just punched in the face, simple as.

"Can't a brother just turn up to surprise his sis? Treat her to a little lunch?"

"Not when the lunch is funded by your ill gotten gains... I'll buy my own lunch."

Now it was Danny's turn to stop. Reaching out, he pulled Celeste round to fully face him.

"Okay, sis. Truce, truce. I know I cocked up. That was not cool stashing something in your garage. I promise I won't do it again. And...wait for it...I apologise."

Celeste let her arms drop by her sides. She tilted her head to the sky, staring at some unseen point in mid-air.

"Danny...I love you. I really do, but you make it soooo hard. I could kill you sometimes. You might have your standards, you've always done everything on your own terms, but you can't just waltz in and out of my life - my family's life - doing as you please. Risk and children do not go together. Especially my kids...my family life. It might be boring to you, but it's my life, my treasure."

Celeste reached out and put a hand on his chest, pushing him gently back on his heels.

"Which is why I'm apologising. I just wanted to let you cool down a bit before coming to see you. Everything is okay at home, isn't it?"

"Yes...yes of course it is. Apart from Dad, of course..."

"I'm not interested in him, just you. You and the kids and what's his name?"

This earned him a sharp look.

"Kidding, kidding...but you're all okay...right?"

"Yes! Jesus, what's got into you? Saying sorry, now acting like some kind of weird family counsellor. Hold on a minute, what's going on?"

It was Danny's turn to look exasperated. It helped cover up his actual sense of relief.

"Holy shit, Celeste. I'm not working an angle here, just asking. I can't win with you."

"Okay, okay. It's just, you don't act like this much. Come on, I'll buy you lunch. I need to go to a cash machine."

"I'll buy you..."

"We've covered that already bro..."

Danny gave in. They walked along the high street near

Celeste's office a little further to the nearest bank.

"Watch and learn, Danny. This is how you get money from a bank the legit way."

"Ha, bloody ha…"

Celeste tapped in her pin number. She had a moment's hesitation as she thought about shielding it from Danny.

"Celeste!"

She giggled. Her face lit up the way it used to on the rare occasions, as kids, they were able to play together, when their father's presence was not heavy over them.

The money emerged from the cash machine. Celeste snatched both it and her card into her handbag quickly, laughter still passing between them.

"Come on. There's a great Thai café just over here. It does good noodles."

They started to walk again, but as she was getting herself sorted, Celeste stopped again.

"Jesus, that can't be right."

She was staring at her receipt from the cash machine.

"What?"

"Naww, the bank must have made a mistake."

"Celeste, what is it?"

"My balance…according to this I have over £82,000 in my current account."

Danny's heart sank.

"I'll have to go in and see them, after lunch. What do you think?"

Danny was thinking only one thing, but he couldn't say it out loud.

Harkness.

22

✧ Puzzle Pieces ✧

In London there are pubs and there are pubs.

Most London pubs are just normal, drinking holes, where tourists and locals gather to have a pint, maybe some food, watch some live sport and socialise.

But then there are the other pubs. These are anything but normal. They are the legendary venues steeped in local colour, history, and with folklore. These are the mixed hostelries where villains rub shoulders with cops, where dodgy deals are done, compromises struck and negotiations conducted all under the watchful eyes of discreet landlords. New York may have its Italian restaurants where mafia bosses eat pasta. London has pubs.

And The Spotted Dog public house in Willesden Green is one such den. An old-fashioned Irish boozer tucked away in north west London, it has long been the scene of many fist fights and riotous drinking. At one point both the local police force and the Irish mafia, the 'Murphia' as they are known, used the pub for private functions as well as regular boozing sessions.

Danny loved The Spotted Dog. It was just a great, sawdust, spit-on-the-floor pub that belonged to a different era, a time of fewer complications. Where a spit in the palm handshake was as contractually binding as any legal document and if you had a dispute it could be sorted out on the small forecourt in front of the pub and then back inside for the next round.

Nobody skipped a beat when Danny walked into the bar. The room was filled with chatter and The Undertones were playing on the speakers dotted around the room. Danny soon clocked the man he had come to meet. He, and his companion, were the next players in his rapidly forming plan, and as soon as he did, he could not help but feel the smile grow on his face. Danny liked this crazy Irish bastard and, more importantly, trusted him.

The ginger haired man stood and gripped Danny's hand with all the strength of a man twice his height and breadth. He shook it vigorously, returning Danny's smile with a grin of his own.

"Danny Fucking Felix...has the devil not caught up with ya yet?"

"Not yet, Ciaran. He's too busy hunting you down."

"Nahh, sure he plays poker with me every fuckin Friday night. That bastard knows just where to find me! Come on, let me introduce you to Big Man Boom. But don't call him that, least not to his fat Fenian face. He prefers Belfast Enda these days."

Danny nodded and followed Ciaran through the body of the pub. His bright orange mop of hair was easy to spot even in the fog. So much for not smoking indoors. The clientele of The Spotted Dog didn't much care for the law.

Finally, he was standing in front of a round table in one corner of the bar, and sat behind it was one of the biggest blokes Danny had ever clapped eyes on. He was huge. Boulders for shoulders, he was well over six foot, at least 20 stone with meaty fists for hands, one of which was now encircling Danny's own hand making it look like he was a kid taking his Dad's hand on a walk.

"I believe you are Danny. Good to meet you. Ciaran says you're a grand lad."

"Nice to meet you, Enda. Ciaran says the same about you too."

"We thought you might be thirsty," said Enda gesturing towards a pint of Guinness on the table, obviously meant for him because there were two others half drunk beside it.

"Sure. Danny always has a terrible druth on him."

Danny didn't know what a druth was but pretty sure it meant thirsty. He didn't really have time to make this a social meeting, but he knew it would be rude if he didn't have at least one round and return the favour.

Mind you, despite his urgency, the black as night beer tasted great as it went down, and once he had wiped away the foam moustache it left behind he went straight for it.

"Apologies for cutting straight to the chase here, Enda, but circumstances at my end have become a touch more complicated. Has Ciaran filled you in?"

"Ay, some. He says you want a variety of surprise packages left at different spots all round London. My only question would be how big do you want these surprises to be? And, even more interesting, how deep are your pockets?"

While this discussion took shape Danny noticed that Ciaran's eyes never stopped sweeping the room, not in an obvious way, but enough to discourage anyone from getting too close to their table.

"Well, it depends. Some of the places will need a bigger surprise than others. Not all need to be the real deal. They just need to look like they might be. It's more about whether you can lay your hands on the stuff and get it prepped...time is tight. As for my pockets...well let's just say 20 upfront, another 80 if I get away with it."

Enda was reaching for his beer. Danny was fascinated by the way his huge fist nearly obliterated all sight of the pint glass. He was then further amazed at how the almost half a pint was downed in a single, swift gulp.

"I'll go if you stand 'em, Danny Boy," said Ciaran, offering to recharge the glasses. Danny peeled off a 20 quid note.

"I was thinking more like 40 upfront and a 100 if you make it?"

"I tell you what. Let's say 30 upfront and 90 if I make the grade. And Enda...I fully intend to make the grade."

"I've heard the likes of you before. You say more than your prayers. But Ciaran says you're some boy at this game. You fuckin' better be."

"And what about people? Can you make sure that the surprises end up where they have to be when they have to be? No slip ups?"

"My lads are like the frigging Pony Express. 'Deadline or dead' is what I tell them. On that matter, you know there will be a few..."

"Casualties? Well, perhaps we can plan to minimise those. Only one surprise needs to be in or around a large crowd. The rest should be like a domino effect."

"I'm with you. Show them the real thing and let them jump to their own conclusions. A scare can be as effective as a big bang. Ciaran was right, you're some boy..."

Danny smiled at the big Ulsterman, nodding and knowing what comes next.

Both men spat in their hands. Danny again marvelled at the huge fist that was now pumping his, neither breaking eye contact across the table.

"Enda, so we understand each other, I have more than just the money riding here so no hitches, please. And I'll pay you out, don't worry on that score."

"Sure, if you don't, I can always beat the living shite outta Ciaran...by the way, you do know if there is any oul nonsense, there'll be more than the Peelers to deal with."

It wasn't a question. It was a statement. Danny nodded thinking if only the Old Bill were the only thing he had to worry about.

"Enda, I don't own a car, but if I did, rest assured I wouldn't want to be looking under it before I drove it."

Ciaran returned with the pints.

"Ah sure, Jesus, we don't do that sort of nastiness anymore. Do we, Enda?"

He winked at both men as he said it, leaving Danny to round off the business end of the talk.

"You better do, or else I might have to try buy the Jihadists a drink..."

Ciaran nearly lost half a pint through his nose at the thought of that.

Freethy had left Christine a message on her mobile asking her to call.

"Mark Freeth."

"Freethy it's me, what are we doing?"

"Hiya, I managed to get us some face time with D.C.I Collinson."

"Great. I thought the pub. I want him in a chatty mood. I want to backtrack all of this. All these jobs have just been too good to be true."

"What if he won't share? These tips have all been pretty high level."

"They came from somewhere. If they all came from the one place then something stinks, mate."

"We'll have to play it carefully, CC. We might have a can of worms here."

"What time are we meeting?"

"Lunchtime. I thought you'd want to get away to see Shauna as soon as..."

"Ok, see you at the usual..."

By the time they were into their third round at The Coach and Horses, Collinson was holding forth with a story that contained at least seven violations of current procedural regulations. Christine wasn't in the mood. She hadn't told her friend about the message from the doctors yet, there would be time enough for that later, and if there was

A. MARLEY

a way to get Collinson to open up quickly, then Freethy would know it.

So for every pint their guv'nor had, unbeknownst to him, they were taking in half in the form of lager shandies.

She hated the taste of it, but she had no choice if she wanted the information to remember it and still make it to the doctor meet with a brain clear enough to function. Collinson was finishing up his latest anecdote.

"And all we did was give him a right good battering and send him home to his old man with a note pinned to his shirt saying: "Sentence served". It was a lot easier in those days, I can tell you that for nothing. None of this oversight and procedure bollocks."

Freethy saw his chance.

"Well, Guv. You know Christine thinks it's all coming a bit too easy to us right now."

"Yeah, she mentioned something like that to me last time we spoke...course she then went on to oversee the demolition of an historically significant townhouse in Knightsbridge the same day. Fucking careless if you ask me."

Some phlegmy laughter and a short bout of coughing was followed by a mouthful of Fuller's London Pride ale to clear his throat.

CC went next.

"Come on, Guv. You have to admit the scoops we've had the last while have all been premier league. All of them. How often has that happened in your time?"

"Swings and fucking roundabouts. You get purple patches. I don't see why you are fucking whinging. I mean, you get the overtime, dontchya?"

Freethy's turn.

"Yeah, but there's happenstance, coincidence and then there's too much of a good thing. Anyone would think the SO15 boys were leaving us to do their heavy lifting. Heathrow, north London gunfight...CC's Knightsbridge redevelopment scheme..."

Collinson laughed at the idea of Christine as a TV makeover host, then swallowed more beer.

CC's turn.

"It's not funny, Guv. Are we getting the run around? I'm thinking there is a connection beyond intel here."

Collinson snapped upright suddenly, like he'd been slapped in the face. At once he seemed completely sober.

"Chance, what are you fucking inferring here?"

His voice was a low growl. CC started to stutter before Freethy did the decent thing.

"Nothing...nothing, Guv. It just all seems a little, you know, action-packed and headline heavy. You know her, she hates the fucking paperwork that goes with this kind of run. Overtime or not."

Collinson snuffed down his nose like a horse who didn't want to wait any longer for its feed.

"I can assure you both that all of that intel was fucking legit. If you must know it came from a very credible source."

CC and Freethy shot each other a look. They both knew what that meant.

"I need to break the seal...'scuse me." Collinson lumbered off in the direction of the gents.

When he was far enough away, CC stepped closer to Freethy.

"He's talking some Masons shit, isn't he? It's the only time he feels so certain about any info we are handed."

"Only one way to find out."

"He'll never tell us that."

"Watch and learn, young Chance..."

When Collinson rejoined them his cheeks were a darker red than before he had broken away from them.

"So, guv. All these recent hits, they've all been lodge leg-ups?"

Christine might have gasped at Freethy's blunt question, but she was too desperate to hear the answer.

"Yes, it was, Mr Freeth. And I am more than happy to admit it. Listen, you fucking babes-in-arms. We got the intel. We did the jobs. The faces are off the streets. What difference does it make? You'll get your commendations. I get my stats and the public don't have to worry about another load of dangerous fucking herberts messing with their home insurance cost."

CC glanced at the clock on the wall. She would have to go soon if she were to make the meet with the doctor. Collinson gave her a break.

"Right, next round's on me."

Collinson wandered off toward the bar. CC turned to her best friend.

"You can cajole him to talk a little more now. He's broken his own ice."

"And you are going where, exactly? This is your bollocks here, Christine. You are the suspicious one."

CC spread her hands in front of herself, pleading innocence and playing her ultimate card all at the same time:

"Doctors want to meet. I can't miss it. It sounded all a bit...well, you know. And, anyway, Collinson's old school. He'll tell a bloke more than a bird."

Freethy relented as soon as the word "doctors" was mentioned.

"Alright mate. I will text you if I can make him spill anything more. And listen, keep me posted on... you know"

CC waved him off, trying again not to let her mind run riot, certainly not now, not in the pub in front of her mate or even her boss if he came back right now.

"I just need to listen to what they have to say. I've been putting off even thinking about this kind of chat for ages now. Right, I need to go."

"No worries, CC. I'll tell the Guv'nor what's happening. Go on now."

It took 25 minutes to drive to St Michael's Hospice. Christine was taking her time leaving the car, gathering herself before the meeting. She felt like she was about to put some kind of final piece of the jigsaw of her daughter's health into place. She didn't want to be the person responsible for doing that but knew that no one else was around to take it on for her.

As she finally stood up, she felt her pocket vibrate. The mobile.

She pulled it out and tilted it to see the screen. A text message from Freethy. It simply read:

I HAVE A NAME.

So, another piece of that puzzle had fallen into place, she thought. If only the one before her right now wasn't a jigsaw she was afraid to complete.

23

✧ You'll Do For Me ✧

The estate agent couldn't help but feel a little nervous. She was on her mobile to her boss.

"Look, Daaaavid. I'm not happy about being here on my own. This ginger chap is a strange one. He's walked round the outside of the unit about five times already. He's not looking at the building itself. He is spending rather a lot of time around and along the street. And he just keeps staring at my boobs, without so much as an attempt to disguise it. Oh, he's coming back in. Call me in five minutes if you haven't heard from me."

She hastily hung up as Ciaran came back in through the side door.

"Are you one of those sloany ponies? You're right an' posh now."

"Ehh, I don't know what you mean. Anyway, Mr...?"

"Aye, so right enough. How long has this been lying useless?"

Her eyes scanned the pre-fabricated shell. There was nothing unusual about the unit. Pre-fab, low level, two garage type roller doors on the front, plenty of space inside, strip lighting and a little cornered off office area in the back right hand corner. It, like the rest of the units nearby, had stood empty for many months. But she wasn't about to let a potential customer know that.

"Well, Mr..."

Ciaran just looked at her.

"Well, the recession has hit this kind of space. These units were normally leased by small retail businesses for storage or distribution purposes, to cater for the boom in online shopping and so on. But I am sure you will agree it is well connected to all the major roads from in and out of London. Park Royal is very sought after."

"Is that right, now? So it's been lying empty for at least a year, like?"

"Not that long...I..."

Just as she was about to lie, Ciaran flicked his shoe at a pile of rubbish on the floor. He revealed a yellowing copy of *The Sun* newspaper, one with a whole page headline bemoaning the performance of the England football team at the 2010 World Cup.

If she had noticed it, fair play to her, she didn't bat an eyelid, thought Ciaran. Not that he was looking at her face.

What she was actually thinking at that moment was: What if my mother was right? What if this was just too risky a job for a young, attractive female?

"So, tell me, girl. The rest of these here units are empty now?"

He had a sing-song accent, talking at a million miles an hour, the sound of his voice reedy through his nose.

"Pardon, sorry, I couldn't..."

"Them ones, the rest of 'em, empty ya say, now?"

"Oh, yes..."

"And been a quare while?"

"A what? Sorry..."

"Stop apologising, love. You sound like a Catholic priest to an altar boy. How long have they been lying idle?"

"Oh. Well, does that really matter? I'm not sure."

"Well, Jaysus. Let's just say your boy, the client, needs the few sheckles then."

Before she could say it Ciaran interpreted for her. Fuck me, he thought, these Brits are thick as pig's shite.

"The landlord must be desperate for a few quid."

"Well, I suppose so. On this occasion I can speak reliably for the landlord because we actually own the units ourselves. You would be leasing directly from us."

The three things that happened next would form the basis of a story she would tell over and over again for the rest of her estate agent days.

Number one: The man with the shock of ginger hair produced a wad of cash, licking his fingers as he counted, all hundreds. He made a sheaf of money that, as he separated it out, formed £10,000. It took a minute or two.

"Right girl, here's ten grand. You said it was 20 a year, so here is the first six months."

Secondly, he seemed to spit into the palm of his hand and then offered it to her. She was so shocked, she actually took it, albeit very slowly.

And last, but not at all the very least, after shaking her hand, he stepped past her into the centre of the storage area and as he did so he gently patted her on the arse.

"Pleasure doing business with you. Sure you're a lovely girl. If I wasn't so busy, I'd buy ya a pint. You'd do for me, ya would."

He started toward the entrance, while she just stood there open-mouthed.

"Are ya coming or not, girl? I'm sure you'll have a shite load of paper for me to sign..."

Ciaran had just found Danny his HQ.

Later that same day, an ad was posted on *Craigslist* London. Its headline read simply...

Wanted: Ruby Red Slippers.

And once you clicked on the ad, it opened to reveal this...

Bring lots of money.

Ciaran wasn't surprised that the bicycle shop was packed. It was late afternoon, and just off Oxford Street in the heart of the West End. He liked the weird mix of customers: tattooed and pierced bike couriers waiting for replacement saddles, rubbing shoulders with be-suited office workers in to pick up a new helmet camera.

What he liked even more was the music playing over the shop speakers. The Waterboys were declaring that they'd seen the whole of the moon. Ciaran wouldn't have minded seeing all of that estate agent girl's moon, but sadly there was no time for play today.

He moved through the racks of hi-vis jackets, reflectors and waterproofs, stopping to admire a bike that looked like it was an arrow. It was obviously built for speed and city cycling, the kind of bike that a courier would favour. A saddle on it that looked like a blade, tyres that were thinner than the width of a good cigar. Ciaran couldn't resist running his hand over the centre bar of the frame. He then picked the bike up with one arm, surprised at how light the whole thing was.

"It's a fab machine, isn't it?"

Ciaran turned to look over his shoulder. One of the assistants was standing there, wearing the orange tee shirt with the shop logo on. But any sense of uniform ended there. He was wearing long shorts, with chains hanging from the belt loops to the pockets. His head was shaved on either side, leaving the top of his head Mohican-style that lead, improbably, to a ponytail. Completing the look, he had one arm and one leg festooned with tattoos. Ciaran thought the one of the snarling wolf on his forearm was particularly good. It made it easy for him to throw the lad off guard with his next words.

"Howya, Howler? Sure it was you I wanted to see."

Howler returned Ciaran's grin with a frown. He stepped

closer in order that he might not be overheard as he spoke through gritted teeth.

"Not just anyone gets to call me that...who the fuck are you?"

"Jaysus, no need to get your gander up, lad..."

"Who. Are. You?"

Ciaran's grin widened even further. He liked this one.

"I'm the boy who is going to make you rich."

"Frankie's Coffee Shop. Round the corner. In 15 minutes. I drink flat white."

"Aww, Jaysus...d'ya not have a pub nearby?"

Howler sighed.

"The Half Moon, two doors down from the café. I still want a coffee...you can get me a takeaway."

And for the second time that day Ciaran found himself saying.

"You'll do for me."

The pint was gloriously cold, both in his hand and as it flowed down his throat. He knew it would be thirsty work talking to all these people.

The most important thing however was that as soon as he had mentioned Danny's name, he had grabbed this Howler's attention. And it was even more focused once he had slipped the envelope under the table. It should have: it had 5,000 quid in it. Danny had said to tell Howler it was a good faith down payment.

"I can't see any reason why I wouldn't be able to handle that."

He had been quiet for a few seconds, staring into the surface of his girly, useless coffee. Flat white. For fuck's sake, what kind of a drink was that for a grown man?

"As long as the numbers don't concern ya, I can get the rest of the detail to you. Well let's see...36 hours notice."

"That will be fine. Do you want my mobile number?"

For the first time since they had met, the smile slipped from Ciaran's face. He reached across the table and put his hand firmly onto the boys.

"Now listen to me, fella. We don't do it like that. We don't use those things. Ever. For anything. Do we understand each other? That is one of our absolute conditions."

Howler could suddenly see that this Ginger Paddy was not to be messed with. His diddly-dee, *Riverdance* demeanour only served to cover determination and ruthlessness. Howler knew that Ciaran would gut him like a fish if it served the overall success of his plan.

"Uhh yeah, sorry. I forgot how Danny feels about mobiles."

Smiling again now. "There's my man..." Ciaran drained his pint..."Right, your round."

"Er, I have to get back to the shop mate..."

The non-grinning Ciaran was back again.

"Well, you can get me one before you nip off now, can't ya?"

It had been as horrible as she had imagined it would be. Gut-wrenching.

It had made her feel enraged and broken all at the same time. A great wave of frustration had crashed over her all the time the doctor, who looked young enough to be her kid brother, had talked. He sat there and detailed the oncoming developments that amounted to nothing more than a timetable for pain.

Shauna Chance was, over the next few weeks or a month at the most, going to go through hell.

The young doctor was only doing his job. He was only trying to brace Christine for what was to come. The last of her daughter's days would be a catalogue of increased medication, long periods of unconsciousness, only waking when the pain managed to cut through the fog of her assorted drugs.

"Towards the end, with the amount of pain control Shauna will require, she may not be able to recognise you, Ms Chance. But you must know that it is all we can do."

Christine could have punched him in the face.

A familiar voice broke her train of thought.

"CC. We're here. Are you alright? Are you sure you want to go in?"

Freethy's words brought Christine back to the here and now.

Feeling awkward, she ran her fingers through her hair trying to look tired instead of distraught.

"Yeah, I'm okay. You got the name, and then you found out where he is, so let's follow the rabbit down the hole."

Freethy paused, looking at his colleague, his friend.

"Look, Christine. You don't have to be here. Not now, not with what is going on for you."

She looked over at him, her face hardening.

"My Dad was a great copper. He always wanted me to be one too. I'm right about this hunch. And good coppers listen to their guts. That fucker is in that bar now. My Dad would tell us to shift our arses in there."

"Yeah, CC. But come on, give yourself a break. Shauna needs you right now. You need to be with her right now. This is just work."

"It's what I do. We do."

"CC..."

"Just shut the fuck up, Freethy. I'm here now. Doing this."

"Okay, okay. Jesus, CC. I just...I don't get it."

"Well, I'll tell you, shall I? It's this simple. It's work. I know how to be here. It's easy here. With Shauna? I don't know how to be...I can't..."

Christine reached for the car door handle, letting herself

out into the air of the street. As she stood up, facing the entrance to the shitty pub they were about to enter, she felt her face set and breath come easier.

Freethy was up and out too.

"CC?"

"Time to ask some awkward questions."

So they did.

24

✧ Directions ✧

As soon as she entered the pub CC thought it was horrible. The carpet stuck to her feet, the smell of stale beer seemed to surround her like a fog and the atmosphere was laden with desperation.

It wasn't so much a pub, as a refuge. A sinking ship filled with people who only came really to do one thing: drink. And this wasn't a 'meet you for a pint and a catch up'. This was drinking for the sake of it.

In one high corner of the long thin bar room hung a very old bulky TV, horse racing flickering weakly on the greasy screen.

A selection of hunched patrons sat before a long galley bar. All nursed various drinks, all studiously avoiding each other's gaze, not wanting to lend anyone a misapprehension that they wanted to chat.

Opposite the bar were a series of small booths. All were cracked faux leather, and had yellowed stuffing bursting through the gaps. In the one furthest from the door two men were in conversation. Whispering, faces close, drinks in front of them, one had hardly touched theirs, while the other was half quaffed and outnumbered by empties, both pint pots and shot glasses. CC nudged Freethy, gesturing with her chin towards them.

They were different ages. The one looking towards the door was young, a big man, confident in his size and stature. He surveyed the room as Christine and Freethy approached. The other man was older, going to seed, thickening around the middle, broken veins blooming across his eyes and cheekbones. Dandruff decorated the shoulders of his old-fashioned tweed jacket. The conversation between the two-seated men halted.

"We'd like a word, mate," said CC letting them see her Met Police brief.

The two drinkers looked up at their visitors. They simply stared at them, as though they were aliens just landed on the planet preparing to invade.

"Always happy to help fellow-serving officers," the older man replied. He was the one who fitted the description Freethy had given her, the one Collinson had told them was the man behind the tip offs.

"Detective Inspector Christine Chance, Flying Squad. This is my colleague, Detective Constable Mark Freeth."

Freethy joined in the badge flashing party now, just to underline his legitimacy.

The younger, bigger man spread his hands in front of him, before shuffling out of his side of the booth.

"Looks like you want some privacy. I'll leave you to it."

CC took a close look at him: big, broad shouldered, dark hair swept back, and eyes that looked like they could cut glass. He wasn't the one they wanted to talk to, but for some reason it crossed her mind to stop him leaving. This thought was interrupted by their main target.

"I'll catch up with you later, Harkness. You can tell me the rest of that story another time."

The Tall Man waved over his shoulder as he left the bar, not even bothering to look back.

"Now, how can I assist you? I don't want my evening taken up with too much chit-chat. I have some drinking to do."

CC sat down where the Harkness bloke had been. Freethy pulled up a low bar stool, sitting perpendicular to the table, pretty sure in his mind that their man would realise this was done in case he should decide to try and make an early exit. Once seated, Freethy took a second to send a text from his mobile phone while Christine started the ball rolling.

"I am speaking with Detective Inspector Murray of SO15, aren't I?" she began, getting a nod as an answer.

"The very same. Has my fame reached all the way to Flying Squad then?"

"I wouldn't call it fame. I'd call it a sneaking suspicion."

"Suspicion...? Officer, you're sounding less than professionally courteous. Need me to clear something up for you?"

"Yes, please. Why am I running around London picking up your shitty work for you?"

Murray lifted his pint glass, swallowing the remains of his beer, suds sliding down his chin as he set the empty back on the table.

"Well now, love. You know the expression...why have a dog and then bark your-fucking-self?"

This chat wasn't going to be friendly.

If Harkness was troubled by the fact that two Old Bill were in a bar bracing one of his little helpers, he didn't show it on his face as he boarded the Tube train at Green Park.

And there, on the train, was Danny Felix. Right where he was supposed to be. Another special little helper. He was the only other person in the carriage...just the way they both liked it.

As the train pulled out, Harkness lowered himself into the seat next to his pet blagger, passing him a heavy padded envelope as he did so.

"There's your pin money, Felix. Don't go spending it all

at once."

"We are getting off at the next station, Bond Street. You will walk across Oxford Street and into the car park at the back of Selfridges. Level three, silver BMW five series. Get in the passenger side. You are going to show me the route."

"Well, well, well. I do like it when you get bossy, Danny. If by the route you mean the route that the dosh will take, then yes, that is no problem. We can do that now. But I will want to hear your plan in full as we drive."

Danny looked at the big copper, making sure his eyes stayed as dead and flat as he could muster.

"I'll tell you fuck all until I am ready. Tonight, your only job is to be my guide."

The squealing grind of the Tube train's brakes drowned out whatever it was that Harkness said in response, but Danny didn't need to hear the words to recognise the word "cunt" when it was levelled at him.

As they exited the pub, both Freethy and Christine felt like they wanted to stand under a hot shower for a very long time.

The interview had been as antagonistic as it could have possibly been. Murray sweated through his shirt while evading any version of truth. He neither confirmed nor denied CC's suspicions that the previous month's work had been nothing more than the bidding of someone much higher up. The bit that really rankled her was the thought that the jobs might have been rotten to the core.

The thought that she and her colleagues had been put in harm's way for some dirty cops plan was just about as heinous a crime as any straight-thinking Old Bill could envisage.

"Well, if being an obstructive, obtuse, drunken fuck was proof of anything illegal, that wanker just gave us enough to send him down for life."

Freethy followed this by pulling fresh air into his lungs, trying to shake the morbidity of the bar from himself.

"What did you make of the big man? The one who left just as the party started?"

Freethy was smiling now. He realised that both he and his friend had exactly the same instinct, the same urge to slap the big fucker in the face and tell him to sit the fuck down and join their friendly chat.

"I didn't like him one bit..."

"Me neither. Something not right there...confident but too cocky."

"Which is why I had him followed as soon as he left."

CC turned to look at her partner, a smile spreading on her face.

"And that was the text you were sending. And I just thought you were being rude in front of our new friend."

Christine was laughing as she said it. She should have known that Freethy would have been on the same page, at the same time as her.

"That's why I asked Little Colin to come with us and hang out in the background. We thought something else might catch our eye - and it did. Listen, it's obvious isn't it? Murray is a pisshead. Too drunk to be anything other than a man counting the days until he pensions out. If he was feeding jobs for a reason, you can near as damn it be sure..."

Christine finished the sentence for Freethy.

"...that he's only the messenger boy. The monkey, not the organ grinder."

"Let's see what Little Colin comes back with. I asked him to try smudge up too...see if we can get an idea who the big man is with some photos."

"He said a name, didn't he? Clarken or Harken?"

"It was Harkness and I think he was job, mate. I'd put money on it."

"Yeah, right! You don't have any money."

"Oh shit yeah, that makes it your round then…"

"Only a cheeky one. Then we'll see if Little Col has anything to report. Then I have to go, you know, to the hospice."

"Deal. But let's go to a nice pub, shall we, CC?"

Once they were in the car, Danny in the driver seat, Harkness beside him, Danny felt much more at ease. He felt in control. To him, Harkness was like a wild animal, given to bursts of unpredictable, almost feral behaviour. It was a real life embodiment of having 'a tiger by the tail'.

He had thought that if anyone was to make a movie version of this job, and God knows his plan would surely deserve it, then they would have to cast Gary Oldman as Harkness. Not the Oldman of the *Batman* movies or that shit mobile phone ad on TV. No, the Oldman who played the villain in *Leon: The Professional*. All crazy eyes and weird behaviour. With an air of violence just there, lurking in the background ready to take your face off without so much as a by your leave. Mind you, Harkness didn't much look like Gary Oldman. He was much bigger for a start. Maybe it was Danny's turn to be unpredictable:

"Do you like Gary Oldman, Harkness?"

The detective just stared at the side of Danny's face, not quite computing the question, and then responded in the only way he knew how.

"Stop talking shit and drive. Take us to New Scotland Yard. It's closer to us from here. We can drive the route in reverse."

"You'll never guess who I had in the back of my cab the other day…" And Danny swung the car out into traffic, snaking down from Oxford Street towards Victoria, passing Buckingham Palace.

Soon they were by the headquarters of the Metropolitan Police at New Scotland Yard. The iconic building that had been the base for so many landmark investigations.

"I've seen this place so many times on TV. All those journalists and their pieces to camera for the ten o'clock news in front of that stupid spinning sign. Makes it look like they sell vacuum cleaners instead of policing the nation. Can't believe they are going to sell it next year."

Harkness huffed his agreement.

"I can't think of anywhere near here that you would want to pull the hit off. Too close to the Yard. No point in making it easy for them to get to you once it's done."

"You said the transfer will happen early morning. How early? What time are we looking at?"

"That kind of shift can be carried out at any time of day. But because this one's such a big amount, they want to go during early morning rush hour. It makes it more difficult for anyone who might want to have a go at them, too hard to make a clear break for it if they did."

Danny was nodding, thinking it made sense. London traffic could cripple a job.

"So aren't you going to ask me then? Or are you playing the hard man?"

Danny wasn't sure if Harkness was referring to Dexy or his sister's suddenly bulging bank account. He knew that his strategy of keeping any emotion out of this deal had been pointless. Still, Harkness was right. He didn't want to give him even a millisecond of satisfaction.

"I reckon you are the one with the problem. Anything happens to her, it won't just be this job that goes wrong. And that doesn't take into account that she is more likely to kill you than I am, given half the chance." Danny didn't look at Harkness as he said it. He just kept his eyes on the traffic.

Harkness responded with a chuckle.

He shifted in his seat. Reaching into his jacket pocket, he produced a flashy mobile phone. A few seconds of tapping and he was then holding it up to Danny. Moving pictures. Dexy, blindfolded. That day's news on a TV beside the chair she was tied to. No way of telling where this room was, but the news on the TV certainly dated it as today. The Dexy on the screen then seemed to realise that she was not alone. Starting to kick and struggle against her bindings, fabulous blue language came out of her mouth, including threats, swearing and oaths of revenge. The whole thing made Danny's guts twist.

"I'm a good film director, don't you think? She is a hard bitch, I'll give you that. But your bravado doesn't fit, Danny. I like the version of you that stays focused. That's why I wanted the leverage."

Danny stayed quiet.

They were now down by the river. The Thames flowed gently in the late evening glow. Industrial units sat cheek by jowl with new executive apartment blocks, built during the boom, trying to tempt people with a view of the river.

Harkness guided them through a few double back routes. He knew that despite the need for the rush hour traffic the Old Bill would still take these short cuts to ease some of the traffic pain. It was in one of these that Danny suddenly pulled the car over to a little side road that led down to the banks of the Thames itself. They were in Battersea Church Road. The water shimmered as it smoothed its own path out to sea, the reflection of the redeveloped Lots Road Studios dominating the water surface and the skyline itself.

To their right was a big ornate church, St. Mary's, which sat on the corner of a tight dog-leg in the narrow road. Down one side was a gap to the river. Opposite was a high brick wall, bordering the residential properties that had stood for years. Georgian probably, Danny thought.

On the same side of the road as the church, and forming the other side of the gap to the river was a new apartment block. Danny parked the car just above the slipway between the church and the new block.

"Let's take a look."

Both men exited the car, Danny clocking the amount of CCTV on the edge of the new apartment building, but realising straight away that they were angled in order to cover only the perimeter fence.

"Those cameras probably don't cover too much of this slipway. Good stuff."

"This all looks a little tight to me," said Harkness, still desperate to know what Danny had in mind. Danny didn't answer. But he liked the spot a lot.

The slipway emerged onto the road right in the middle of the dog-leg turn. It was by no means a wide road, making it easy to block off if necessary. Danny turned and walked down towards the water's edge.

To his right was a smattering of houseboats. They were moored up, right on the edge of the river at the back of the church. There was no gate to the slipway, the route to the water was unguarded .

Crossing now towards the church, Danny was further encouraged. In the church's courtyard he could see a pathway that led onto a riverside path, obviously meant to afford walkers and cyclists a safe passage away from the narrow road. The path seemed to go all the way to Battersea Bridge.

"Is this your spot then, Danny?"

"Harkness, you tee'd the job up. You forced my hand, and you focused my mind with Dexy, so now you can fuck off out of the way. This is my bit of the game. I will not share with you. Like you said yourself, you don't play well with others."

Harkness could see that Danny meant every word.

"If you don't share with me, Felix, this will not end well."

"Really? Are you so sharp that you're confident you can keep that promise?"

Harkness just returned Danny's stare.

"Because if you are all that, how come you didn't spot the geezer who followed you out of the Tube and over to the car park at Selfridges earlier?"

Danny walked back to the car, leaving Harkness to deal with that juicy little one.

25

✧ Fail To Prepare ✧

Ciaran knew his red hair could be a problem. It was, after all, fucking bright.

This meant that whenever he was engaged in any questionable pursuit he always had to make sure that he was fully hatted up at the very least. Witnesses had an irritating habit of remembering his fiery beacon at the scene of a crime. This wouldn't normally be such a big deal except that Ciaran had a tendency to sweat like a pig when under any degree of pressure. Not that he didn't behave cool under fire. But he did sweat. A lot. To the point that it would leak from under his chosen headgear and at various points would render him almost blind.

And here he was, in one of those situations. Middle of the summer. North London. The dead of night in a knitted balaclava, wiping his eyes like crazy as he tried to hotwire the heavy-duty dumper truck.

Enda had given him all the information he had needed. Where the storage yard was. How many security guards and what time they were likely to be either asleep or busy downloading porn to notice that someone was about to fuck off with one of their biggest vehicles. The storage yard was huge. About the size of five full size football pitches, and just off the M1 motorway. There were three exits, which included the security hut at the main gate. Ciaran fully intended to leave by the gate furthest from that point...if only he could keep the sweat from running into his eyes long enough to see the ignition wires.

"Holy Mary, mother of God, it's fucking hot," he whispered to himself in the truck's cab. Ciaran had to pause every 30 seconds to stop from drowning in his own gravy.

When the huge German Shepherd dog came sniffing, Ciaran was neither surprised nor frightened. Once again Enda had warned him about the massive dog and how the night man usually let it run wild all evening round the yard, chasing cats, urban foxes and, when it was really lucky, flame-haired Irish truck thieves. The lump of minced beef with veterinary grade tranquilizer crushed into it sorted the animal out in about ten minutes. This delay, however, only served to sour Ciaran's mood and make him sweat even further. Eventually he thought, fuck it, and dumped the balaclava on the passenger seat in the cab of the truck. If anyone clocked him, he'd rather just kill them than have himself melt down to a puddle on the truck floor. Witnesses were a pain in his hole.

Finally, after about twenty minutes, he managed to start the huge truck. Enda's exhortations to him to be careful beamed into his mind as the diesel engine growled into life and coaxed the young Irishman into a fit of conscience. He pulled the woolly hood over his head again before gently starting to ease the truck out of the line of vehicles it had been parked in. No point in tearing off at 50 miles an hour and making too much noise at this point. Downloading porn or not, why rouse the security guards now? And, anyway, if it came to a chase, should the paid-for-plods discover his theft quickly, there was no way he would be able to outrun a police patrol car in something like this.

And that was the bit Ciaran didn't understand. Who needed a big rumbling truck for a robbery? Surely you needed to escape quick? I mean, for fuck's sake, the get-away drive was always the best bit as far as he was concerned. But, to be honest, he didn't have the first clue what it was that Danny was planning. All he knew was that it was a robbery. That they needed Enda and his skill set. They needed Howler and a load of his mates. They needed an industrial unit and that they needed to steal a dumper truck.

The rest of it was all in Danny's head. At least, it was going to be that way until they were all to meet at the unit later that evening. Excitement was already building in Ciaran. Jobs always did this for him. Especially as Danny had hinted to him that it was a job that would make the headlines.

Ciaran had always fancied being a bit famous...or better still, infamous.

This made him gun the engine of the truck just a bit too much and for a second he considered just barreling through the gate at the rear of the storage yard. But then he saw Enda's face again in his mind's eye. Not yet, young Ciaran...save the excitement for the big day. So he stopped and cut the gate open with his huge bolt cutters instead.

And best of all, nobody was around to see him or his ginger nut when he did it.

Christine had a problem.

"Here he is leaving the pub. Another one of him going into the Tube. Crystal clear, as good as any I've taken." Little Colin had done a cracking job and he was proud of it. His compact five foot six inch frame, clean-shaven head with a somewhat everyman face allowed him to disappear in a crowd. He was someone you would look at once but never twice, and barely recall having seen him at all. And this was why he was so good at following suspects and even better at getting surreptitious photos of them.

"You'll like this one even more," squealed Little Colin, his nasally whine of a voice peaking as he got more excited about his handiwork.

Christine was now looking at a photo of two men. It showed the big bloke who had left the pub earlier with another man, this time exiting the Tube.

"Top work, Col. Thanks for all this." She blew out her cheeks as Freethy started to rise from the café table, pointing at Colin's cup.

"Another, mate?"

"Nah, nah, I have to do one. The Mrs...waiting for me at home. We're into that *Game of Thrones* series. She can't get enough, so we watch one every Wednesday, no matter what time I roll in at. So, I'm off. Anything else, just shout, lads."

And with that he was gone, melting into the crowds like a pro.

These photos would of course be invaluable in getting Christine closer to whatever it was that was going on but they also presented her with a huge hurdle.

Freethy came back with two more coffees for them.

"Jesus, Freethy. We are going to have to tread lightly here."

"You thinking what I am?"

"The big man was Old Bill too..."

"Yep..."

"Where is this going to take us?"

"We can't share info with anyone now. We don't know where the rot starts and stops...unless we are jumping to conclusions."

"Our friendly chat with Murray was too antagonistic to be just brushed off as professional rivalry. We just need to confirm who this Harkness geezer was, and now, who this other one is too, coming out of the Tube with him."

"But who the fuck do we ask?"

"Computers are out...electronic trail and all that...

"Even pressurising Collinson may have been a risk."

"No, Collinson's old school...he may be a lot of things but he's not dirty. Jesus, why am I the suspicious type?"

"Bit late for wishful thinking, CC."

Her coffee tasted particularly bitter.

✧✧

"You look tired, Mum."

"I look tired?" said Christine, rolling her eyes at the irony.

She was sat at Shauna's bedside. The machines bleeped softly. Technology was ticking over. It was telling them, and whoever else was interested, that all was still okay with the world.

"It's just work stuff. I think I've stumbled into something a bit...messy."

Shauna's eyes took a beat to focus.

"What's going on?" she tried to shuffle up in bed. CC eventually helped pull her up, once again heartbroken at how light her girl's frame had become.

"I think I may have rumbled some Old Bill who are playing both sides...corrupt."

"Oh...sounds tricky."

"Pretty much..."

And suddenly she was laying the whole picture out for Shauna, knowing that her little girl was probably only taking in about 60 per cent of it. Also knowing she was retelling it for herself. Feeling her gut as she stepped through what she thought she knew of the conundrum, gauging where her instincts were triggered the most.

By the end of it Shauna was dozing and CC felt just as drained. The hypnotic thrum and beep of the ward took her off, into sleep. A deep sleep, the likes of which CC had not allowed herself for some time.

She didn't know what time it was when Shauna's voice woke her.

"This could be dangerous for you, Mum...Mum?"

It took a second for CC to compute, but Shauna was

continuing the conversation from where both had let it trail off.

"Umm, yes, I suppose. In fact, no suppose about it. It will be. I feel so stupid. Stupid for being nosey, letting my suspicions lead me and Freethy to here. I have put both of us at risk."

"Yeah, but...it's what you do, Mum. And you're not stupid. Never have been."

They looked at each other, silence settling between them.

CC broke it.

"I don't know, Shauna. I don't know how to do this."

"You'd be a pretty weird Mum if you did...you mean me, now, don't you? All this crap."

She lifted her arms in the air, gesturing at the paraphernalia of illness.

"It's just dying, Mum."

"Don't..."

"No, it is, Mum. If you think about it. That's what I'm doing. It's something we all get to, but I'm just ahead of schedule. The reason you don't know how to be is that we didn't expect it. You only do this a few times, so we aren't supposed to be used to it."

CC sighed, nodding.

"The important thing is, just because I'm stopping, it doesn't mean that you have to as well. If anything..."

She didn't need to finish the sentence, she could see her Mum understood. And she felt better for having said it.

"I was always a better copper than a mum. And now I'm not even doing that right."

"You were just good at being Christine Chance..."

CC felt a flutter in her chest, her shoulders relaxing.

"Mum...?"

"Yeah..."

"Are there any Haribo left in my locker?"

"Let me look..."

CC stood. As she opened the drawers of the white bedside cupboard looking for the sweets her daughter loved so much, she rummaged passed countless magazines covered in boy bands and young, bare chested actors.

At the bottom of the drawer she came across a newspaper and a bag of the sweets. It was the newspaper Shauna had shown her a week ago, the one that covered the Heathrow job where this had started. The page was still folded over at the article. CC once again recognised herself at the scene in the photo.

"Bingo, one bag of Haribo."

"Cool…"

"You kept this from the other week."

"It's not every day your mum makes the papers."

"Shame it's not a nice photo of me. Mind you, every time I have had my photo taken for *The Job*, it's been a bad one."

"Yeah. The one you showed me that time, of you graduating from the cadet school…your hair…you look like a furby." Laughter passed between them.

"That was a long time ago. And my hair was very trendy. I must look that out, see what Freethy looks like as well."

And then she went silent.

"Mum? You okay?" The question was asked through a mouthful of gummy cola bottles.

"Yeah…*The Job*."

"What about it?"

"No, *The Job…The Job* magazine."

"Now you're not making sense, Mum."

"No…no, I am. The Tall Man, I told you about…if he's a cop…a senior copper, his picture might be in *The Job*, our internal magazine at work."

Shauna thought she understood, but she knew her Mum's brain was off and racing, and soon so would she be.

"Before you disappear, Mum…I'm going to need more Haribo next time you come."

CC was already grabbing her mobile phone and car keys.

It was the fifth time Danny had walked this part of the route. The impact site. Checking, re-checking all the details that had first excited him about this spot when he had driven it with Harkness.

He paced out the distance from the slipway to the edge of the road. Then again from the slipway to the opposite side of the road, making mental notes, assessments for timing. He spent a bit of time jamming a huge, sharp-ended stone into the bollard that was meant to rise and fall to prevent access to the turning circle in front of the church. It didn't look like it had been operational for a long time, but there was no sense in leaving that to chance. Soon, he had ringed the whole outer tube of the bollard with a series of stones, wedging them down with his boot heel repeatedly, hoping that it would stop the mechanism grinding into life any time soon...or in the next few days at least.

Once he was satisfied with his survey, he climbed into a car that he had stolen for the night, and drove the few short miles back out to west London and to the industrial unit that Ciaran had leased for them. He took a circuitous route to make sure he didn't have any unwanted hangers-on after clocking Harkness' shadow earlier.

That was one major concern. Two actually. Firstly, Harkness hadn't spotted the tail. Admittedly Danny was in no doubt the short man who was following was good, but still, Harkness should have been better, should have had "eyes about". Secondly, if Harkness was under scrutiny, was Danny also attracting attention? Ordinarily, under such circumstances, Danny would have postponed the job. But this was not an option for him now. Not with the Dexy factor and the ticking clock on the movement of the money. It was Hobson's choice...and Danny didn't like it one bit. The next conundrum for him was whether to share the presence of the tail to the rest. Common sense almost certainly dictated a 'yes', but Danny was hesitant. What if the tail was the result of a leak? A leak from within his team, not at Harkness' end? Also, he didn't know the team really well, so didn't know how they would react to the news. Enda was the biggest concern to Danny. He was a new face to Danny's band of merry men. And for this job he was also the most vital. If Enda didn't weave his magic, the rest of the gig was as good as fucked.

This jumble of thoughts were still bouncing around in his head as he finally turned down the potholed lane towards the industrial unit, satisfied that he didn't have any company behind him.

As he pulled the BMW up to the garage style doors, they started to open, clattering as they went. Ciaran was grinning like a mad man behind them. Danny eased the car in. He parked it next to the huge dumper truck that would prove invaluable in the coming days. The rest of the team was there already, all waiting to hear what was what, when and how...all waiting to be clued in. They were all waiting to hear Danny tell them they were going to change London forever. Harkness was right...cities don't stand still.

The Job was a typical internal communications maga-zine. Sterile. On-message. It was not widely read. By producing it, the Met could always say we told you about this or that change months ago...it was in the *The Job*.

The high esteem the publication was held in by the men and women of the Old Bill was accurately reflected by the fact that a huge pile of them was used as a doorstop in CC's office. Each month, when the new edition came out, it was promptly placed on the top of the doorstop pile, until such times as the pile became too big and half of it was binned straight into recycling.

Now, here in the wee small hours, Christine was sat at

her desk having lifted the top thirty magazines from the doorstop pile. She was leafing through them, looking at every group photograph she came across. Group photos were almost always taken at one of two things, a PR opportunity announcing some new initiative...or a charity function.

She had already gone through one pile and no luck. No photo of the man, Harkness, in any of them. In fact, she was beginning to think that her gut reaction had been wrong. That he wasn't Old Bill. And if that was the case then Christine needed to enjoy more of that sleep she had had earlier.

She finished flicking through the last magazine in this latest pile. Nothing. Fuck it. Time to sleep.

She stood up and carried the pile over to the doorway, allowing them to return to what she figured was a much more useful application than the one they were actually published for.

She made her way into the locker room, realising she needed the toilet. Pushing her way into the ladies, she picked the cubicle closest to the door. It was in a right state so, while pulling a face, she had to go to the next one, pushing the door and stepping in.

She caught herself laughing out loud as she locked the cubicle door behind her. There sat on the top of the toilet cistern was another copy of *The Job*. As she sat down, CC lifted it, noting that the date showed it was the very latest issue.

Might as well, she thought, scanning it for photos again.

No. No. No. No, then...hold on.

She went back a page. A big group photo. A load of Old Bill in suits. Among them were some men, kitted out for what looked like boxing.They were bare-chested with shorts on. And one of them, to the extreme right of the picture, was beaming right at the camera. Claret all over his big wide-boned face. His nose had obviously received some special trauma. But he must have come off better, as he was holding a trophy in one hand.

The by-line beneath the photo read:

Congratulations to the Mixed Martial Arts Fundraisers! Freemasons Grand Trust make Charity Thousands in One Night.

And then a list of names, from right to left. But the name Christine was most interested in was the last one listed:

Detective Inspector James Harkness.

"Fuck me, I've got him."

26

✧ Listen Up ✧

Danny looked at them. All their faces were turned to him. He always enjoyed this part of the game. He always liked having people to work with, to rely on. His job, as leader, was to enable them to do their best, albeit illegal, work.

He had been talking for about 60 minutes now, using a blow-up map of London that they had pinned on the back wall of the unit. Red rings were littered across the face of the map. Times were beside them and then a green line picked out the route from the Barnes Flying Squad all the way to New Scotland Yard in Central London. Drawn at the point where this green line met Battersea Church Road there was an even bigger yellow circle.

Danny felt sure he had been pretty clear with the instructions. Some of the points he had made had been greeted with looks of incredulity, the odd intake of breath. But by the time he had expanded and expounded, understanding and acceptance seemed to bloom on the faces of the men in front of him. This was followed closely by nervous excitement as they began to realise that this plan could...might...just work.

A question and answer session had followed. Clarifications were delivered, adjustments suggested. Some were taken up, some rejected.

And now all that was left was to make sure they were

all up for it. Ready to put their backsides on the line, to take the risks and see them out to the end, bitter or sweet.

"Gentlemen, all I can say now is I am ready," announced Danny. "If any of you feel you can't execute your part in this plan now is the time to speak up. If that is the case we all walk away. The job doesn't get done, and we all get to lie on our death beds thinking what if..."

Ciaran, Big Enda and Howler all sat, staring back at him, knowing that they really had no choice. Coming this far into a job of this size and potential, they would be mad to back out now. Plus, they would probably spend the next few months hunting each other down if they did. Loose ends were never an attractive proposition.

"Enda. You and your men, do you feel you can achieve what we need you to?"

Big Enda took a deep breath, his gaze never leaving Danny's face.

"Well, ye have some fucking out there ideas, Danny, but I am clear. Me and my boys will deliver."

"Howler. You feel the same?"

His answer was straightforward and confident: "Ready to rock, ready to roll, Danny."

Finally Danny looked at Ciaran.

"Danny, I'm in, fella. Can't wait," was the response, accompanied by a wink.

Danny weighed up what he was about to say next, deciding then that it was right that he shared.

"Okay, we are a go. One last word, gents, though. Eyes about. I don't trust our friend, Mr. Harkness. Neither should any of you. He has been attracting some unwanted company of late, but I don't believe that has spread to us. I have one more meet with him, later today. After that, it is our gig until divvy up. But keep your wits about you. Fuck knows what he might be planning or thinking. Last but not least, here are the remaining payments for your boys and don't forget to pick up your transistor radios and earphones on the way out."

Ciaran spoke up.

"Harkness is being followed?"

"I think he might be, yes."

"If that is the case, what do we do with him?"

"You mean after?"

Ciaran nodded.

"Don't worry. I have a special treat planned for the Detective Inspector."

That brought a grim chuckle from Ciaran, but silently Danny wondered to himself if they would ever get that far.

It wasn't what you would call a comfortable night's sleep.

The cot was lumpy, the locker room drafty and Christine's tossing and turning and crazy dreams added to her suffering.

It was about five forty in the morning now. She decided she'd had enough lying around.

Routine. Habit would help about now, so she indulged in one of her own. She changed into her gym kit, grabbing her skipping rope from the locker she kept there. Once in the courtyard, with the early morning sun creeping across the concrete towards her, she started to skip.

It felt good to her. The rhythm of the rope. The flexing of her arms. Her muscle memory kicking in. She varied her tempo and steps. The sweat breaking on her forehead. Feeling it run between her shoulder blades. She whipped the rope over her head and down to her feet. She constantly tightened her core muscles. She enjoyed the rush of blood through her veins. It was hypnotic to her: meditation at 200 skips a minute.

She used the time to run all of the facts about the conspiracy once more though her mind.

The ease of the jobs. The large amounts of money recouped at each one. Being fobbed off by her boss. Harkness. Murray. With each slap of the rope at her feet she counted off each factor.

What should she try to do next with regard to Harkness, Murray and the whole damn thing? She needed some kind of indicator, a signpost that showed her the way to concrete proof or a fact that would burst the bubble.

Shower.

Trying to wash away some of her anxiety.

As she dried herself, beginning to feel a little more human as she did so, CC began to feel foolish. Was she on a wild goose chase? Was this notion of a grand conspiracy of cops tipping off criminals and in turn directing inform- ants so that other cops would intervene just the stuff of Hollywood movies? After all, the recovered money was safe. It was residing here in the building under lock and key and, she believed, due to be moved to Scotland Yard any day now? Where was the benefit?

Doubt crept into her mind, then her bones, then her theories.

As she dressed she realised she was hungry. When had she last eaten?

By six forty-five she had bought a paper and was settling into a seat in her favourite local café. She knew the bacon, sausage, beans, fried egg and toast was not good for her, but they tasted more delicious than any other food she had eaten in months. She abandoned any notion of dietary guilt in favour of sheer indulgence.

At seven thirty, she was enjoying a third cup of piping hot tea and was most of the way through *The Times* when her mobile buzzed.

Text message. Freethy.

"Where U?"

"Caff," was her simple reply. He'd know which one.

Five minutes later Freethy walked in. He looked down

at the damage CC had done to her plate.

"Bleedin' hell, Christine, there is a Third World out there you know!"

She laughed. She was pleased to see her mate. He ordered his own fry-up and coffee. But when he sat down in the seat in front of her, Freethy started to put his serious face on; CC waited for it.

"Have you heard?"

"Heard what?"

Just at that moment, CC's phone began to chime out again. This time her ringtone gave out some ridiculous pop song programmed in for her by Shauna. She held a hand up and took the call, leaving Freethy to pour sugar into the coffee the waitress had set in front of him with all the grace of an all-in wrestler.

"Detective Inspector Chance here."

"It's Ayoade. I've just come in to find the final test results from the post mortem in my in-tray for your friend Mr Fisty."

"And…?". She held her breath.

"Toxicology levels show he overdosed, by a lot. My examinations show no sign of any force majeure or coercion. Plus…he was a ticking clock."

"What does that mean?"

"He had fairly advanced cancer of the liver. Untreatable. They say only a few weeks to live. There's no way he could not have known. His pain levels must have been off the chart but the amount of drugs he was using…and the amount of evidence of sexual activity on him, he was determined to go out in a blaze of debauched glory."

"And that is what your report will say?"

"Absolutely."

"Right, okay, thanks. I owe you one." CC was deflated. It sounded like her doubts had just all come home to roost in one fuck off fell swoop. She ended the call.

It was Freethy's turn to look puzzled.

"Well, I've heard now. So Fisty had advanced liver cancer and he OD'd."

Freethy looked even more confused now.

"What?"

CC took a swig of tea before she replied.

"Isn't that what you meant when you asked me had I heard?"

"No, mate. But what was that about Fisty?"

She told him, also how foolish she was beginning to feel with her mad conspiracy theories and gut instinct so far off it was on another planet.

But Freethy started to shake his head.

"No CC, no. The news I was referring to was about Iggy Adesina. He was found late last night in his cell. He'd hung himself using pillow cases and the end of his bed."

"Is he dead?"

"As a big fat dodo. And now I am beginning to go as crazy as you. This is adding up."

"But Fisty..."

"Our killer wouldn't have known Fisty was sick. He couldn't have known and even if he did know he couldn't leave that loose end to take its natural course."

"But Ayoade said no signs of coercion or force majeure."

"Yeah, but, as you and I both know, where there is a will, a criminal will...there is always a way."

Danny looked across the table at his sister. She was fidgeting. This only ever meant one thing. She was worried.

"This has got to be something to do with you, Danny. I mean for fuck's sake. First trouble, then guns, now a shitload of money in MY bank account that isn't mine!"

"You have to be the only person I know who is pissed off because they found an extra eighty grand on their bank account."

"If you do not tell me what you are up to right now, I am going straight to the police about this. This is all too much for me, Danny. I am not joking...my career and therefore my family are at risk."

"Listen up, Celeste."

Using her name with such a stern tone she sat up and sat still.

"Where did the bank say the money came from? What account?"

She spread a page of paper in front of him, her bank statement, printed off at home.

She had run a highlighter pen over the deposit that was causing her to lose sleep.

"Have you told the husband?"

Celeste shook her head.

"Anybody?"

Another shake of the head. She knew Danny was in his no nonsense mode. This was exactly when she was a little bit scared of him. She could never tell him that. Nor could she ever say to him that in these moments he reminded her most of their Father. That would just about make him freak.

Danny laid his hand on hers.

"Okay, Celeste. The truth is the bank will already be investigating this and they will flag it all the way up their chain until it reaches the police."

"The pol..."

Danny cut her off. Her shrill voice was starting to attract attention.

"Shush. Yes. And I already know who in the police will be handling it. So don't worry. Do not tell anyone. Do not go into your bank, unless they summon you. If they do, talk to me first."

"I...I...I don't want the money. Whoever owns it can have it back. Jesus, Danny. I just want to be left alone. They must know this is nothing to do with me."

She was beginning to unravel. He grabbed her hands and without anyone being able to tell he began to squeeze them. Hard. Celeste didn't shut up until she registered the pain. She tried to pull her hands from him, but Danny didn't let go.

"Listen. To. Me. Celeste," he snapped.

She finally focused on him.

"What if I was to tell you that there is a way that this can all go away?"

She looked at him. Distrust flashed in her eyes, but only for an instant.

"I know you don't trust me, sis. That's okay, because I love you. I know, in your world at least, I'm not easy to trust."

"Danny..."

"But I will make this go away. And...you will get to keep the money too."

A puzzled look crossed her face. Danny let go of her hands and nonchalantly took a sip of his coffee.

27

✧ Cat and Mouse ✧

Little Colin was fairly sure he'd been rumbled by the bloke with the tall man he had been following from Bond Street Tube over to the car park at the rear of Selfridges. It was time to change tack...and for a bit of ingenuity. So, today, he had donned his long-haired heavy metal wig, put the boots on with the lifts in them and applied a beard where one had never been before.

What interested Colin the most was Harkness. He didn't seem to be behaving in an over-cautious or deviant way. He hadn't tried to dry-clean Little Colin. There were no extra double-backs or wariness in his movements as he travelled.

Now he was outside the Finchley Road nick where the tall bloke had just arrived. He had been with him since before dawn. He was careful not to be too obvious, having to call on all of his surveillance experience to avoid being spotted two days in a row. Not easy when you are on the follow on your own but he couldn't change that right now.

So Little Colin was able to put his feet up in a Costa Coffee right opposite the front entrance to the nick.

Colin didn't like this very much. The thought that he was on the trail of a fellow copper for other Old Bill made him uneasy. However, he knew Christine and Freethy well, and as far as he was concerned they were good police. If they wanted someone looked at, there must be a very good reason. He trusted them, having had to rely on them to get him out of a few tricky scrapes in the past. So now, if they needed his help, he gave them it. And here he was. Waiting...watching.

Harkness had spotted his tail too now. He didn't think it was the same one as the day before, but nonetheless, he was there.

And that angered him.

How could he have been so lazy? How had he not seen him before Danny Felix had?

And who the fuck was following him in the first place? He could think of only one possibility. Who were the coppers who had braced Murray in that shithole bar of his? He needed to find out.

A quick phone call to Murray furnished him with a name. Two names in fact. Chance and Freeth. Out of Barnes. Close. Too close for comfort. Murray was dispatched to do a little more digging...with orders to text over anything else he might find out.

Harkness sat looking at the names he had written on the post it note on his desk. He sighed and then muttered to no-one in particular: "Well, Ms Chance and Mr Freeth, you do know what happens when you try to corner a rat? It gets very aggressive."

Little Colin was given the runaround all day. New Scotland Yard. A café off Wigmore Street in the Marylebone area that looked like it still inhabited the 1950s. The British Museum in Holborn, and finally an apartment block in South Kensington. Harkness liked to travel. But now Colin had a problem. He knew the apartments. He had been to them before a few years back on a previous follow, tracking a team who liked 'home invasions'. He knew this particular building had more than one main entrance. The building straddled the entire block, with roads going down both the eastern and western sides of the building. And despite how good he was, even Colin couldn't be in two places at once. There was only one thing he could do. He called Christine.

Harkness liked her. Not that he would ever tell her, but he liked her all the same. The defined Eastern European cheekbones, slender frame, long legs and the fact that she knew when to speak and when to shut up. And today, he most definitely didn't want to talk. He was tense. It was all knitting together now, he could feel that the end-game was in sight. He knew what the next steps needed to be, what he had to do, but he was still on edge. Not nervous. Not worried. No he was just...edgy. He was buzzing, waiting for the bell to ring. For his opponent to come out of his corner, face him for the first time, to throw the first swing of his fist, then calm down and go about his work. That's what it was...an overwhelming desire to start, an itch to start scratching.

And right now, this young lady could help him ease the tension. She could help scratch the itch until such times as he really started, which would be tomorrow. And anyway, he liked the idea of making the wanker who was following him cool his heels for an hour or so; see if he could work out that this place had two doors.

And at that, she walked into the bedroom, a vision in very little...Harkness felt his mouth go dry. My...he did like her. More than he realised.

223

It took CC just 45 minutes to reach South Kensington. It took her a bit longer to find Little Colin, especially as she wasn't used to looking for him in his disguise...the bearded heavy metal look.

Once that barrier was overcome, Colin gave her the full bill of the race. She was always impressed by his work. He was the best cat-and-mouse man she had ever worked with.

"I've been circling the block every ten minutes, but I can't be 100 per cent that he is still in there, CC. It takes more than three minutes to do the block and if I go too many times, I begin to stick out like a sore thumb."

"Yeah, no worries. So you backed off how long ago?"

"Twenty minutes? But he'd gone in about 20 to 25 before that."

"Okay, I'll take the east side. You the west? Is that how you want to go?"

"Easy by me. There's a Carluccio's restaurant on the east side, so you can enjoy the better coffee."

"Shame, that," grinned Christine, and off she went.

CC had just ordered her second coffee when she saw The Tall Man. Harkness emerged from the double doors on the eastern side of the apartments. Bollocks...she'd been enjoying her drink. They were off and running.

Harkness took them to the one place they hated. The London Underground.

CC cursed him. She knew a follow is fucking difficult on the Tube. She couldn't get too up close and personal, especially as CC had met Harkness.

So they sandwiched him. Christine in the carriage down

from Harkness. Colin was one up from him. District line. Going eastbound. Until they got as far as Westminster, then Harkness looked to change. Before now, CC had always liked the look of Westminster Tube station. It was all metal struts and shiny surfaces, like something from a science fiction film. The walkways and escalators snaked around the interior, linking the District, Circle and Jubilee lines. They made for a labyrinth of grey steel. But today, she hated it. It was a maze, and trying to keep track of Harkness without getting clocked was a fucking nightmare. At first it looked like he was heading street-wards. Maybe to join the tourists as they "oohed" and "aahed" at Big Ben and the Houses of Parliament, but at the last second he switched direction. He went back into the bowels of the station.

He's dry cleaning. Christine could spot it a mile off. Which was weird, as Little Colin had earlier told her he hadn't bothered. She felt her stomach tighten. He didn't care earlier. But now he was going somewhere that he did care. Or going to meet someone he wanted to keep under wraps...

She hung back. Looking around carefully, she finally spotted Little Col, leaning against the station wall, trying to look nonchalant. As if he was waiting for a friend to catch up. So she acted like his friend.

"He's dry cleaning..."

"I think so too," agreed Colin. "It means he wants to be all alone. He's looking for me more than you. I'll leave you to take the lead. He won't be expecting to see your face. Then when we see who or what he is trying to protect, we might need to split again."

Christine nodded. It made sense. So that is exactly what they did.

Harkness boarded the rear carriage of the northbound

Jubilee line train at Westminster, this being his turn to wait to see if Danny Felix joined him at Green Park. He thought he had shaken off his "new friend" at the Tube station. Westminster was excellent for that sort of thing, lots of escalators and big open landings. Contact could be lost easily. He suspected it had.

So all he had to do now was keep his eyes peeled and wait to speak to Felix. And at the next station Danny appeared. However they weren't alone in the carriage, causing a delay to the start of their conversation. Harkness didn't mind, it gave him more of a chance to keep his eyes peeled. He needed to make sure he was clean before starting to talk.

CC's breathing was shallow. She was tense as she fought to keep her eyes on Harkness. He had taken her all the way to the Jubilee north platform. She had to time her last minute hop onto the train carefully so as to avoid being spotted. She could only hope that Little Colin had managed to keep up. At least she still had her eyes on the prize.

The carriage didn't empty until they were quite far north, in fact as far as where the train left the tunnels and came out above ground at Finchley Road. Once they were alone, the two men sat opposite one another.

Emerging into daylight, Christine felt her pocket vibrate a couple of times. Text messages. The first was one from a friend, asking about Shauna and a drink later. The second was far more interesting. From Little Colin.

Harkness joined by guy. I spotted him other night at Bond St.

Christine edged forward in her seat slightly, snatching a glance down into the next carriage. Harkness was sat opposite the man. They were talking.

CC quickly tapped out a message back to Colin.

Col u take new guy I take Hark if poss. Might be tricky as stations quiet from here out.

She pressed send...at least they had a plan.

Danny was staring blankly at the adverts on the inside of the Tube carriage until the two of them were alone. That took a while. Finally, as the train pulled out of Finchley Road they had the carriage to themselves. Harkness made the first move.

"Are you ready?"

"Yes, we are."

"Tell me..."

"No. Be at the unit. Tomorrow night. Ten o'clock. Have her with you."

"Or?"

"Have you ever seen a film called *Man on Fire*?"

Harkness was looking intently at Danny now, puzzled by the switch in subject.

"No."

Danny gave him a wry smile, the first emotion he had shown since boarding the train. He paused while the train stopped at West Hampstead, making sure no-one joined them. The train pulled away again.

"Denzel Washington. Plays a bodyguard who is charged with protecting a little girl. He fails. But he makes sure she isn't left un-avenged...Watch it. You might like it. If Dexy is not there safe and sound tomorrow night..." added Danny, letting the words hang.

The train squealed. Metal wheels screeched against metal rails. The sparks threw splashes of light onto Danny's face, creating shadows around his eyes. They made him look, for a split second, cadaverous.

"You bring the money. I bring your precious redhead."

Harkness then reached inside his jacket, Danny tensing as he did, but the hand emerged holding a sheaf of papers.

"These, Danny boy, are the investigation orders for Mrs Celeste Winslow. A financial matter, possible proceeds of crime. It says I am to be the investigating officer."

Danny gave him nothing back.

"Of course, if this paper was to disappear, or I was to report that I had found nothing untoward...I just thought you might need another little incentive. Keep you between the lines, Danny. Now I want to know. How exactly are you going to pull this off?"

Danny managed to keep the hatred he felt for Harkness in that moment from his face, the jolt of the train helping.

The train pulled into Kilburn station. Danny stood up.

"Watch the news, Harkness. Watch the news...oh and by the way, does my sister get to keep your money?"

Danny got off the train.

They split up, just as CC's text had suggested. But Christine's end of the deal was a short one. At the next stop Harkness simply switched platforms. He took the train south again, alighting at Finchley Road. From there it was straight to the police station where he entered and stayed put for at least an hour.

Little Colin on the other hand had a far more tricky time of it. His lead took him on a merry dance, doubling back, ducking in and out of dead ends, retracing steps then deviating from them a third time around. All the while though, Colin managed to keep the target in his sights...but only just. Almost an hour and a half after exiting Kilburn Tube station, Col gave in and texted CC. Seconds later his own mobile rang. It was her.

"I need your help now," said Colin. "I'm getting tired and this guy isn't dry cleaning, he is positively fucking with me. It's like he knows I'm here and he's almost willing me to be bold and front him."

"My boy's been inside Finchley Road nick for a while now," explained CC. "Where are you?"

"He's got me all the way down in Holborn now. About 15 minutes ago he went into the Chancery Lane Hotel. There is only one main door in and out, but no sign of him yet. I need to eat, I need to pee and I need you to come now or I will break off."

"I'll come down now."

It took her 20 minutes to get there. A coffee shop, a little way along from the grand frontage of the hotel. Little Colin look wrecked, dead on his feet with fatigue. Nothing CC could do but let him go and take over herself.

Half an hour later it all started again. Christine was in pursuit, snaking her way down, on foot, through Covent Garden. Over to Leicester Square, which was a nightmare as the summer funfair was in residence. There were huge crowds, the noise and light of the rides adding to the confusion and then, after a wander through China Town it was back up to Covent Garden.

In the piazza a street performer had a large crowd applauding his fire-eating karaoke act. Any other time CC would have found it funny but this evening it was all just more irritation, watching the back of her target's head appearing then disappearing, until finally she'd lost him. Nowhere to be seen.

After all this time, Christine felt gutted. Both she and

Colin had been on the go for hours and had learned next to nothing about their targets. Fucking Pointless!

Fatigue then hit her too, like a sideswipe from a giant's fist, making her head feel too heavy for her neck. Exhaustion dragged her shoulders down, and her spirit with them. She took her mobile out, she was going to call Freethy, update him on the days wasted efforts as she headed to the Tube station and home. She was fishing in her pocket, the phone not co-operating with her, snagging on the lining of her jeans, when she walked right into someone. Christine looked up. It was the man she and Colin had been following for most of the afternoon and evening.

"If you want to talk to me, all you have to do is ask."

Christine was lost for words; all she could do was gawp. And just as she finally put her brain in gear and was about to speak, her phone rang in her hand. Dumbly she looked down at it, expecting to bounce the call, until he saw it was the hospice.

Shauna.

She held a finger up in her quarry's face, gesturing the phone with her other hand.

"One second, please."

Her target just shrugged.

"Christine Chance here..."

"Ms Chance, it's your daughter. Can you get here as soon as possible? Her condition has deteriorated considerably over the course of the last two hours."

She felt like she'd been kicked in the gut, not this. Not now. Not right now. Fuck, fuck, fuck.

"I...I'm on my way."

She ended the call.

"I suppose this means you don't want to talk to me."

CC stuffed a business card into the man's hand.

"I have to be somewhere else. Now. But if you are involved with the man we saw you with earlier today, you need to think again. Call me. Tomorrow. Whatever trouble you are in I can help get you out of it."

"Who said I'm in trouble?"

"I...I don't...look, just call me tomorrow. The man..."

Christine just stopped. She'd blown it. Everything that could have gone wrong with this follow just did...and then some. All she could do was step aside and start to run. Run. Run to the Tube, run to the hospice. Run to the one thing she wanted to run away from.

For his part, Danny stood still for a second, looking around, trying to see if he had missed a second follower. Where was the one who had been on him earlier? After a while he was fairly sure he had been left alone. He had knackered the first one and then freaked out the second one. But no, he wasn't stupid. Something in the phone call had spooked her...not just Danny's bold-faced cheek.

He looked at the card. Metropolitan Police. Barnes. Flying Squad. Det Insp Christine Chance.

Well, well, well. If they did suspect that their money van was going to get burned tomorrow, there was no way that Danny would be stood right here right now.

Fuck me...they're fishing. They have no idea. Fuck me. This might just work.

It's amazing what you don't see, even when you are looking.

You could be stood on a Tube platform, looking at a huge poster in front of you of a beautiful young couple walking on a beautiful beach having a beautiful holiday somewhere ...well, beautiful. But as soon as Freethy's train clattered into the station, he wouldn't have been able to tell you where the advert was imploring him to go. He had been looking, but not seeing.

Not surprising really. He was absolutely exhausted. The events of the past few weeks were enough to make anyone's head swim.

The carriage was one of the new Metropolitan Line trains, all open plan, flip seats and brightly lit.

The passengers all looked as miserable as sin, jostling against each other as the train sped out of London, out towards the leafy Hertfordshire countryside.

A young Asian man, furiously tapping on his smart phone was battling some electronic monster. A business woman, had obviously had a wine or two. Her business suit skirt showing a little too much leg as she gently dozed through her journey home. Three blokes in army fatigues and rugby shirts, looking like they were on their way to meet mates, passing a can of cider between them. Countless other commuters, all with varying degrees of urban numb plastered across their faces, enduring the Tube train and the proximity of strangers. A means to a destination end.

But even with all that looking. Freethy didn't see it.

Didn't spot the threat.

He needed to piss. So at his stop he didn't go straight to the exit gates. He went to the gents. He didn't look over his shoulder to see the three lads in combat trousers and rugby shirts delay their exit from the train until the last possible second. He didn't see them quicken their pace to come through the door of the gents a split second after him.

But he did feel the first boot square in his back that propelled him into the wall over the urinals. He did feel the thrashing of six fists and six boots as their blows rained down on him from behind. What he did see was himself, in his mind's eye, disappearing down a long, black hole, with the taste of blood in his mouth and the sensation of his own urine flowing down his legs. They decorated the walls with him and his blood.

They left him for dead. Or they assumed he was. The paramedic certainly thought so when he first arrived.

28

✧ A Moment of Quiet ✧

Coming through the doors of the hospice like a hurricane, Christine almost took out a nurse and had to catch a grip of herself, embarrassed by her haste in a place where speed was the last thing anyone really wanted.

Apologising profusely to anyone in her path she finally reached Shauna's room.

This was it.

She knew it. Instinct was telling her. She could feel it, like a heavy cloak that had wrapped itself around her, pulling at her. She stood still, her thoughts were thrashing around inside her head. She felt like she was walking out onto a frozen lake, knowing the ice was only thickest and strongest at the edges, but still striding out to the middle anyway, just waiting for the crack and the give, waiting to plunge into icy blackness.

But from somewhere, Christ knows where, she found the strength to reach out and push the door open.

She caught her breath. If it was possible Shauna seemed even smaller in her hospital bed. Her breathing rattled unevenly in the silence of the room. The usual barrage of monitors had all been silenced. It was as if they knew, with all their technological wizardry, that there was nothing left to do.

Christine stepped up to the bed. She took her daughter's hand and just held it. She sat like that for a very long time. Shauna's breathing was sporadic at best, long gaps forming between each draw. At some points CC wondered if the moment had finally arrived, only for another gasp to emerge and take her back from the brink.

They sat together.

"I love you, Baby Boo."

Christine whispered it, barely out loud.

It was strange to her. She had feared this moment for so long. From a distance it had always looked insurmountable to her. But, with the advantage of time and love, it simply was a moment of quiet and simple acceptance of how things are.

She had been dreading a tempest. But she found herself, now, in a space of calm, feeling, respect and love.

It was alright, it really was. Shauna had to go and Christine was happy to let her. And that is exactly what they both did.

Danny sat on the grass in the park at the very top of Primrose Hill. It was, many believed, one of the best views of London. He agreed with them. The city spread out in front of this little patch of green, like an apology to nature. It was simply a small reminder of what London would have looked like had man not excavated, built, concreted and developed.

Danny just sat, creating a space within himself. Finding a moment of quiet before the upheaval to come. He was not nervous or doubtful. He knew he could pull the job off tomorrow. He also knew that Harkness would try to kill him once it was done and dusted. And Danny had thought about that too. He had thought about it many times over the last few weeks.

Was he afraid to die?

What unnerved Danny most was his answer; not really.

However, what angered him most was the thought that he might not shuffle off on his own terms. No, that was very different. He had never viewed death as a finality, rather just as a fact of life, a development. He wasn't religious, like his parents had been. He didn't think there was a bearded man in the sky waiting for us all to clean up our acts. But he did like to think that there might be another space, another form of consciousness that you could morph to after this collection of atoms, chemicals and biology had taken you as far as it could. It was a process, and like all processes it moved forward, whether you liked it or not. Like a job. The moment you pulled out your shotgun or grabbed the security guard, you were in a process, and even if you started it, it would finish with or without you.

Just like London would, as with any big city. Whether you rolled out of bed, the city still cranked up, still went about its city state business, still moved forward with its own processes. Like Harkness had said, a constant state of forward flux.

Except, Danny knew that tomorrow would be different. He might indeed die tomorrow. Maybe not on his terms and perhaps even because of them.

Who knew?

So he sat there taking the city in. He could feel its rhythms, its heartbeat. He could predict how it would react to almost any given situation. He was able to spot its patterns and behaviours.

He smiled to himself; it made him think of *Highlander*. Connery describing to Lambert how the quickening felt. Showing him how to tune into the heart beat of the stag on the Scottish moor, feeling its life force course through both of them simultaneously.

Just as he could with systems. And a city, London, any city was a huge lumbering system. That is why he knew he would succeed with the robbery tomorrow.

Tomorrow, London would be his. His process would

crash into this city's. It would be a day London would never forget. What was it the villain in *Highlander* said? "Listen up, I have something to say. It's better to burn out than to fade away..."

Danny agreed. He nodded his head gently to himself as he sat still, feeling the late evening breeze on his face. Atop Primrose Hill, he enjoyed the moment, enjoyed the anticipation. For tomorrow, Danny would bring a stillness to the whole of London.

29

✧ A Moment of Disquiet ✧

Once the doctors had officially pronounced Shauna's death, there was the inevitable flurry of activity.

The questions about arrangements and information about the process now kicked in. The death certificates, funeral directors and a myriad other things seemed to pass Christine in a blur.

In the middle of all this one nurse spotted that CC was on the verge of becoming overwhelmed. In a quiet moment she came and found her, bringing with her a cup of tea, an act of kindness.

"Your daughter was a lovely girl. I'm so sorry for your loss."

Christine took the cup from her, smiling vaguely at her words. It took her a little longer than she normally would have. She looked at the clock on the wall for the first time since she had arrived there. It was almost five in the morning.

"We see a lot of loss here, but also a lot of hope. Your daughter was so proud of you. She always talked about you and the work you do. She wanted to be a detective too, she told me, just like her mum."

"Eh...did she...she never told..."

"It was nice that one of your colleagues came to see her too. Very late, last night. Your colleagues obviously think a lot of you."

It took a second to understand what the nurse had just said. But when she did, it made Christine sit bolt upright.

"What? Sorry, what did you just say?"

"The other policeman, who came to see Shauna. Last night. In fact, I think he left an envelope for you."

She beetled off to the nurses' station. She returned with the envelope, handing it to Christine.

"Such a big, handsome man. I know police have to be able to handle themselves, but he was very tall. Once he showed me his badge, I knew it was okay to let him visit."

CC was now practically clawing at the envelope, pulling it open, taking the small card out from inside. It was a Metropolitan Police business card, standard issue, with the name and contact details printed on the front. On the back, a handwritten note that simply said...

Just so you know I was here.

"What was the policeman's name again?" The nurse broke into the blizzard of her thoughts.

CC looked up at the nurse's query. She held the card in mid-air as though that was the answer. Her blood ran cold and her guts turned weak as water. The nurse took the card from her, not registering the look of panic that was now growing across CC's face. She read aloud.

"That's right...Inspector Harkness."

30

✧ Surprise ✧

For Enda, it had been relatively easy to acquire the explosives.

All his life he had always been able to sense where to look, which palm to grease, which favour to call in, and which threat to dole out.

Even now he could hear his Da's mantra, ringing in his ears as it had done during his childhood. "Ye can get a howl of most anything so long as ye know where ye shud be lukking."

It was advice he had taken to heart ever since.

The years of service in the everyday world of construction and demolition gave him the right kind of connections to stock up on his favourite fireworks in no time at all. And given also his years of service in the not so everyday world of Irish insurgency, he was an expert at putting them to use.

Danny had been very specific in his instructions. Enda was to produce two actual live devices. The rest were to be nothing more than a good old-fashioned 'flash, bang, wallop'. Enough to cause havoc and panic, but no actual harm.

Standing over them now he felt satisfied with his handiwork. Each separate device clearly marked up in his own code. At a glance he knew which was which, each for a different destination. No-one else would know the difference. No one dispatcher would know where the others were bound for.

He had spent the last few days visiting the places where each of these dark parcels would be deployed. All those car journeys in different, often stolen, vehicles. Pretend breakdowns while wearing a variety of outfits and head coverings.

Then there were the walks around the train stations and, most unnerving of all, Heathrow. Looking without seeming to be looking, trying to spot likely locations, trying to make it easy, trying to make it possible even.

Using a flashy camera with a sizeable lens, he had taken a series of photographs that went from a wide shot to slightly closer then closer then closer still until the last picture was an extreme close up of the very spot he wanted the package placed. Each of his despatch boys would be left in no doubt as to exactly where they were to make their drop.

All was going according to plan. Danny's plan. Thus far.

But it didn't have to stay that way now, did it? Sat here now in his Willesden Green lock up, Enda eyed the little packets of mayhem in front of him. A dryness was developing in his throat with a familiar tightness in his chest. His tongue clicked in his mouth as he reached for the hip flask in his coat pocket hanging on the back of his chair. The familiar smoky slide of the 'Green Spot' down his throat was a welcome distraction from his thoughts. But as he lowered the flask from his lips, he was strangely unsurprised to hear the three sharp knocks on the metal door of his lock up.

Opening the heavy door with one hand on the gun tucked into the back of his waistband, Enda didn't recognise the big man standing there, but he was pretty sure he could guess.

"You're a polite one for a fuckin copper."

"And you are casual for a man who is about to participate in the job of the century..."

Enda revealed the handgun by letting his hand drop loosely at his hip, gun and all.

"You won't be needing that this evening, I'm here under a white flag."

"When did rules ever stop a fucking British copper from doing what he wants?"

"Ah, Enda...a life of bitterness is so unbecoming...I'm James..."

"Harkness. I know who ye are."

By way of acknowledging Enda's perception, Harkness reached slowly into a black holdall he was carrying, his hand emerging with a bottle of Jameson 12 Year Old. The amber glint in the dim room was enough to make Enda involuntarily run his tongue over his bottom lip.

"Can we play nice, Enda? Even for just a little while?"

Enda answered by stepping to one side, allowing Harkness to step into the room.

Two dirty mugs were briefly run under a tap at the back wall of the workspace. Enda set them on his table. Harkness broke the seal on the bottle as he pushed a wooden box in front of it to sit down. The pair didn't clink glasses or even make eye contact as they shotgunned the first measure. Harkness instantly poured more into the mugs. He surveyed the array of devices on the table and the floor around him.

"Quite some night's work...but then you are Enda Crilley. Or should I call you Big Man Boom...?"

Enda didn't react.

"Omagh...Enniskillen. Rumoured to be involved in the bombing of Horse Guards Parade in 1982...you have quite a CV for a man who builds motorways."

"Am I supposed to feel scunnered that you know so much about me?"

"Feel what?"

"Scunnered. Embarrassed. Off kilter. Because, right now, I couldn't give a shite."

Harkness chuckled softly. "Not at all. I just wanted to meet the man, the legend. Wanted to see whose hands were getting ready to do my work for me."

"Your work, is it? I think you'll find I only answer to me. The money will be my reason for being sat here."

"Ah, filthy lucre. The root of all evil, or so they would have us believe. But surely a man like you has more than just a few quid to motivate him."

Enda raised the mug to his lips, giving Harkness a look as he did so.

"If you're so fucking smart, how come you are being followed?"

The attempt to throw Harkness didn't have the desired effect. A smile spread across his wide-boned face.

"I was the one who walked into your lock up unannounced, Enda. Being Anti Terrorist Squad has its advantages."

"But will ye get out alive?" asked Enda, nudging the gun in front of him for emphasis.

"Oh, Enda. I come in peace."

"Brits don't know the meaning of that word."

"Well, I am the exception...I brought you some gifts, besides decent whiskey." Harkness hoisted the black holdall onto the only free corner of the worktable, setting it down carefully. Enda reached out to pull the mouth of the bag wider, peering in.

"Semtex. Now what would I need Czech Semtex for?"

"Very good Enda. I'm impressed." Harkness leant forward, a conspiratorial look on his face.

"You see, our boy Danny may not have shared his plan with me, he may not have shared it all with you, but it doesn't take Stephen Hawking to work out that if you are involved, which I know you are, then something is going to go bang. And if that is the case then I just wanted to lend a helping hand. Make sure you have enough...supplies."

"D'ya think I'm completely stupid? You are fishing. I

don't have a fucking clue why but...you are fishing."

"Not at all. Call it more like insurance. Danny strikes me as a cautious type. He wants or needs a distraction for London tomorrow, and I am more than sure you will be the one to provide it for him. I want to make sure the job gets done...properly, not cautiously. He'll need all the time he can get tomorrow. I want the job to come off. I am just giving you this bag of supplies to make sure that the distraction is as eye-catching as possible."

"And what makes you think I might choose your orders over Danny's? I don't know you from Johnny Fucking Ga-ga."

Harkness stood slowly, his full height blocking out most of the light from the strip neon above his head, casting his shadow across Enda and his handiwork.

"Because you are Big Man Boom, Enda. An artist with a tripwire. Because you aren't done with whatever version of the Irish Troubles that gnaws away at your heart. How many times was your house raided in Belfast? Was it the Paras or the SAS who shot your brother coming out of that betting shop on the Falls?"

Enda was up out of his seat, faster than Harkness would have believed a man his size could move. A smash reverberated as the mug of half drunk Jameson's shattered against the far wall.

"You don't fucking talk about my brother, you English bastard...every last one of you has blood on their hands, your own people and mine."

"Which is exactly why you will take that bag and make every last one of these go off with a proper bang. Give London what you always felt it deserved, Enda. Do it for me, do it for the success of the job or do it for your brother. Whatever your reason, just fucking do it. I want this city distracted. I want this job to play out just like Danny's imagined it...and then some."

Harkness turned on his heel, walking towards the door.

"Enda, do you know who Robert E. Lee was? He once said that you should always try to mystify, mislead and surprise the enemy, if at all possible. You have your chance to do that tomorrow."

Enda mumbled something in return. Harkness was now stood in the doorway, not quite catching it.

"Something to tell me, Big Man?"

"Ay...it wasn't General Lee said that...it was Stonewall Jackson. Now fuck off, you cocky bastard."

Christine was reeling. She had often heard the expression but never expected to ever feel it herself.

But there was no doubt. Christine really was reeling. Driving like a woman possessed, she was desperate to get to Collinson, to Freethy and quiz them about this Harkness bastard and to tell them what had happened and where she had been.

What she didn't realise was that she was actually in shock. She had been from the moment Shauna had actually died, a state that was only deepened by the note from Harkness, and was now being hammered home by her blind rage and panic.

She reached for her mobile for the third time, trying to ring Freethy. Voicemail again. She needed to share, needed to tell someone. Needed to talk it out.

She punched the 'on button' of her car stereo. Perhaps music might help. Some human babble, some background mindless noise might steady her.

The first station to appear was a news talk one, some idiot blathering on about what the government was or wasn't doing for the taxpayer. She hit "seek", watching the frequency change at a rate of knots until it settled on what sounded like a seventies rock song. That would do, but almost immediately as the station locked on the DJ's voice kicked in.

"Great tune there, a little blast from all our pasts. *Touch of Grey* by the Grateful Dead."

Christine felt liked she'd been slapped. Dead...grateful? Fucking grateful? Dead? Fucking Dead? Dead...my Shauna is dead.

And that is when it truly hit her. Crashed through the shock, crashed into her consciousness and really hit home.

And she could feel the wind being knocked out of her, the bile rising in her stomach. She didn't know it but she was letting the car coast. Taking her foot off the accelerator, thankfully somehow remembering to knock the car into neutral, she let it drift until it came to a halt of its own accord. She opened the driver door and leant out, vomiting onto the road, her chest and stomach heaving, salt tears wringing from her eyes.

And then she sat upright. Just sat there. And then one emotion battled to the fore, began to rise up in her as surely as the bile and cups of tea just had.

Rage. Pure white, hot rage.

Rage for Harkness.

Harkness, who had inserted himself into one of the most private moments of her life. He had come between her and Shauna's passing. He had put himself into a memory that she should have been able to look back on as some sort of relief, a release from the suffering her little one had endured. And now, here was this fucker Harkness making Christine think that her child's death was not just her own experience but was maybe hastened on someone else's terms. Played out according to their agenda, not God's or love's or nature's.

"You cunt."

She actually said it out loud.

"YOU FUCKING CUNT."

Screaming it now. Starting the car again.

But before she started to pull away, her mobile phone

was ringing. She snatched it up, expecting to see Freethy's name, her friend returning her many calls. But the screen showed a number she didn't recognise. She hesitated, until the earliness of the hour made her realise that this might be no ordinary call. Clearing her throat, she hit the receive button on the handset.

"Hello, is this Chance?"

The voice wasn't one she recognised, but what it said made her sit bolt upright.

"Detective Chance, can I talk to you about a very bad man. His name is Harkness."

31

✧ Pick of the Pops ✧

It was obscenely early in the morning. The birds had no right to be so fucking cheerful. His missus had snored so loudly last night that even the dog had left the bedroom. But Collinson was still walking into his office at precisely the time he wanted to. He was a stickler for never being late to work. Ever since he had joined as a cadet, aged 16, and now at 55-years-old was still clocking in before most of his team had woken up.

Frankly, Collinson would be glad when today was over. He wanted the pile of around 22 million pounds gone...and gone today. All that money gathered in a short, six week span had been stored in his evidence room, all under plain packaging after the counting team had come in and checked it, wrapping it in bundles of 50 grand each. More money than he had ever seen in his life.

The sheer amount made him feel dizzy and nervous. Ever since Christine Chance and her mate Freethy had started whining about the intelligence which had led to its gathering, Collinson had had a dull ache at the back of his old copper's brain.

He sighed to himself, peering out of his glassed-in office as the first few bodies appeared in the squad room.

He looked over one job sheet in front of him, the fingers of his left hand playing along the roughened edge of his leather brief holder. A habit he had developed when he first received his police badge. The once black leather of the holder now looked almost silver, his fingers had passed over the black surface so many times, burnishing it with years of nervous energy. That brief had seen almost forty years of service. Now he was so close to the end of it all.

He hoped his fellow police would recall him as a "copper's copper". He loved the job, but there was no doubt it was changing. Everything was changing. One second you were a fresh faced cadet. The next you were old, labelled a dinosaur and being investigated for 'improprieties', even though in the intervening blink of your eye you had given your entire life to the job.

Time.

Collinson looked at his watch. 5.05am. He wanted that load of money on the road before six. He would feel better then. He would feel relieved once he had watched the three junior detective constables, Young, Sharp and Imbeki, drive that money out the gate. He could see them now, preparing to load up the white unmarked Luton van they had hired for the job.

It was a joke really. Shifting all that money with no protocol in place to handle such an event, no way to use an armoured cash van or a secure alternative. Cutbacks, rare event, the usual blah blah blah explanations. Just restrict the movement order to those who need to know and use unmarked...it'll all be fine.

The bigwigs...they didn't give a shit, beyond what box they could tick and how many corners they could cut to make their budget look tight. And that included doing everything they could to remove the experienced, and therefore more expensive, old boys off the books. By hook or by making them all feel like crooks.

Well, if you were going to be made to feel like a wrong 'un...

Collinson swept his fingers over his brief once more.

A copper's cop.

And yet as soon as he watched those boys pull out the gate he would make a call the likes of which he never thought he would make. He even had a throwaway mobile to make it on. Time had caught up with another old school Old Bill.

Time. It marched on, and sometimes it took you places you never saw yourself going.

DJ Johnny Dearie had never even received so much as a speeding ticket in his whole life. That was at the very heart of his appeal. He was the whiter-than-white housewives' choice.

It was his boundless optimism and enthusiasm that went a long way towards making him the most popular radio host in Great Britain. His breakfast drive time show was a ratings juggernaut. Nine million people chose to tune their dial to his station every morning between 5am - 9am. He filled the airwaves with genial music, positive musings on everything good about the world and had a stubborn resistance to anything that might be seen as even slightly controversial.

This, of course, won Dearie as many trolling haters as it did doting fans. Once, on *Facebook*, a page had been set up calling for the extradition of Johnny Dreary (sic), for crimes against entertainment. It went viral and within 24 hours it had over 30,000 members and twice as many 'likes'.

Not that Dearie could give a toss. He knew exactly why his audience liked him. He knew exactly what it was he liked about himself and his show and he never swerved from that course. After all, he had one and a half million reasons a year to stay true to that formula and every single one of them had the Queen's head on it.

He had always known that he wanted to be a disc jockey. To be the man who would fill the airwaves with the right song at exactly the right time, bringing little slices of musical joy to a commute or a moment of isolation for even just one listener. That's what drove DJ Johnny Dearie on.

And that is what he had done, Starting at hospital radio, Then moving to local, local to network, late night to lunchtime and finally the Holy Grail: the breakfast show.

He was a radio genius. He knew what people wanted to hear and when they wanted to hear it. It was why they kept listening. It was like he was some kind of radio Pied Piper. This laced with his sunny attitude and willingness to avoid becoming cynical had made him a star.

Which made this morning, this day, even more ironic.

Not that Dearie would ever know. Nor would anyone ever know.

"Ahhh, good morning Great Britain, another Faaaabulous day on our planet earth."

An imaginary crowd cheered for him at the touch of a sound effects button.

"What time is it, DJ Johnny?" his Greek chorus of sidekicks all yelled in unison.

"Glad you asked, gang. It's that time, the time where we cheer up Chingford, smile down on Solihull, tickle Tewkesbury and give Glasgow a giggle..."

More sound effects. A giggling little boy with a bicycle bulbhorn on the end.

"It's time for our regular sunny song, the music that makes your commute that little bit easier. And today, just like every Thursday, it's my all time fave..."

"*MR BLUE SKY*!!!"

"That's right, gang...if this song doesn't make you smile, you need to see a Doctor!!! Who doesn't like to hear The Electric Light Orchestra singing about *Mr Blue Sky*?"

Johnny Dearie started the track.

The drums. The throbbing bass line. The opening strains of *Mr Blue Sky* filled the ears of every single one of Danny's team.

Today, as the song poured out of the little portable transistor radios he'd handed out, Danny Felix and his team used it as their joint cue to swing into choreographed action...

At approximately 5.50am it was their synchronized signal to rip London's head off and shit down its neck.

"The sun is shining in the sky..."

And they began their dark work...

32

✧ Boom Bang A Bang ✧

As soon as he heard Jeff Lynne's opening lyrics Big Enda knew it was game on. Party time. All of his planning and work was about to be put to the test.

Enda both loved and hated this bit. He hated the thought that he might have missed a detail, missed a crucial connection or misjudged a position. But once the chain of events kicked in, he was always...well, Enda didn't have the words to express it other than a rush of blood to his head and other parts that left him feeling a little dizzy and more than a little thirsty. If he had the words they would have been ones like "elated"," euphoric", "orgasmic" and perhaps even "deific".

In the end, it all came down to what Big Enda knew best. Danny had told him: "Play to your strengths, Big Man Boom. This is your moment in the sun...so make it work, make it count...play to your strengths and then play them fucking sure."

So he did. All of Enda's devices were packaged up in very traditional ways. Fairly dated technology that still worked. Old school knowledge that still packed a punch. A hell of a punch, and for London, today, it needed to be a straight knockout. And the impact would be so much heftier with the help of the extra Semtex that Harkness had given him. Now he could give the Brits the kicking he had always dreamed of delivering. Danny Felix may have wanted to cause a modicum of real damage and then use misdirection and natural panic to do the rest. But there was room for doubt, happenstance and failure in that plan.

And after Harkness had intervened with his wishes, Enda had thought about it all. Why not be sure? And why not be brutal while you are at it? Two birds, one big fucking stone.

And so as Enda listened to ELO asking why *Mr Blue Sky* had to hide away for so long, he was busy pushing a series of buttons on some low frequency transmitters arranged in a very particular order in front of him.

As the rush engulfed him, he could only begin to imagine the chaos those little commands were unleashing, but he would savour every second as his revenge rocked London.

Enda had done what was asked of him...and then some.

Enda's explosions tore into London in a brutally choreographed manner.

The first took the M1 and M25 motorways out of the equation. A 2010 Mercedes family estate that appeared broken down had been parked up on the southbound side of the M1 at 4.45am, the hazard lights left blinking. A shop dummy dressed in a waterproof jacket and jeans had been left in a seated position with its back to the safety fence about 20 feet behind the car itself. The car sat right on the hard shoulder just at the start of the bridge that took the M1 over the M25. When the bomb loaded into the back seat received the radio-signalled green light, the blast was hot, loud and almighty.

Luck can play its part in absolutely anything, and depending upon your point of view, luck, of a kind, showed up here. As the blast radiated heat, energy and debris up, out and away from its core, an articulated lorry had just come alongside the site. One of the Mercedes' alloy wheels was ejected sideways at about 100 feet per second, punching into the base of the drivers cab, just where the wheel arch and the chassis of the truck meet, causing its own wheels to skew and lock. Covered in glass and debris, the driver of the 40-footer suddenly realised his huge transport was jack-knifing. The giant vehicle was folding in on itself, the smell of burning rubber, squealing of air brakes filling the void around him.

The massive juggernaut took out two more alongside it. Firstly a car containing three Eastern European lads on their way to a day's labouring in London. Their tiny, relatively unprotected 1990 Skoda got swiped to the side as if it were made of nothing more than paper. It eventually flipped onto its roof in a shower of sparks, glass and screams as it slid for at least another 50 yards, actually going under the fuselage of another vehicle. This one was the second casualty of the jack knife.

The second one was way more serious; it was a fuel tanker. Freshly loaded and barrelling on its way to refill a north London garage. The jack-knifing 40-footer swung out in front of it. The tanker driver watched like he was in some kind of weird slow motion dream. He felt his calves cramping as he stomped on the brake pedal with all his might. All to no avail. The back end of the 40-footer smashed into the very front of his cab. Their joint momentum created what was essentially a five ton out of control bomb. Both vehicles careened down the carriageway, at an angle that brought them to and then through the safety barrier. The sound of metal squealing and shearing, giving way, bombarded the 40-footer's driver. Flinging his door open he tried to avoid being pulled over the edge with his truck and the tanker. He made a vain attempt to leap to safety only to be swatted over the edge by his own vehicle, as it pitched over the freshly broken barrier. The only consolation was that he didn't have time to feel anything as his truck landed on him just as he hit the M25 below.

And less than half a second later the fuel tanker hit too. The resulting blast could be heard up to 12 miles away. Not that it mattered, for all over London the sounds of exploding fireballs were drowning out everything.

There were other M25 explosions. The worst of which happened on the eastern side of the circular roadway, where it met the M20. The car bomb took out a minibus full of French students on an exchange programme. Their van disintegrated in the hot slam of the blast, casting metal and bodies into the air like burning feathers in a whirlwind. A total of 17 cars cannoned into each other as a result. Passengers were thrown about like rag dolls. Twisted metal and debris scattered across the carriageway. Everywhere was filled with the funk of gunpowder and charring rubber. The air was sucked away from the immediate surroundings of each blast as oxygen fed the flames. The resulting plume reached 30 feet in the air.

The M4 was blocked off in a similar fashion. Except here the bomb was not in a car, but a metal trunk left just over the verge of the road. As it went off, roads and routes into the capital city were being shut down faster than you could say "boom".

The metal trunk packed an impressive thump augmented as it was with Harkness' extra ordnance. The explosive was packed around a firing pin and normally used to excavate pathways for new roads through hills and mountainsides. It created a firestorm that melted most of the facing road surface in, literally, a bright instant.

The human toll was less here. A brief respite in traffic was caused by an accident just two miles further down the motorway and doubtless saved lives. As it was, only one car felt the full smack of the explosive. A pensioner in a little Nissan Micra, on her way to London for an art exhibit. She had been gently singing along to a song she remembered from the 1970s on her radio, a record her son had liked if she recalled correctly, about the sunshine. It was a nice song. Then nothing but a hot white blaze in front of her car and she knew nothing else.

The first thought that crossed the businessman's mind when he first saw the mangled fingers flying through the air in front of him was, "Oh, my God, some poor devil's hand." It was only afterwards, much later when he came round that he was informed that they had been his fingers. He was the poor devil in question.

He had been reaching up into the luggage rack for his bag as he travelled on his 05.35 train into London's Waterloo. At precisely 06.01 the bomb packaged tightly in a rucksack next to his briefcase went off causing the train carriage to lurch to one side, throwing him back onto the seats and the aforementioned fingers to break free from their knuckles and into the smoked-filled air. His was double bad luck really, as this was one of the devices Danny wanted to be nothing more than a flash bang rather than an actual bomb.

At just about the same time a coach arriving into London's Victoria Bus Station was lifted four feet into the air by what should have been another dummy package. A bomb in a suitcase jammed in amongst the luggage was the cause. The crack reverberated around the coach station and up into the adjacent train station, like some kind of cri-de-couer telling the early commuters to get the hell out.

Panic soon began to set in among the early morning rush hour crowds. Word was starting to spread, across email, radio, TV, social networks and frantic phone calls from loved ones. London was under attack, London was under siege. London was the one place on earth that no one wanted to be this deadly morning.

Similar scenes played out in other stations across London. Most notably in Cannon Street Station and Clapham Junction, where the devices that brought fire and death were both hidden among deliveries to newsagents on their respective concourses. Here the victims and casualties were showered with burning paper and debris.

And as if all this wasn't enough chaos and carnage, Enda had reserved his best until last. The knockout punch. At 06.08.

Heathrow Airport. The short-term car park was lit up like a firework display.

A brand new Ducato van was parked on the top level of the Terminal One structure, the rear of which was packed with enough roofing tar and petrol to blow away a whole building. Which is exactly what it did. Firing the surrounding parked cars out onto the adjacent road as though a giant had decided to upend a box of toys. The worst of this was a rental car coach carrying 14 passengers...in the wrong place at the wrong time. A Range Rover Sport landed on their transport just as it felt the secondary blast wave from the explosion rumbling out of the parking garage.

Destruction.

Death.

Mutilation.

Shock and shockwaves.

And this had been done within a space of exactly ten minutes to one of the world's most important cities.

Emergency services were dashing into action across the entire length and breadth of London, immediately stretched and swept up into a panic that had not been experienced since the Tube and bus bombings of July 2005.

And now the city would go into spasm. No-one would be let in...or out. It would contract in on itself in fear and desperation. The police would be pulled in all directions. Suspicious packages would be identified on practically every street corner by frightened members of the public. The city's heart would be crippled.

And that is exactly what Danny Felix had asked Big Man Boom to do. It had been his final, whispered words to him when he first told him what his plan was to be. "Bring this city to a shit-scared standstill, Enda. You know how to. You are Big Man Boom."

And, as Big Enda took the cap off the first of his one litre bottles of super strength cider after locking himself into a storage room at his construction company workplace, he retuned his little transistor radio away from the fucking droning shite music played by that wanke Johnny Dearie and onto the news radio station he liked best, *BBC Radio 5 live.*

A Standstill.

What a thing of beauty. London streets ground to a halt. A smattering of traffic where there were usually hordes. A concerto of emergency sirens were echoing off the concrete canyons of the financial district and beyond.

What a shame that he couldn't just go and walk for a while to enjoy the pause that he had created. What a crying shame that he couldn't take pleasure in his own vengeful masterpiece. But never mind, he hoped that Danny Felix would make the most of it.

And at that Enda took a big, long drink and sat on the concrete floor with his back to the wall. And soon the tears of joy came, running down his face. Just like the tears of pain his planning and expertise had caused his myriad victims in that ten minute spell of destructive misdirection.

33

✧ Stick 'em Up ✧

Imbeki had been prattling on for at least five minutes now. The only reason that Collinson had put three of them on this job was because there were so many packages to be lugged around. Loads of them...and if the office gossip was to be believed every single one of them was full of dirty, cold cash.

"Boi, this is not what I got into the fucking Old Bill for, playing at being a glorified removal man."

Grant Young just kept driving the Ford Mondeo estate through the sparse, early morning traffic in west London.

Young wished that Imbeki would shut the fuck up. He didn't much like his fellow recent recruit. He was chippy about almost everything and didn't mind telling you about it either. To drown him out Young reached for the radio, flicking it on just as The Electric light Orchestra's *Mr Blue Sky* was starting. Just as Young was thinking he liked that song, it made him smile, the car was flooded with the sound of some god awful hip-hop crap.

"Sorry mate, had to change it. I can't stand that wanker Johnny Dearie on the radio."

"Bloody hell! You're even chippy about the radio."

Young glanced in his rearview mirror to make sure that their colleague Graham Sharp was still behind them, driving the Luton van with its unbelievable load in the back.

"What would you do with all that dosh?"

Imbeki sat forward in the passenger seat, twisting to look at Young.

"It IS cash! A shitload!"

"Yes, mate. That, I believe, is the official job term. M'lud, we entered the premises and found what can only be described a suspicious shitload of cash. The prosecution rests."

Imbeki let out a soft whistle, followed by a sucking of the air in through his teeth.

"What now, Chippy?"

"Boi, who says crime don't pay?"

"I've been daydreaming about what I'd do with even one of the millions I helped pack into the van. I fancy a trip round the world but would do it in style, like, take in the sights, go to some of the big events. Real Madrid against Barcelona at the Bernabeu. Or that mad horse race they have in Italy, round the courtyard of that ancient building. What's it called? The Palio? In Siena?"

"The one James Bond fucked up in that movie?"

"Yeah, that's it..."

"All I would want, blood, is a suite at the Dorchester, champagne and that booty off of the dancing show...the judge...Darcy thingummy...lock the fucking doors...sweet as..."

"She'd only end up giving you no points."

The car filled with laughter.

Meanwhile in the Luton van, Sharpy was chuckling, congratulating himself for his speed at picking up the van keys and suggesting that Imbeki hop in with Young. He couldn't bear the thought of that whinger going on and on in the van with him. He could see them now, in the car in front. It looked like Young was mainly silent while Imbeki's head was bobbing and weaving, doubtless bitching about this, that and the fucking other. He had only been in the office barely a month and already everyone had him down as a tricky dickhead. It wouldn't surprise Sharpy if he thought that the fact that the Luton van was white was some kind of coded racial slur.

Sharp turned the radio up, enjoying Johnny Dearie's music choice this morning, just like he always did. He could-n't remember what today's smiley song was, until he heard the opening notes of *Mr Blue Sky*...not bad, not bad at all...

Sharp began to sing along at the top of his voice

And if they all hadn't been so intent on other things, one of the three of them might have noticed that since leaving the office, they had been accompanied by a variety of cyclists. Nothing unusual in seeing commuters on their bicycles in London, but if they had looked closely they would have noticed a pattern to how the bikes were keeping pace with the van.

Like some kind of mad peloton, a mix of about five cyclists were swapping the lead as they either rode just behind, between in front of the two vehicles making their way from Barnes to Scotland Yard.

And in case they were taking notice the riders would occasionally break away, into a side street, change a top or bag or helmet. They kept their sunglasses on though, pulling their cycling bandanas up round their noses, as if they were in place to filter out the car fumes and not just obscure their faces.

The riders jockeyed for position in the light traffic next to the Mondeo and the Luton van, measuring their progress across the city, swapping, rotating, tracking.

Following.

Ciaran and Danny had been parked up since five am. The lumbering dumper truck had proved to be surprisingly comfortable, the big sprung seats bouncing the pair of them as they meandered their way down towards the Thames, over Vauxhall Bridge and along to Battersea.

Once in situ, the first order of the day was to neutralise the one and only closed circuit camera that overlooked where they wanted to execute the hit. Watching Ciaran shimmy up the balcony to where the camera was fixed, Danny thought of Cheetah from the old black-and-white Tarzan movies, with Johnny Weismuller yodeling the Tarzan call at the top of his lungs while the mischievous monkey was up to no good. Probably best not to share that thought with his ginger-haired mate.

Once Ciaran had spray-painted the glass fascia of the hanging security camera, a feat that took no less than a minute and a half start to finish, the pair settled into their respective seats, waiting for the big show.

This was the part that Danny hated the most. A pause just before the game began. The tick of the clock, the space between him and the job, a gap filled with unknown circum-stance, happenstance and endless permutations of what might or might not go right. Once he had started, he always itched to begin, to start. It didn't matter to him if he was about to rob a cash replenishment van or creep a flat to retrieve a mobile phone clip. As soon as the job was moving he wanted, no, needed, to keep moving it along.

He also realised that this type of wait, one that came immediately in the teeth of a job, was the kind of pause that made him sharpen up. It put him in a heightened state of awareness. He could feel the root of every single hair on his body. He could detect the flutter of birds' wings from a hundred feet. He could sense subtle atmospheric changes. For instance, right now he knew that Ciaran was gagging for a cigarette but he wouldn't want to risk anything drawing attention to them. Not even the flare of a match-head struck or a plume of sweet smoke carried on the wind to one of the residential balconies directly to their right.

Their dumper truck was parked on a small service ramp that lead directly from Battersea Church Road down to the river, the one that he had scoped out with Harkness just days earlier. All was as before when he and Harkness had pulled in from the road. He had come back a few times, and he had sat watching the road, the apartments, the river houseboats. He particularly liked the quiet, almost anonymous feel, to this little slice of London. The longer he stayed the more he knew that he could pull the job here, and maybe, just maybe get away with it too. Of course a lot of that would be down to how well Belfast Enda fulfilled his part of the process.

Danny was sat with an earphone bud stuck in one of his ears, listening to the Johnny Dearie show, waiting to hear the signal that they had all agreed was the one to start the festivities. And when it came, Danny felt the rush of heat into his face as he looked sideways at Ciaran.

"*Mr Blue Sky*," is all Danny said.

"Well, I hope the sun shines on the not so fucking righteous today, Danny." A smile as wide as the River Thames split Ciaran's face. He clapped his hands together gently and then started to rub them together.

Danny retuned his transistor radio to *5 Live*, just as he knew Enda would, and started to listen for word of their little symphony of chaos. Not suspecting it would be more chaotic than asked for.

At just about the time that Sharpy had yelled his last ear-splitting note as he sang along with the radio, his own rover walkie-talkie began to go mad with emergency calls. Sharpy turned his van radio down and his rover up; almost rear-ending the Mondeo carrying Imbeki and Young because of a sharp stop. They had pulled to a halt at the lights beside Smugglers Way in Wandsworth. At that his mobile went. He answered to hear Imbeki's voice crackle from the handset at him.

"You hearing this, Sharpy?"

"Yep, sounds like something's kicking off."

"Something? A lot of things, mate...Young reckons we should check in."

Sharp thought about this for a second. Check in and do what? They were on a specific duty, one that the guv'nor had been very clear about in his briefing, right down to specifying what route they should take to Scotland Yard. He had looked like he'd meant business when he talked to them this morning, and Sharp didn't fancy crossing swords with his new guv so early in his stay at Barnes.

His move to the unit had been one of convenience given that he had fallen out so dramatically with his last guv'nor just weeks before the transfer. He had visions of spending a life investigating domestics when the new orders had come in, and Sharp just wanted his grace period to go as smooth as possible. And anyway, if the rumours about their cargo were true, he wanted to deliver it as safely and as quickly as possible and return to base, no dramas, no worries, no possibilities of a fuck-up.

"Check in and do fucking what exactly?" snapped Sharp. The rover sitting on the seat next to him was going proper nuts now. Dispatch traffic was going back and forth at lightning pace. What the fuck was going on out there?

Holding the phone away from his lips, he could hear Imbeki share his opinion with Young. Some kind of reply, a little muffled to-and-fro.

"Listen, Sharpy. This sounds like it is escalating, bruv. Have you actually got your rover turned up?"

"If something is kicking off, all the more reason for us to get this drop finished and jump back onto the radio when we are proper done and dusted. That way we can help then, whatever mess is developing."

He could hear sirens across the city, faintly but definitely there, and he could feel a dull ache starting in the pit of his stomach. He didn't like this.

"Good enough. Lights changing. Let's get to the Yard,

then see what's occurring."

Imbeki cut the line dead, and Sharp tossed the phone next to his rover on the seat beside him. But he now couldn't ignore the increasingly urgent chatter that was emanating from the handheld radio. What the fucking hell was going on? It sounded like war had broken out or something.

Just as he was about to pull away, he had to slam his brakes on again for a second time, blowing his horn hard and heavy at the cause of the latest disruption to what should have been a straightforward drop and return job.

"Fucking cyclists!"

It sounded to Danny's ears that Big Man Boom Enda had done his damnedest. The radio was flooded with breaking news, travel alerts and instructions for all commuters to stay home and not try and enter London. It was exactly as they had envisaged, or rather as Danny had hoped.

But his first feelings of satisfaction started to darken as more reports emerged. How many casualties? How many explosions? He'd insisted on only two real ones.

The way Danny saw it, if you were going to steal from the Old Bill then you had to keep them occupied. Plus, if you were feeling like making doubly sure, shut the city down to keep the streets relatively clear. Danny had never forgotten how quiet the city had been in the immediate aftermath of the July bombings in 2005. London had emptied like a chamber pot down a sewer. The rush to put distance between the city workers and the terrorist threat was instant and dramatic. And here was just such a panic again. There wouldn't be a cop for at least a 20-mile radius who wouldn't be either shitting himself at every empty paper bag discarded on a street corner or trying to marshal panicking punters away from the centre of the city. By his estimation, Danny reckoned he had at least a good 30 to 40 minutes of wriggle room once the actual hit had gone down...now if only the wriggling could fucking start. He shook his head slowly, bringing his focus back to the here and now. Rolling news always got the details wrong at the start of a major incident. Concentrate on the job.

Young and Imbeki could feel an urgent panic rising between them. They had been debating putting a call back into their Barnes HQ. They were starting to imagine the trouble they might be in professionally if they stuck to their course and ignored what appeared to be the outbreak of a major terrorist incident in the city around them.

Just at that, Imbeki's mobile chirped into life, the screen telling him it was Sharp calling.

"Just had the guv'nor on the line. He says we make the drop and await our next move once we are clear of the load."

"What the fuck is going on out there?"

"He says we aren't heading directly for any of it at this point, but we have to listen up to the rovers. If that changes then he will call us or if we get caught up in anything we are to call him."

"Yeah but, seriously, what the fuck..."

Sharp cut him off. "Listen Imbeki, Old Man Collinson was very fucking clear. Keep our wits about us. We are less than 15 minutes from the Yard. Once there, we can start into it, whatever it is. And watch out for those frigging cyclists, they seem to be the only ones who don't know what's going on. I've nearly killed two of them this morning already."

Imbeki saw Sharp was right. They were about two buses away from a set of lights just before a dog-leg bend on the road ahead them just where Vicarage Walk joins and turns into Battersea Bridge Road. As the light changed, a cyclist ahead of them, one of those crazy, courier types put his body and his bike between the two buses, then up the side of the lead bus. He cleared the front of it as the light changed again from green to amber, like a man possessed. Imbeki didn't care what anyone thought or said, if you were mad enough to cycle in central London you deserved every near death experience you got...which, judging by the guy ahead of them, added up to a lot.

"Okay, we'll stay the course. Bell us if the guv'nor comes back."

The line went dead, and Young looked sideways at his companion.

"We have to make like Curtis Mayfield," offered Imbeki by way of reply.

"What?"

"Guv says, "Keep on keepin' on"."

Young put the car in gear and followed behind the bus. It made it through the lights but they didn't. They could have done, but it would have meant leaving Sharpy and the Luton van behind.

He glanced into his mirror and had a lightning, reflexive thought that he immediately forgot as soon as he had it: no cyclist there now.

To be honest, Danny's inspiration had come from the words of Harkness. An uncomfortable thought, but still the truth. He had told Danny that he would be his "chaos".

Chaos.

Despite all his bullshit philosophical warbling, Danny wondered if Harkness knew where the word had come from; the Greek's used it to describe a gaping void, or more precisely the gaping void before the creation of the universe. What Danny suspected was a better word for Harkness was crisis, which the Greek's used firstly to describe the turning point in a medical condition or disease.

Danny had needed to create a turning point, one that would turn this situation in his favour, or at least the circumstance and context within which he could steal this money. And as for Harkness, disease was a fitting word to describe him in Danny's mind.

Radio 5 Live was now feverishly spewing out the rolling news' version of the chain of unfolding events. They were simultaneously offering conjecture with the odd scrap of fact and dressing them up as both.

In his ear, Danny was hearing tales of fireballs over the M25, commuters caught in panicked crushes and emergency services struggling to keep up. There were flying flaming cars at Heathrow and a train derailing just as it reached its destination of Waterloo.

So far, Danny had tried to sequester any thoughts of the human casualties that would result from his plan, but even he could see now the collateral damage was unavoidable. But as he listened to the radio he became sure that there had been way more live devices than he had ordered.

"Big Man Boom..."

Ciaran looked at him.

"Wha?"

"How crazy is your man, Enda?"

"When you say crazy, what do you mean? He has spent a life hating the Brits and thinking up ways to blow them the fuck up..."

"I think he may have taken up his role this morning with more gusto than I required."

"Huh? I thought we were only going to mean business with one or two. The rest were for show and panic."

Danny handed the radio earpiece to his wing man.

After a moments intent listening, Ciaran turned, wide eyed, his face paling.

"Jesus, Mary and Joseph. What has that fucker done?

Danny wanted to disappear. Withdraw from this fame

obsessed, unjust and unbalanced, so-called society. And one big job, one like this, could make that happen for him. A sum of money that could magic him away to somewhere warm and balmy, where Amazon delivered movies by mail and the drinks were funky colours and always came with little umbrellas. That would do for Danny. And all he had to do to get there was to pull this job and put Harkness back in his place. Not such a small picture to paint, but one worth attempting.

His biggest job ever. His masterpiece. And if you are going to paint on a canvas as huge and dramatic as London, then he realised his primary colour would have to be red. But not anywhere near as much as seemed to be splashed all over the streets this morning. He felt sick to his stomach.

And at that thought, in a burst of yellow hi-vis jacket and speed that would have been more appropriate from a moped rather than a pushbike, a courier cyclist came round the bend of the dog leg corner. He raised his arm above his head, pumping it in the air once, twice, three times and then he was gone as quickly as he appeared.

"Three waves. The target is three vehicles behind whatever comes round that corner next."

No time to think about anything else. They were about to move forward, the job was on.

Ciaran was pulling his balaclava down over his face. Danny tightened the bandana he was wearing around his nose, mouth and chin. He reached down between his feet in the cab of the truck and grabbed a cowboy hat, screwing it firmly onto his head. Lastly he double-checked his seat belt was securely fastened. Were the pair of sawn-off shotguns safely wedged into the adapted carpenter's tool belt cinched around his waist? The answers to both were "yes". A bus was coming into view, followed by a second. Ciaran and Danny didn't realise it, but they were both holding their breath.

✧✧

Harkness was being a good boy. He was doing what he was told. He stood in his apartment, naked and newly awake, overlooking what was once Highbury Stadium. But he wasn't ruminating on the footballing glory of Arsenal Football Club. Harkness was listening intently. He had put his television on as soon as he had the call on his mobile, and now he was taking in the stream of consciousness that 24-hour news traded as reportage. He always marvelled at how minutiae and speculation was presented as crucial fact. The ever-hungry monster of airtime to fill and not a lot of truth to fill it made for a strange mistress within an industry that once prided itself on reporting the truth at all costs. To his mind, journalism was now nothing more than entertainment. A sport just as much as the one that used to be played out on the grass below. Who can get the next nugget of possible fact first? Which channel can find an eyewitness that no-one else has? Eyewitless was more like it most of the time though.

And so it was now. A delivery driver who had narrowly avoided a fireball on the M4 was repeatedly answering the staccato questions of the journo with a mantra that comprised of nothing more than "I thought I would die" and "It was like the *Die Hard* films with that Burt Willis bloke". The line of investigation was quickly becoming circular but that didn't deter the reporter or her bosses from their persistence.

What was most definitely true though was that Big Man Boom had put his gifts to devastating use. Action? Christ, there was plenty of action.

Harkness turned to face the television. The graphic scrolling at the foot of the screen carried the all important bullet point headlines. Multiple explosions across London. At least 33 dead and hundreds injured. The city in lockdown, and the mobile phone signal was suspended across the central parts of the city. Emergency services were at full stretch. The public were advised not to travel into or around London. Other cities of the UK and indeed Europe had been placed on high alert. It was a suspected major terrorist event.

The ticker then started to repeat itself and Harkness tuned it out.

"Terrorist event."

Misdirection more like. Sleight of hand.

Harkness started to laugh. A chuckle at first, now growing to a giggle, ending in a gale of his own laughter. He had to set his coffee cup down for fear of spilling it, or burning his own bollocks if he wasn't careful.

He had challenged Danny Felix to write his own moment in London history. If he could pull off the robbery he would be writing his name big among the capital's criminal elite. But with his intervention this job wouldn't write Danny's name in the history books, more like it would tear it up and piss on it. All to nick a few quid.

What a legend. What a fucking legend.

Harkness laughed again. Gently this time as he approached the low set bed in the middle of the room. Watching the form under the duvet stir at the sound of his amusement, a whisper of red hair on the pillow, the slender calf protruding from one corner.

Harkness grasped the ankle, firmly at first, but then more tenderly, running his hand slowly up under the covers, finding what he was looking for, achieving the response he wanted.

"Wakey, wakey love. It's another beautiful day in the big city. We ought to start it as we mean to go on..."

It's fucking agony when you practically bite your own tongue in two.

Charles Imbeki regrettably knew this to be a fact, because that is exactly what he did when the huge dumper truck struck the front side of the Mondeo.

The force of the jolt caused Imbeki to be flung forward, his seatbelt arresting his progress like hitting a brick wall, his tongue involuntarily pushing between his teeth as the wind was knocked out of him, only for his jaw to be wrenched firmly shut as his body slammed back into the seat. An airbag added insult and further injury to an already nasty turn of events. It was at this point that his tongue gave way to the force, his blood exploding in his mouth with a coppery taste just as his nerve ends did their duty and communicated the pain signals to his brain at lightning speed.

Young didn't fare much better, but the fact that his seatbelt was more snug across his solar plexus meant it winded him. His fight to inhale sent his tongue backward not forward. But needless to say he didn't come away unscathed. The impact whipping the steering wheel, which he had been responsibly holding in the quarter to three position, dislocated his left thumb and broke his right index finger. The next gift was the shower of windscreen shatter that found his face before his airbag could go off. Like a bout of sandpaper to his eyes, he caught multiple frag-ments in both, the world turning an excruciating watery red as the car settled back onto its suspension after the initial full frontal smack. Finally, the popping noise that he had heard go off in his head wasn't actually the airbag but the music of his own body, as his right shoulder tore free from its ligaments, dislocating like a lid being flicked off a tube of Pringles. The real joy coming as his body crashed back into his driving seat, pressing the shoulder into the space where it should have been but couldn't actually fit into anymore. A red-hot knife of pain.

They hadn't seen the truck until it was on them. A big, metal object, stopping them in their tracks as efficiently as one might stop a fly from hitting one's face.

Ciaran had judged his take-off perfectly. As soon as the cyclist had rode past them, he held the big truck on the bite of its clutch. He could feel the power of the big fuck off vehicle beneath his touch like a wild horse trying to break free. All he had to do was release that clutch at precisely the right moment. Then they would be up over the brow of the little slipway that lead down to the Thames. Up over into the narrow road, stopping anyone and anything that might be there...an unmarked police convoy perhaps.

Ciaran screamed as they took off.

"JESUSMOTHERFUCKINGHOLYSHITFUCK!"

He had executed the collision perfectly. The crunching impact with the Ford Mondeo felt as satisfying as landing the punch on the point of the jaw at the moment of maximum effect. The kind of blow you struck and instantly knew that this part of the fight was won. He had a hard-on the size of Thames Ditton and a snarling smile plastered across his face to match. Not that anyone could see that beneath his balaclava (or trousers), but he knew they were both there.

"Jaysus, but I love my fucking job," was his cry, for anyone who could hear.

Danny was out of the door of the truck as soon as the smash tinkle tinkle had stopped. Being careful, he had to jump away from the big vehicle as Ciaran had already thrown it into reverse, pulling it away from the wrecked car. Danny knew he was making sure they could still drive it. They really would need to be out of here in the next three minutes. If they were too entangled, the job would be simply fucked. However the motion of the big dumper reassured him that the stolen juggernaut had been well chosen and more than fit for purpose.

Danny was making straight for the Luton Van. It was directly behind the Mondeo with its brakes slamming on hard, tyres sending the dark delicious smell of burnt rubber in the air. Too little too late. It rear-ended the Ford. Poor bastard Imbeki coughed a lump of his tongue onto his own chest at this point.

Danny was sprinting now at full tilt.

The act of braking had sent Sharp's mobile phone and rover radio into the footwell of his cab. He was thrown forward, the seatbelt doing its job, but his impact was much less than the car in front meeting the truck. His airbag didn't go off, a blessing to his nose, and also to Danny. It would be easier to get this done if he could pull the driver and snatch the keys out of the van as fast as fuck.

By the time Danny had leapt over the roof of the Mondeo using the rear tyre to leg him up to reach the driver's side of the van, Sharp was coming to terms with what was happening. Although it all looked more than a little surreal, a construction truck had just stopped his mates dead in their tracks. He had then smacked into the back of them and suddenly someone who looked like 'Jesse frigging James', complete with Stetson, was coming at him, from the driver's side. As the Cowboy yanked the door open he pulled a pair of sawn-offs out of what looked like holsters. Sharpy suddenly had a lot of gun in his face.

Did this fucking nutcase just scream: "Stick 'em up pardner!"?

34

✧ Saving the Planet ✧

Within half an hour of the first explosion two different militant Islamist groups had claimed responsibility for the whole damn show. Not that they were responsible...or Islamist. It suited their own insane misanthropic agendas.

This was exactly as Danny had planned. There was nothing like the vanity of a bunch of madmen to help misdirect investigations even if it was only for a few hours. But those few hours were all he and his crew needed. They were more than enough to get this show on the road.

And the show was going like clockwork.

The copper in the Luton van was wise enough to play ball. He allowed Danny to plant him face down across the seats of the cab while he wound insulation tape around his hands at his own back, then his ankles and finally around his eyes. He then picked up the police rover and the mobile phone off the floor of the van.

Three men leapt out of the back of the huge dumper truck and lined up in formation, making up the middle and end of a human chain. It was completed by Ciaran and Danny after they had finished with their tape and the coppers in both vehicles. They now formed the chain running from the Luton Van to the back of the dumper truck. They then began to play the world's richest game of pass the parcel, taking the packets filled with money out of the van and ferrying them into the rear of the dumper. The whole operation took less than five minutes, by which time a few pedestrians and a smattering of cars had come upon the scene. Everyone acted sensibly though, the sawn-offs at Danny's waist enough to inspire timidity. Danny could see them reaching for their mobiles to dial 999 for the police, but again his foresight proved correct. The bombs had forced a shut down of the mobile signal, hadn't they? Even if they wanted to report the crime, right now they couldn't and those in the flats adjacent found that when they tried their landlines, the emergency number was constantly engaged. Not that it mattered. Even when reported there simply weren't enough Old Bill to react. They had their plates full.

Once the transfer was complete, they jumped back into the truck.

Ciaran could feel the heat of excitement rising in his chest with the huge adrenalin kick that had flared up there as soon as he had put the truck into gear for the initial impact. He also knew that when the job was done that adrenalin rush would be replaced by an almost inescapable exhaustion. But for now, fuck, he felt good.

Danny was in the same mindset. Elated that they were now climbing back into the truck having not had to put anyone, copper or punter, down with the sawn-offs. And while he could hear siren after siren in the distance, he was fairly sure they weren't coming for them.

Ciaran, still wearing his balaclava, put the great truck into gear and pulled away from the wreckage of the Mondeo. He took to the little sliver of pavement on the right-hand side to navigate their way past the small knot of cars that had come upon the scene. Danny couldn't resist a tip of his cowboy hat at the staring public, about 12 people in all, as they passed them on the dog-leg corner. He reckoned that if he had been chewing tobacco he could have spat on one of them like Eastwood in The Outlaw Josey Wales...but no sense in leaving unnecessary DNA at the scene of a crime.

They were now retracing the route the money van had already taken, driving back towards Wandsworth. As they did so, with their precious cargo on board, the peloton of cyclists appeared alongside them. This time their numbers were a little larger. Danny watched them materialise behind the truck, telling Ciaran they were all there, present and correct. And among them was Howler. Even with his disguise on, his helmet pulled low, Danny recognised him. He saw the slight wave of the hand, the acknowledgement that the next part of the process was about to kick in.

At this point London was treated to another surreal sight. The bike team now formed an orderly line across the rear of the truck, maintaining speed along with the lumbering workhorse. One by one, each cyclist went forward, gripping onto the back of the lorry, using its momentum to pull them forward. This allowed them to sit upright in their saddles for an instant, taking their other hand of the handlebars long enough to receive a backpack stuffed full of cash from inside the rear of the dumper.

Then it was a super fast sling over the shoulder and a let go, some of them pulling away and going left, some right and others doubling back, returning from where the truck had come.

Dispersing.

Two of them had to take a couple of goes at the tricky manoeuvre, but they managed it. Danny was watching all this from the side mirror, breathing out as the last rider pulled away from the rear. Another part of Danny's plan was completed. No sense, he thought, in rocking up to the industrial unit with the entire twenty two million ready for Harkness to drool over. And anyway...why would you expect a thief to do as he was told?

"Done and dusted?" Ciaran said, now looking at Danny.

"Yep...at least some of the dosh is safely away. Now, let's rendezvous."

How could Danny and Ciaran not do this at Smugglers Way? Firstly, it actually served their purpose well, a side street in Wandsworth that was right off the main road. Blink and you could miss any vehicle turning into it. Secondly, it was populated by some drab industrial units and a huge council-run domestic waste site. And thirdly? Well, Smugglers Way for fuck's sake. It was too delicious. The clue was in the name.

Ciaran guided the truck into the dead end street, marvelling again at how light the traffic was, and how Danny's huge gambit had paid off. As he made the turn, he couldn't help but look at the McDonald's drive thru. Wouldn't that have been the ultimate 'fuck you' to the Old Bill.

Nodding to the fast food joint. "Jaysus, I could murder one of those now. Can you imagine? Yes, Officer, they pulled in at about half six. There were five of them. I knew they were desperate men, they all ordered black coffee with their Sausage McMuffins. That and one of them was dressed like Woody from Toy Story, cowboy hat and all. Funny, what you think about as you're committing the crime of the century."

But Danny's face was grim.

"How many has he killed, Ciaran? What have we done here?"

They drove down Smugglers Way just far enough to be hidden from the main junction, but also not so far that they would be seen on the CCTV cameras around the waste site.

Waiting there were two parked vehicles. One a car, the other a small white van. The five of them leapt out, repeating the unloading and loading job they had just executed earlier. Only this time they were even quicker because there was less, and also as they were desperate to get the job done now. The remaining money went into the white van. The three who had ridden in the back of the truck stripped to their underpants, flinging their clothes into the back of the dumper, reaching into the waiting car and fishing out new clothes. Once dressed in what made them look like painters and decorators in overalls, they climbed into the car, each of them now carrying a money packet.

"Don't spend it all in the one shop now, lads...or should I say the one strip club, ya dirty hoo'ers," laughed Ciaran at them through the driver's window as they prepped to drive off. Danny just nodded at the driver.

"Thanks, lads."

A broad Belfast accent replied: "Sure it was, wee buns. A pleasure doing bizness with ya, mucker. Hope you get the rest to your piggy bank safe now, like." And they drove off.

Ciaran and Danny now did the strip, staying close to the dumper as they did so, pulling on a change of clothes from the white van.

"Are you good to go?"

Ciaran nodded back, smiling eagerly at his fellow thief.

"Aye, now, ready to fucking rock. I'll just move this into the recycling centre, flick the switch on Big Enda's bit of gear...sure Danny, did ya not realise we were saving the planet? I'm going to recycle this here dumper and then later I'm going to help you recycle that money we just nicked."

"Saving the planet...but what about Enda? We'll have to deal with that."

Ciaran's expression turned grim.

"Leave that to me..."

"Just let me know where he is when you find him."

"No Danny, I recommended him. I brought him in. I feel like he's mine."

A look of understanding passed between them.

"Okay, Ciaran. See you as planned. Keep your head down until then."

Danny finished by throwing the police rover and mobile into the dumper truck.

Ciaran checked that the bicycle was where he had left it,

chained to the fence further down the street on Smugglers Way. It was. He jumped up into the cab of the dumper truck and started the huge engine up. He then positioned the truck so that once he jumped out of the cab, he would be mostly shielded from the centre's CCTV cameras by its bulk. Just before he jumped out, he reached under the driver's seat, between his own legs, flicking the switch on the timer.

He vaguely wondered if he should have been concerned that he had spent the whole time driving sat on top of enough industrial Semtex to take out a whole street.

As he rode away on his bike, Ciaran heard the blast clearly enough. He imagined as he pushed himself away from the scene. All those tin cans, reams of newspaper and wine bottles flying through the air, along with the charred remains of their clothes and the truck they had so profitably used to stop a Ford Mondeo.

I tell ya. We're saving the world, he thought...

35

✧ Settling Dust ✧

Danny was satisfied with the way London's systems had reacted to his plan.

To say that the city had been "thrown for a loop" was equivalent to suggesting that the marriage of Prince Charles and Lady Diana had been a tad unsettled. The chain of events that he foresaw in his mind all came to pass. Like dominoes, each development had knocked the next one into place.

There were instantaneous raids. Specialist police units crashed hostels, flats and flophouses in every corner of London and its outskirts. Every suspected nutjob preacher, acolyte, internet militia man, bedroom blogger and blind follower was on the end of the policeman's knock. It began to resemble some kind of bizarre Haj in London's holding cells, with every stripe of militant religious mad dog all being slung in together until such times as alibis could be checked, questions asked and flats and laptops searched to within an inch of their very existence. The process of bagging their hands while awaiting forensic swabbing for traces of explosive, gunshot residue or even so much as a smidgen of fertilizer under the fingernails slowed the process the most.

There was a huge influx of journalists and commentators from all over the world, all piling in to cover the

'Shutdown of London'.

In the following days it seemed that the streets carried more TV crews and international news correspondents than actual inhabitants. The populace seemed reluctant to trust the authorities really had the situation back under control.

In the midst of all the clamour, Danny's team managed to reach their respective boltholes easily. This had been another facet of Danny's thinking. With the exception of himself in the white van and the three loading boys, everyone else had departed the scene of their deeds on push bike.

To say that the police would not be looking for modern day highwaymen on bicycles would have been an understatement. They were simply too busy.

But Danny knew this hiatus was very much a temporary one. The forensic geeks would soon do their work. The explosives used by Big Enda would, ultimately, be traceable. Also, it wouldn't take forever to see that all the jihadists and part-time terrorists would have, largely at least, solid alibis.

So the clock would once again be ticking. He had his escape route planned. He knew where he would go, and how he would get there.

Except there was Enda, first, and then Harkness to deal with. Plus the small matters of Dexy, the money and some payback.

So as he made his way to his own bolthole, Danny also carried out a few minor chores. A few little bits of preparation. Ciaran may have thought that this morning had been the 'big show', but Danny had always felt it was only the ticket to the 'big show'. This evening would bring the 'main event'. Anyone in their right mind wouldn't want to miss it.

Barnes Police Station was like a ghost ship when Christine finally reached there. Her shock had been growing as she heard the reports of what was taking place around the city. Almost all personnel had been summoned to other duties, like rodeo cowboys gathered to throw a rope around every wild horse in the land. She worked her way through the empty locker room and ground floor offices.

It took a few minutes of wandering around until she was beckoned up into the back of the squad room, to Collinson's office. It was the sweet caress of cigarette smoke that drew her upstairs, like a beacon from another time. The heady aroma at first seemed entirely normal, like background noise until Christine finally computed that it was her boss and his aversion to the fact that it had been forbidden to smoke indoors anywhere in Britain since 2007.

The boss was snoozing. Asleep. Feet on the desk, a cigarette burning between his fingers, an open bottle of Bells whiskey on his desk, a good eight inches missing from it.

"Guv?"

She said it gently at first, like she was waking a sleeping child. She then realised that she wasn't waking a kid. Her boss was asleep while London burned.

Another "Guv"...then a kick of the table to accompany the greeting made Collinson wake. Sitting upright, he flicked the cigarette away from himself, having burned himself in his rude awakening.

"What the...Chance? Fucking Chance."

"Guv, what are you doing? Do you know what's happening out there?"

It took Collinson a few seconds to meet her gaze. His eyes looked like they needed rounding up and pointing in the right direction and it wasn't an easy job.

"Of course I fucking know," spat back Collinson. Literally, flecks of saliva hitting his desk.

"Guv, you were asleep. Have you heard about Freeth?"

"It's all a fucking mess. The whole thing, burning down round me. Just burning."

"Guv, I got a call. Do you know that Freethy is in hospital? He is in intensive care. I need to ask you a few things. Do you think you can sit up and answer?"

"The world has just gone mad, luv, just fucking mad. Who would blame anyone? Eh? Who would?"

"Who would blame anyone for blowing up the city? Sir, is that what you are saying?"

"What? No, no, no, I'm talking about the rest of it. The other fucking shite that is going to land right here." Collinson pounded the top of his own desk and then reached for the bottle, but CC got there first, sliding it a few inches away from him.

"Guv, what did you do? Is this to do with Harkness? Guv?"

Collinson's head snapped up at the mention of that name. His rheumy eyes tried their best to harden. He started to cough, but he fought it down.

"I knew you would work it out. Part...part of me hoped you would."

The rapid truth now, tumbling out of Collinson's drink-laced words.

"He had me. That fucking bastard had me. You have to know that. They have to know it. He had me. What could I do? They were going to do me over. No pension. No fucking life after I gave them mine. How could I tell my Mrs that? What would my girls think of their dad then? But he said he could make it go away. All I had to do was help him..."

Christine couldn't believe what she was hearing, but at the same time she could. The letter handed to her by the nurse, Freethy, Fisty, Iggy, and now Collinson. And worst of all herself.

What a fucking joke. She had been running round London as a bag carrier for Harkness. She had been gathering the money into one handy place. Harkness had a finger in every bit of this, even to the extent of manipulating Collinson...and also possibly hastening her daughter's end.

"Guv, the money?"

Collinson just shook his head. "Gone already". Collinson reached the bottle this time, not bothering with the glass, tilting it straight to his head. Then he started to cry, babbling in between the sobs about his life and career. How he was a good copper, bending the odd rule, kicking the odd arse but never anything like this.

"In for a fucking penny, in for a pound. They make you feel like a fucking blagger. You might as well act like one."

"Guv, we'll get him. We'll get this cleared up. You just need to tell me a few things, that's all. A few details and we can get this settled."

Collinson looked at her, sat back, and really looked at her.

"Settled? Are you fucking mad, luv? After today, it'll take a long time for the dust to settle in London...a long fucking time."

CC hadn't seen the gun. It was wedged under Collinson's crotch, but by the time it was swung up and under her old guv'nor's chin, it was too late to do anything. It was too late to try and launch herself across the desk, knock the pistol out of his hand, stop him in any way she could.

The shot went off and CC's ears went dead. The bullet caught Collinson under the soft part of his throat, travelling up through his mouth into his brain, laying waste to tissue, veins, arteries and all in its path. It finally exited through the top of his skull, punching a flap the size of a CD in the top of this old cop's head. A vivid splash of blood, flesh and brain coated the wall behind, and made Christine think of a rotten tomato being crushed under foot.

Ciaran had little trouble locating Big Man Boom. Having been discovered completely pissed in a store room at work, he was driven home by one of his fellow workers, except he had insisted on being dropped off at The Spotted Dog pub.

All Ciaran had to do was wait. As the bomb expert emerged from the pub into the afternoon light, he carried a bottle-shaped brown paper package under his arm. It was a short walk to the lock up, although it did take the Big man a few goes to unlock the heavy door. Ciaran was close enough to hear the swearing, Enda's hangover causing him more than a little grief.

As he finally managed to open the door and went to step through, Ciaran strode quickly up behind Enda, using his momentum to push them both through the metal door.

Ciaran shut the door behind him, Enda staring at and then recognising the small ginger lad instantly.

"It's you, is it?"

"Ay, Big Man, tis."

Enda turned, walked over to his work bench, and plopped himself down into the battered old seat he kept behind it. He put his elbows on the bench, his face in his hands, running his fingers through his hair.

"I couldn't pass up the opportunity."

"And why would that be, Enda?" said Ciaran softly, the musical lilt to his Cork accent stronger than usual.

"All those times. All those jobs. We never really stuck it to them. And then, those fuckers, those slimy politician fuckers, they just gave in so that they could become respectable and fill their own bellies. Suddenly, none of it mattered. The Hunger Strikers, Bloody Sunday, the torture, the history. All fucking forgotten. Brushed under the carpet."

Ciaran slipped his hands into his pockets.

"But when they work it all out. When they realise that a Paddy finally made them pay, that there was at least still one Irishman willing to still fight them. It will all be worth it."

"You're dead right, Enda. Chucky Ar La an' all that."

Enda nodded at this. "Our day will come...our day just did come. What made it even sweeter was that the extra explosives came from that fucking copper, Harkness."

"Is that right now? How'd that happen?"

"He just showed up. Right where you're standing. Called me an artist, he did. I called him a bastard. But I took his semtex, and I did what I do best."

"Went a bit further than we were expecting, Enda."

The Big Man looked up at Ciaran, reaching for the brown paper bag. He took the bottle of Jamesons out of it, opened it and took a long swallow.

"Ciaran."

"Yes?"

"Would you ever just get the fuck on with it and kill me. My work here is fucking done."

So Ciaran did exactly as he was asked.

36

✧ A Dog Having His Day ✧

It was growing dark, the late June sun finally giving up and beginning to shrink in the inky city sky. The industrial unit in west London was practically empty. Every shred of any time that the crew had spent there was carefully, meticulously disposed of. Ciaran even took the time to put so much drain cleaner down the toilet that Danny suspected that there wouldn't be a rat left alive in Acton.

But now, the big space was exactly that, just a big, low-lit space except for a single chair right in the middle with Danny sat on it. At his feet were piles and piles of packets. Packets of money.

Glancing at his watch, he was unsurprised to see the door in front of him open, just as the second hand brought itself and the others into line at 12 o'clock exactly. Midnight. Danny noted to himself the lack of vehicle noise preceding this. Had they been parked up for ages?

Harkness entered. Tall, imposing, almost swaggering, but seemingly alone. Danny knew that would definitely not be the case, watching as the big cop spread his arms expansively in front of him, a grin slicing across his face, the hands coming back together now. Harkness started to clap.

"Well, fuck me, Danny Boy. You are the king of misdirection. I mean, I knew you were good. I had high hopes and ambition for your endeavours but you even made me feel... how would I describe it? Proud? Yes that would be it, proud. Like a doting, fucking father."

Danny just watched him, sitting passively in the seat, surrounded by the objects of all their affections.

"You knew that the crazies would jump in, claim your fine work as their own, give you the time and a little bit of room, didn't you? Fucking genius, Danny. I have to applaud that kind of chutzpah. Harry Truman once said that it's amazing what you can accomplish…."

Danny cut him off with the rest of the quote "…if you do not care who gets the credit."

Harkness was stood opposite him now, ten feet away, smiling.

"Always full of the surprises, Danny. I am sure you have one cooked up for me right now. But first, business. I take it this is the fruit of our labours?"

Danny nodded, trying to strain to hear beyond Harkness. He was trying to look for clues as to who was with him, without looking like he was doing it.

"If you don't mind me saying so, Danny, that doesn't look much like twenty-two-point-four million to me. Have you had some tucked away?"

"I'm a thief, Harkness. Shake my hand and be sure to count your fingers after."

Danny's breathing was shallow now. He could feel the heat rising in his body. The tension notched up in the space between the two of them. He could tell that Harkness was feeling it too. He had shifted his standing position, ever so slightly, also imperceptibly, but Danny knew that Harkness was on his mettle, bracing, feeling ready, ready for…what?

"I'm offended, Danny. Did you think I would try and keep it all for myself? Cut you out? Are you suggesting I am not a gentleman of principle?"

"We are about to find out, I feel. When's Dexy going to show up? This is her game after all, isn't it?"

"Ahhh, Danny, Danny, Danny. People are not always what they seem. Are they? Bravo for working it out."

And at that, Danny heard the unmistakably expensive

click-clack of high heels. His eyes snapped to the doorway as a vision of cascading, red hair sat atop a beautifully tailored double-breasted dark suit stepped into the big room.

"Hello, Gorgeous. Did you miss me?"

Her lipstick was blood red and flawless. Her hands deep in the pockets of the jacket, making the neckline plunge a little further than it should, giving just an extra hint of her outrageous sense of style and glamour. Especially as she wasn't wearing a blouse underneath the jacket.

"I want to thank you, Danny. You have exceeded even my expectations. When James first came to me with his... little plan, I knew you would be the only man who could pull it off."

It had all started to stack up for him a few days ago. How else could Harkness have come into his life? Who else could have talked about Danny, pointed him out for this kind of work, given so much detail so as to gain just exactly the right amount of leverage? It could only have been the one person he would have suspected last: Dexy.

"So, this is what it feels like to be the stitched up kipper then?"

"New experiences are only sent to make us better men, Danny," chuckled Harkness. Dexy joined in.

"Oh, darling, that's not the way to look at it. After all, every great musician needs to play on an equally fabulous instrument...and you made London yours. It was a virtuoso performance. But now, for your encore darling, where is the rest of my money?"

Dexy took her hands out of her pockets, revealing a beautifully crafted one shot derringer hand gun, pointing it squarely at Danny's head. This was Harkness' cue, which he took gleefully. He closed the space between him and Danny in a flash, one big hand encircling Danny's throat with a grip like a vice, the other giving his balls the same, unwelcome treatment. Harkness pulled Danny up out of the chair, up off his feet, holding him in place like you might do with a coat that you are about to put on.

"Darling, I have gone to a lot of trouble in my life," continued Dexy. "I have built up my club from nothing to what it is today, the venue of choice for the most respectable and unrespectable men of their generation. I have made sacrifices and I have made compromises. But this job was to be my cherry on the top. It may have been your finest work, Danny, but it is my job. You want to live Danny. I know you do. You like fine bourbon, expensive and beautiful women and most of all you love the thrill of the steal. You want to live, Danny, so I know you will tell me where the rest of the money is."

Harkness loosened his grip a touch on Danny's throat, allowing him to take in some much needed air. It allowed him to speak, even if it was painful given that he felt like his balls were about to be ripped off.

"It's mine. I did what was asked, there is enough for..."

Harkness rearranged his grip on Danny's neck, hissing into his ear as he did so.

"What do you think I spent my time doing in the Sandbox, Danny? I wasn't making tea for the ragheads. I was squeezing their deepest fucking secrets out of them. I will afford you the benefit of that experience and it will not go easy for you. I will know where the money is. You. Will. Tell."

The last three words were each underlined with a twist of his lower hand, sending shards of hot pain up into Danny's guts.

It was at that moment that Ciaran chose to come crashing through the suspended ceiling of the unit.

The plan had been a simple one. Ciaran was to secret himself up there, in a section where they had reinforced it to take his weight and when the time was right he was to put a bullet squarely in the middle of the forehead of whoever deserved it first, which hopefully would have been Harkness.

Sadly, when Ciaran fell through the ceiling, he was not alone. One of the Harkness crew came with him. But one bit of luck. Ciaran actually landed on top of Harkness' man, using him as a gym mat, protecting him from the concrete greeting below. He didn't move after landing. His head had taken most of the brunt of the impact.

At the same time as the impact Ciaran's chunky desert eagle pistol went off. The bullet filled the air with the bitter-sweet smell of gunpowder as it ricocheted around the warehouse.

Instinctively, Harkness dropped to one knee. He let Danny go as he did so, giving Felix the time to barrel-roll back up onto his feet. Before Harkness could stand upright Danny's right boot connected with the side of his face, laying him flat out. Danny leapt onto the object of his aggression. He gripped his hands around Harkness' head, thrusting his thumbs into the eye sockets. Immediately he pushed them down with full force, trying to make a path with them to the back of this bastard's skull. Harkness was bucking like a raging bull, trying to shift Danny's weight off him, trying to loosen the tightening grip around his head.

Ciaran meanwhile had recovered his gun and his balance, firing twice beyond Dexy to take out the two heavies who were now bundling into the space. Dexy flung herself to the side to avoid the shots.

Feeling as though he was about to lose his grip on Harkness, Danny changed tack. He switched his position and let Harkness' head go. He enjoyed the crack as it hit the con-crete floor. He shifted to a sideways position and brought the full weight of his body, knees first, down onto Harkness' throat. He could feel the windpipe crush as he did so, most of the fight going out of the man in that instant.

And then Danny was pitched forward, not voluntarily, but by a blow to the back of his skull, delivered by another of Harkness' crew, summoned into the room by the sound of Ciaran's gunshots.

There was suddenly a moment of stillness in the room. Danny managed to climb to his feet, despite the hot sticky flow of blood he could feel from the back of his head that crept down his neck and the dizziness that went with it. The only sound in the room was that of Harkness, dry clicks emitting from his mouth as he struggled to get air into his lungs. His boy trying to roll him onto his side into the recovery position.

Once Danny could manage it, he could see that he and Dexy had been joined by two other heavies now both holding Ciaran, plus the one attending to the big cop.

"Are you quite finished with the macho nonsense, darling?"

Dexy was looking at him, like one might look at an errant child who had just delivered his parents a school report that was less than glowing.

"Danny, the money was never yours, my love. The job wasn't even yours. Now if letting you live is not enough reward, I don't know what is. You can't begin to doubt my word. We have disposed of every major stumbling block in our way, especially the ones that might have stopped you from doing such a fine job across this city of ours."

"Dexy, you are just like Harkness. You both think you glide on a cushion of free air. Your arrogance is your weakness."

"Darling, being able to do the things we do is not arrogance, it's merely ability. Force of will, vision some people call it. You either have it or you don't."

"Yes, Dexy, but then you have to factor in uncertainty, chance, happenstance, even Harkness' favourite: chaos. They all play a role too. You have to think like a system. You have put everything in the right order. You know the expression, every dog has its day, don't you?"

Dexy, looking at him now, curiosity brewing in her eyes.

"Well, today, that's all I am. A dog having his day."

And with that, the room exploded into noise and movement. About twenty Old Bill came into the space. Through the doors. Through a section of the pre-fab wall that Danny and Ciaran had loosened earlier. Loads of the fuckers, the leads carrying automatic rifles, shouting for everyone to get down on their knees, hand's behind their heads. These were followed by plainclothes men in little police caps, chequered strips down the side of them. Some had their warrant badges strung round their necks, some of them armed with handguns and some not.

Dexy's roar was like that of a banshee. For a split second she actually considered loosing off her one shot Derringer in Danny's direction. However, as she raised the deadly little gun one of the cops calmly put a shot squarely through her clavicle. The bullet went 'through and through', clanging off a steel girder in the opposite wall. The shot caused her to scream even more loudly. She crumpled to the floor and commenced a tantrum fit made up of pure rage and frustration. Her whole body thrashed as she beat the floor with her feet and one good hand, snarling, screaming, bitching like a thing possessed.

Christine Chance entered the room just behind the armed officers. She made a beeline for Harkness, rolling him onto his back, frantically checking for a pulse as the others busied themselves with the heavies. It was obvious that they were professionals, no resistance was given whatsoever once the coppers entered the equation. They were resigned to the awful knowledge that they were well and truly fucked.

Finally, CC crossed over to where Danny was standing, watching it all. She had to usher away one of the plainclothes men who was preparing to cuff the thief.

"I'll look after this one."

Danny exhaled, long and low. Breathing normally for probably the first time in what seemed like a lifetime but in reality had only been a few short weeks.

"What's your name?" CC looking into his eyes, thinking

the man in front of her looked like he'd done ten rounds with Tyson.

"No, sorry, Detective Chance. That is not how this is going to work."

"It will eventually. Is the money all there?"

Again, Danny shook his head, looking almost sorrowful about it.

"Jesus, not you as well. Everyone seems to be obsessed with the fucking dosh. Like I said, Detective, that is not how this is going to end."

"And why would that be?"

"What time is it?"

Christine was puzzled but she felt that she was indebted to this guy. She knew he had made the call, he had invited them here. He had been able to give her the opportunity to get Harkness in a room. She could find out the answers she needed and not just about this whole fucking mess. And once she had those answers? Who knew?

CC looked at her watch.

"12.25."

"Ok. You and your men have, I think, three minutes to leave."

"What?"

Danny brought the small switch out of his pocket, it looked like something you would open an automatic garage door with. He purposefully pressed the button at the centre of it and the room was filled with a hissing noise, and the sudden smell of butane.

CC's eyes widened as she started to yell. The others clocked the smell of the gas as she did so, and suddenly there was a scramble for the exits.

Christine tried to keep a hold of Felix as they exited, but to be honest it was always going to be a tall order in the confusion. That, plus the deft elbow to the side of the head that Danny adroitly delivered to her.

And suddenly, in the road leading to the unit, there was

Ciaran. He was on a big Triumph Daytona, screeching to a halt by Danny, gathering him onto the bike. He gunned the engine and they took off like a rocket. The big bike wobbled beneath them as he almost over-throttled it. He just managed to get it back under control as they shot out onto the A40 West Way and off into the night.

Instantly an explosion filled the night sky. It was exactly as Danny had asked Big Enda to supply...all heat and flames, perfectly contained, pushing force, prefab and roofing sheets up into the night air. The blast wave knocked a few of the cops off their feet, one taking a piece of sheet metal in his leg, but otherwise, it was all noise and light. Enough to scare the shit out of anyone, but not enough to wipe them out.

And as they raced up the dual carriageway, wind rushing past his ears and through his hair, Danny couldn't resist the urge, screaming at the top of his lungs as they flew past the light traffic around them.

"HARKNESS, YOU FUCKER...I AM ALIVE!!!!!"

37

✧ After the Mardi Gras ✧

The cat! The cat! The fucking cat!

Barry Blount had been awoken, yet again, by the fucking cat. It wasn't even his. It just showed up one day, about a year ago, decided it liked the look of the place and had moved in. It regularly terrorised him out of bed in the mornings with demands for food, or water or just the game of 'you try to pet me and I take your fingers off with my claws'.

Barry took a look at his bedside clock. It was 9am already. He had already fed the frigging cat an hour ago. What was its problem? Then Barry heard the buzzer go at his door, a long held buzz, like it might not have been the first go.

Barry shuffled to the front of the flat. Opening up to find another cycle courier. It was the third one this week. Barry accepted the packet, heavier than the last couple, signed for it and mumbled his thanks.

"Shit! 9am…"

He'd just remembered. Holy shit, he was due on location in the centre of London by 11am. Today was a big day. The first day of filming on his new television series pilot. The show that was going to put Barry Blount back on the map, back up there on the Google pages and the covers of the magazines. *Barry's Brotherhood* was the show to do all that for him.

Okay, it was a self-funded pilot, but still, it was his big shot. You made your own luck in showbiz, and since he had come in to a little money, he had to put it to the best use.

It had all been a blur since that day, that awful day in London a month ago. The man he thought he had dreamt up until he discovered his mobile was gone, he had come back. He had dumped a load of packages in Barry's flat. Had given him a load of printed labels and given him strict instructions of when to start sending them on, in the post. The address was some kind of Post Office box in America. Florida, by the looks of it. Barry had never been there. Didn't like the sound of it ever since he had watched re-runs of The Golden Girls. He saw Florida as a place where Americans just went to grow old and die. The place must just stink of pee and lavender.

He had started the process this week. And now, like the man had said, couriers were turning up with more packets and Barry was to use the extra labels to post those on too.

And he had given Barry an envelope, a big jiffy one, stuffed full of money. Told him there was more once he had sent on all the packages. All he had to do was post and promise not to look in the packets when they came. If he did, the man would know. He would come back again. And Barry didn't want that, did he? No, he didn't. People who could just come and go out of other people's homes as they pleased were not the type Barry wanted to see very often. It wasn't natural.

The money had looked fabulous. He had emptied the jiffy envelope onto his bed, and then rolled around on it, like Julia Roberts did in Pretty Woman. It made him feel dirty, but in a good way.

And now, he was spending. Spending it on some good things, and on some bad. Well a little ounce, or seven, wasn't so bad, was it?

"Right, better hit the shower...it's a big day, after all.

Showbiz doesn't stand still for anyone..."

Celeste was just puzzled. The police had been to ask her questions about her brother on five different occasions. They never once gave her an indication of where he might be or what they thought he might have done this time.

She was out of her mind with worry at first, but as the return visits mounted up she just resolved herself to being cross about it. Thinking what has that useless brother roped me and him into now?

But soon her anger and worry both subsided and the police questions stopped. She began to chill out about it. Especially as, despite all those visits and all those questions, not one of the Old Bill had ever mentioned the money that had showed up in her bank account. The money that Danny had told her to not worry about and that she would be able to keep. The money that was paying for the conservatory on the back of her house. If Danny wanted to show up, she felt sure he would when he wanted to...

Christine stood over Shauna's grave. The earth didn't look so fresh any longer, and the headstone had finally been ordered.

"Right Little 'Un, time I was going. I think I will find out today. I hope to anyway. I'm going to enjoy my time in a room with that bastard today. They have finally finished all their top level shit. Now I get my go. Don't worry, I'll be the Old Bill you would want me to be, but I will get my answers, I promise. You try and rest now, Shauna. I'll see you at the weekend."

She stood, taking in the peaceful surroundings of the cemetery, letting the breeze touch her face, enjoying the stillness of it all.

Stillness. Just like that day. When London went suddenly loud and then, just as suddenly, went quiet. At a standstill. Just like CC's life was in the moment her daughter had finally given in. She would never forget the experience of just sitting still with her child, as she breathed her last, as she took her leave and moved away.

On reflection, it had been on her own terms, whether Harkness had intervened or not. Christine had been there. CC and her daughter, both, in the stillness. No-one could ever rob either of them of that fact.

Her phone chirruped. It was Freethy's number. Hopefully his wife had news on her friend's progress.

"Hello, Agnes, give me the good news..."

She started to walk away from Shauna's last resting place.

It had been quite a journey, but somehow they had managed it. Changing cars a couple of times, switching drivers, both of them shaving their hair off to put people off any descriptions or CCTV footage there may have been.

At first they had laid low for a few days, both of them in a safe house Ciaran had arranged. Not going out, not taking any chances. After that they made it to a remote part of Wales, where Ciaran had a fisherman friend. They took his boat overnight to Ireland, making land at the Ardglass harbour.

From there they parted ways. Ciaran wanted to take his chances in the Old Country. There were places he knew in the south west of Ireland where you could hide forever, no-one ever asking awkward questions or wanting to know too much.

Danny had kept going. He blagged his way onto a freighter all the way to the Dominican Republic. Then after a few weeks rest and a visit to a good passport man, he was off again. He made the short hop across to Florida, finally settling down in Isla Morada in the Florida Keys.

And there, waiting for him was a post box. It was stuffed full of packages. The old guy who looked after the place complained that there were so many he had begun to store them in a safe out back.

Danny apologised and made some space for the ones he knew were to still to arrive. A healthy tip smoothed that one over.

Danny Felix's days were easy, long and enjoyable. He got himself a little place right on the beach front. He bought a modest boat and began to feel himself settle. He opened a quiet business of his own, taking tourists deep sea fishing off the Gulf coastline. The sun. He enjoyed the sun, sea and especially the sky at sunset. Danny liked to drink in the orange light of the evening sunset with an expensive bourbon in his hand, the smoky taste of it dancing on his tongue.

He could hide here. Secret himself away from the majority of the world. He could ignore what he loathed of his London life. He could hide from prying eyes and uncomfortable questions, even the ones he was asking of himself. Yes, there was remorse. Too many lives had been snuffed out after Big Man Boom went rogue. But Danny knew in his own heart that was as much a part of the system playing itself out as anything he might have inspired. He would deal with his own regret a little at a time...that would work for him.

He started growing his hair out, on both his head and his chin. He put on a little weight, formulating a backstory about himself that included a dotcom windfall and a desire to drop out. It wasn't such a big lie when you thought about it.

No doubt he was on all manner of wanted lists. Number one with a bullet on some of them. But, he firmly believed that "long runs the fox" and he was a fox with very long legs.

And in the meantime?

Well, Danny loved it here. He adored the solitude when he had it. He even took a strange enjoyment in meeting the different people who turned up at his door wanting to catch some fish and drink a few beers out on the Gulf of Mexico. Amazon even delivered to him here, a burgeoning Blu-ray collection of movies beginning to form on the shelves of his little bedroom. All paid for from a credit card he had cloned from a particularly drunken, obnoxious tourist, who, nearly a year after discovering it had gone, had yet to get around to cancelling the account.

But what Danny loved most was the stillness. When he was alone on the boat, out on the Gulf, feeling the craft gently shifting under him, the sound of water lapping against the craft, his face tilted to the heavens, breathing in the stillness.

Yes, he loved that, he loved the stillness. Danny had time, time of his own now.

Time just to stand still.

ACKNOWLEDGMENTS

As with every creative endeavour, this book has been helped by many hands and minds.

Firstly, let me thank the fabulous KT Forster, who knocked the myriad 'Irishisms' out of my prose when needed, and gave much encouragement.

My sister Josephine deserves credit for always inspiring me to write and Maggie at Chorleywood Bookshop, who was generous with both her time and comments after reading the early versions.

There was some incredible help with authenticity, especially with the tricky business of making my coppers act and sound like coppers. My gratitude goes to Detective Chief Inspector Sarah Staff, Detective Inspector Caroline Clooney and Detective Inspector Keeley Smith. I now know what to do if I drop my bullets down a toilet...

But my most thorough cop collaborator was Detective Constable Mark Freeth (Ret'D) who bravely battled through every draft and kept me focused when my imagination was getting out of control! I owe him at least one pint of Quadhop...

And last, but never least, a huge debt of gratitude and love to my wife, Helen Jane, who put up with 4am writing bursts. She kept my chin up when I couldn't face another re-write and always told me not to focus on how far I have to go, but rather on how far I had already come.

J.A. Marley 2016.

J.A. MARLEY

ABOUT THE AUTHOR

John A. Marley was born in Belfast, Northern Ireland. Following early success as a film journalist and radio broadcaster in his homeland, he embarked on an accomplished career in television production in England. An avid film fan, John is addicted to crime and mystery thrillers and is passionate about walking his two dogs, discovering new music and travel. Find out more at **jamarley.com**